GOD'S CHILDREN

GOD'S CHILDREN

by

Mabli Roberts

HONNO MODERN FICTION

First published in 2019 by Honno Press, 'Ailsa Craig', Heol y Cawl, Dinas
Powys, Vale of Glamorgan, Wales, CF64 4AH
1 2 3 4 5 6 7 8 9 10
Copyright: Mabli Roberts © 2019

A catalogue record for this book is available from the British Library.

Published with the financial support of the Welsh Books Council.

ISBN Paperback: 978-1-909983-95-3
ISBN Ebook: 978-1-909983-96-0

Cover design: Kari Brownlie
Text design: Elaine Sharples

Printed in Wales by Gomer Press

This book is dedicated to:
The teachers who thought I could,
The friends and family who believed I could,
The editors and publishers who knew I could,
And all the people who said I couldn't.

ACKNOWLEDGEMENTS

Many thanks to Felicity Aston for her encouragement. Her insight and enthusiasm helped sustain me through the long trek of writing this book.

Grateful thanks also to the Royal Geographical Society for the image of Kate Marsden in the author's note.

To all at Honno, sincere gratitude for your faith in my little book, and for bravely sharing my vision for the way I wanted to tell Kate's story.

Thanks, not for the first time, to friends and family who have supported me in my determination to write *God's Children* and see it go out into the world. You know who you are!

And heartfelt thanks to the spirit of Kate Marsden for staying the course with me, and for whom I will always have the utmost admiration.

You remember the snow was blue. So many years have passed, and yet you can clearly see it, can't you? The light so sharp, the air so pure, the day so cold, that the surrounding whiteness was transformed to the palest shade of shimmering blue. The colour of a baby's bonnet, you said, or a fine china tea set, or the eyes of a saint. Instead of blankness and nothingness there were a thousand different thoughts and memories held in that blue-blue ice. The longer you looked, the more revealed themselves.

From where I sat, beneath the shelter of the opening to my tent, I could see the vast expanse of frozen tundra that stretched away west, north and east into impossibly distant horizons. My mind would struggle to make sense of the scale of what it observed. We live our lives for the most part in close proximity to our surroundings, our vision taking us no further than the middle distance; across a street, or a river, or a field. We see in measurements we can comprehend with ease. To be in such wilderness as I travelled through, to feel the insignificance of one's own being amid the glory of God's earth, was at once both terrifying and tremendous.

And what did God want you to find there, do you suppose? What secrets were to be shown you?

Secrets are shy things. They are not easily discovered, for their nature is to hide.

To hide themselves?

To hide the truth.

But in such an open place, surely the truth was easier to see.

You have to wish to see it. Not all do. Is that really what you came to ask me? Is that what you want to know?

1

I want to know all there is. I want you to tell me everything.

Then you should have come sooner. It was all so very long ago.

Tell me what you are able to recall. You said you remember the snow was blue. The light was sharp, the air pure...

That is how I remember it today: tomorrow it may come to me differently. I cannot promise you consistency.

You do want to remember, don't you?

My memory is no longer a matter of volition. I have no choice in what moments appear, what experiences I revisit. My past is not a neatly packed trunk through which you may sift for items of interest. It is an unravelled ball of wool, tangled and confused. You will have to coax out the knots. I cannot guarantee order. I cannot even be certain of sense.

Let's go back to the tundra. It always seems to spark something, starting with the wilderness. The snow was blue, the light sharp...

It hurt my eyes, to begin with, until they became accustomed to it. In the coldest months, while I slept, they would freeze shut. I would have to rub the frost from them before I could open them in the mornings. And then I would view the world through the icicles on my lashes. The glare of the day, the brilliance of the sun upon the snow, would cause flashes of light, like the flare off a diamond, or from the crystal chandeliers in the Winter Palace in St Petersburg. Such chandeliers they were! Grander than any I had seen in England, even when I visited our own dear Queen Victoria. St Petersburg was a place of dazzling spectacle at every turn. There was never anywhere to match it. The week before I set out on my expedition the Tsarina held a grand reception, to make people aware of what it was I was trying to do. She invited every wealthy person in Russia, or so she told me, and of course they came. How could they refuse? I am not sufficiently foolish to think for one moment that they came for me, nor that they truly cared about my mission.

They came for her. To see her. To be with her. Some of them travelled for days to be there. Many spent money they did not have or could ill-afford, simply for the opportunity to be in her presence for a brief time. That was the effect she had on all who met her. There was such a sweetness to her nature, and a beauty about her person – to sit beside her was to know happiness. To receive her attention – her smile! – was to feel blessed. And there was never a person less vain. It was as if God had endowed her with equal measures of charm and humility, so that, aside from her natural bearing and the requirements of her position, she gave the impression of never setting herself above others. It was a gift. A talent too, perhaps. She shone as brightly as those glittering chandeliers. As brilliantly as the diamonds she wore at her throat. Every bit as prettily as the light that danced off that far distant ice-blue snow.

'Nurse? Nurse!' I simply cannot make my voice any louder. I cough, clearing my dry throat, and try again. 'Nurse, are you there? Nurse!'

Now footsteps, and a white-clad sister strides into the room. She is not the young and gentle one. This one is much older. World weary. Her patience long ago used up.

'What is all this noise about?' she wants to know.

'My book,' I tell her, indicating my empty bedside table. The words are clear enough in my head, but I fear they reach her as slurred and jumbled. 'It is not where it should be. I left it here, in its place...' I lean over the side of the bed, causing the nurse to bark in alarm.

'Have a care, Miss Marsden!' She takes hold of me and pulls me back into the bed. 'Are you determined to have a fall? You will break bones and find yourself in all manner of difficulties.'

And make more work for you, I think but do not say. 'My book,' I repeat, while I still have breath to form the words. 'Where is my book?'

With a tut she peers beneath the bed. 'It is here,' she says, bringing it forth. She slaps it down on the little table. 'You must have fallen asleep whilst you were writing in it.'

Did I? It is possible. I am too tired to argue the point. And it is found. That is all that matters.

'You will make yourself ill if you insist on staring at those pages at all hours of the night,' she warns me.

I cannot find the strength to remind her I am already ill. But then, perhaps I am not. I am merely old, and my body is failing as all old things do. And what mind I have I will not waste on her. Many years ago I learned that it does not pay to expend effort and time on those who are not worthy of it.

When I am weary it is to St Petersburg I find my mind travelling. To the Winter Palace. To the Empress. It is strange, I think, that I should find comfort not in thoughts of home or family or past loves, but in that particular variety of beauty.

How my mother would have frowned at such a thought.

'What have you to do with beauty?' she'd have asked me. Plain. She'd describe me as such. She did not believe in the artifice or confusion of tact. 'You are the way God made you, child. It is not for you to change it. He has his reasons,' she told me.

But, what were they, I wanted to know. Why had God seen fit to make me as I was, when other little girls had dainty noses, small faces, sweet smiles? What possible plan could he have had for me that would have been hindered by a modicum of delicacy in my features? It matters not now, of course: old age is a friend to the unattractive.

We are all diminished, those of us who live on to our later years. What we look like is of less importance. Who we are still has a bearing, yes, but it is what we did with our lives that matters at the last. How did we spend the time God granted us on this wide, wide earth? This is not to be confused with how we will be remembered. I care not, any longer, how I am perceived. Had my goal ever been to curry favour, to win approval, I would be a bitter woman now.

Some believed that was in fact your driving force, your greatest wish. They were wrong.

Some ventured to say it. There she is, hobnobbing with royalty. Empresses and Queens. Palaces and titles. Rubbing shoulders with the high and mighty, the rich and powerful. Letters from Her Majesty, notes from Her Highness. Can turn a girl's head, all that attention, all that la-di-dah. Isn't that what they said?

Some did. I took no notice.

Perhaps you should have. Your life would have been so different if you had.

My life was not important. I was not important. I was God's instrument. The little girl grew up and knew what He wanted her to do. Where I came from, what I looked like, none of that mattered. Out there, in the open expanses of Siberia, or in its dense wild forests, or on its icy rivers, there was no time for vanity. Warmth and practicality were the watchwords when choosing items of clothing. Strength in a woman, an ability to endure and to remain in good humour, these were qualities that counted. My build stood me in good stead, but even so I more than once found myself wishing I had been born a man. How much easier my chosen path might have been. But then, would the Tsarina have taken my mission to her heart in the same way? Was it not as women that we forged our friendship? For friendship it was. No, I would not trade a moment of dearest Maria Feodorovna's kind attention for anything.

5

Might you not be fooling yourself? You were a passing distraction for the Empress, perhaps, nothing more. A curiosity. Another way for her to be seen as Little Mother of Russia, caring even for those wretched outcasts you devoted your life to.

They needed me.

She did not.

She helped me.

She helped herself at the same time, used you to make herself shine all the brighter. Sent you off across that terrible wilderness in her name. Save her the trouble of leaving her lovely palace.

You did not know her as I did. She was incapable of sacrificing another for her own gain.

But you were sacrificed, weren't you? Out there, with those men, those ruffians, all that way, all that time. Dirty. Sullied. Body and name. Never got it back, did you? Didn't think about that when you planned your mission, did you?

I would have gone all the same, even had I known the price. I would have paid it willingly.

How that martyr's crown must chafe!

Hush now. Hush. I was where I needed to be. I was doing what needed to be done.

We would try to reach a post-station, a village, or a farmer's cottage for the night, but when this was not possible we pitched our tents in the wilderness. Our camps were simple, and offered the most basic of comforts, for we would spend but a few hours in them. Each day we would move on, forwards once more, and the wind and snow would quickly obliterate our traces. Those camps, which at first appeared to me to scarcely provide human comforts enough to sustain us, I came to regard as the most luxurious accommodation.

In truth I preferred them to many of the lodgings we found along the way, for they were free of vermin, and I was not required to share my sleeping space with strangers. There was always a fire in the camp, and always hot food. My guides and horsemen were men of the landscape we crossed. They were at home there. They did their best for me, though I know at times I slowed our progress woefully. Close by, the horses would dig at the snow in search of grazing, their thick skin and dense coats rendering them impervious to the cruel cold that worked its way through my many layers of clothing. At night they would close their eyes and rest standing. They always slept so, without cover or shelter. Indeed they appeared more at ease in the winter months than in the summer, when they were compelled to endure the relentless attentions of horseflies and mosquitoes. Our guides were natural horsemen and understood their animals. An English eye might have seen sternness in their treatment, but it was merely a lack of sentimentality. Despite this characteristic, Yuri, a Cossack and most excellent guide, was never without his huge black dog. The animal was scruffy and missing an eye, but Yuri assured us he would offer exemplary protection. He told many stories around the camp fire of how his companion came to lose its eye. Some involved wolves, others a bear, all painted the ragged creature in a heroic light.

My legs pained me greatly, even then. Months of travel, including weeks of horseback trek over difficult terrain, being jolted and bruised in a tarantass and on sledges, having one's limbs scraped and bashed against trees, all had taken their toll on my tender skin and muscles. I suffered contusions and abrasions, particularly on my knees and lower legs, caused by my horse bolting repeatedly into the deep forest, forcing himself where there was scarce room to pass. I was in places rubbed raw or sporting open wounds. My determination not to be dismissed as a weak and foolish woman made me reckless with my own health. Had I seen one of my patients in such a condition, the nurse in me would have chided them for their stubbornness. But a physician often makes a poor recipient of his own treatment. I had pressed on when I should have rested. Ignored the protestations of my own body when I should have heeded them. The results were such deep wounds and damaged tissue as I was unable to effectively remedy, so that my progress thereafter was to the loud and relentless accompaniment of pain.

At the end of each day I would sit gazing into the empty vista, too fatigued to speak or sometimes even think clearly, warming my hands around a cup of hot tea. I had become accustomed to the Russian way of serving the drink – black, strong, and sweet – during my time in Moscow and St Petersburg, but it tasted curiously different on the trek. I recall experiencing a dizziness and thickness of the head that was both unpleasant and unhelpful.

Having been a supporter of the temperance movement all my life, I did not recognise the symptoms of mild intoxication. It took a great deal of talking, in my halting Russian and increasingly urgent French, before I could convince them they must stop this practice, as it was against my beliefs and not beneficial for my health. I would sit with my back to the tent, seated on the reindeer skin which I used in a largely unsuccessful attempt to pad my saddle. My coat was also skin, the fur turned innermost, the hood pulled low. It was my habit to wear a woollen scarf tied about my face, so that all that could be seen were my eyes. My one good feature, my mother used to say. Might it have made her happy, then, to see me so covered? I doubt it. I did not cut a pleasing figure. The coat – to which I am certain I owe my life, such was the depth of the cold at nights on the Siberian plains – was so thick and long and heavy that I was unable to bend my knees sufficiently to mount my horse, and at times I had to be lifted into the saddle, or onto the sledge, by my guides, in the most undignified manner. At such times I told myself that dignity was a luxury I was fortunate to have known, and I should not pine for it. How much dignity did the lepers have when their families abandoned them to the forest? How much dignity was there in a disease that rendered a person disfigured and reviled? It was for them I made that journey. Nothing I endured could compare to the lives they suffered. God had blessed me with a strong constitution, a quick mind, and a purpose. I had no business complaining.

In the spring of 1890, St Petersburg was filled with blossom. The trees along the banks of the Neva were doubled by their reflections in the sun-spangled water of the river. The city looked very fine, and I recall thinking, on the day I arrived, that any country in which such a place existed would not knowingly allow its people to suffer. This was a place of light, and fresh air, and life. Its people were vibrant, welcoming, strong. They could not leave their fellow Russians to the mercy of a disease so terrible as leprosy. Surely here I would find support for my mission. The Tsarina had agreed to see me, that was the first step in a journey of many thousand.

Her Imperial Majesty Tsarina Maria Feodorovna, Empress of all the Russias. Such a name to live up to! She liked to call me Katerina.

In this room there is often quiet, but never silence. At night, the unremarkable sounds of the hospital are muted by slumber, by the hour, by the dark, it seems. But they are sounds still. Footsteps outside my door, marking brisk strides along the corridor. Soft moans or muffled snores of neighbouring patients. And whispers.

Many whispers. Not all of them audible to anyone other than myself. At times there are gaps between these noises, but each one is merely a hiatus, and as such it contains the chiming anticipation of the next, imminent sound. So there is no silence here, where I lie, waiting for my body to relinquish its grasp on life. Will there be silence when I am with Him? Will there be no need for anything so clumsy as sound? Will He still lay his wishes upon my thoughts as He has done all my long life? I do hope so. I do yearn to be with Him.

By the time my mother and I arrived in New Zealand my sister's condition had worsened considerably. We had made the slow journey harried by the urgency of knowing dear Annie might not live to see our arrival. How long it was since we had been together, and what sad circumstances would reunite us. The consumption that had claimed my father had her in its icy grasp and would not now release her until it was into God's own care.

Wellington was a pleasant enough place, but for me then it meant only Annie, only her, only her bedside and her fading. When father died our family had been scattered across the globe in search of a living. And of course the disease would not let her slip quietly from this life. The little house in which she had been living her unremarkable life contained an atmosphere devoid of hope, tainted by the smell of encroaching death, heavy with the weight of sorrow. My mother found herself unable to endure witnessing the fierce attacks of coughing where her child was compelled to fight for every breath, and took herself off to another part of the house. She would visit only when Annie was calmer and resting in a laudanum-laced slumber. Mother would sit and hold her hand, stroking her daughter's skin and humming to her softly. I do not know if Annie was aware of her presence, but I convinced our mother that she was, and saw my heartsore parent draw some comfort from that.

She was sitting thus when Annie died. My poor sister had spent a long, embattled night, and needed only a little medication to bring about sleep. Her body was failing, her heart worn out, her will diminished. I put the spoon to her blue-tinged lips and she smiled at me after she had sipped, though she had not the strength to speak.

'There, Annie,' I said, brushing her hair back from her damp brow with my palm. 'There. All shall be well.' Her smile did not falter. I knew she shared my deep faith, and that she was ready to go to Him. 'I will fetch Mother,' I told her.

And so we sat, one either side of the bed. Sisters. Mother and daughters. An hour passed thus. And another. And then Annie drew in a breath that she appeared never to release.

'Ooh!' my mother wailed, as if her passing was an unexpected thing, though of course it was not. She fell to silent weeping then. I urged her to pray with me, but she would not.

After the funeral there was the question of what we were to do. Mother was ill with grief, and I feared that the long sea voyage home would tax her beyond endurance. Better that we stay, at least until she regained her strength. And so it was that I took up the position of Superintendent Nursing Sister at the Wellington Hospital. It was a fine building, with good sized rooms and tall windows, and sufficient funds to provide more than adequate care for its patients. I was to be in charge of three wards, one surgical, one general, and one which would serve as a final place of care for its resident patients.

On my first morning I summoned the nursing staff to my office. I was to oversee all of the nurses, but my particular remit was to supervise the work and training of the newer recruits. In all, there were three of these more junior nurses, and nine more senior. I had them gather before the day shift started, so that I might introduce

11

myself. My office was large enough for all the nurses to stand while I gave a short speech. They were well-turned out and able to stand without fidgeting, though I sensed their apprehension.

'I am both delighted and honoured to have been appointed to this post,' I told them. 'It is a privilege to be asked to work at such a fine and well regarded hospital as the Wellington. From what I have been told, I am to take charge of a nursing team every bit as excellent as the hospital itself. This comes as no surprise to me, for it is the nurses that make the hospital, not the other way around.' The women before me relaxed a little beneath such praise. I did not give it lightly. I believed it to be deserved. 'You will, I hope, find me fair and approachable, though I will not tolerate sloppy work, nor laziness. A lazy nurse puts the health of her patients in jeopardy and it is her fellow nurses who must do the work she shuns. We shall work as a team, together, supporting one another. I trust you will feel able to come to me with any concerns you may have.' My aim was to put them at their ease, whilst still maintaining the formality befitting my post. Looking at the wary faces, however, I suspected it would take time to win their confidence. 'You may have heard a little of my nursing experience to date. I am happy to answer questions on that subject now. Better openness than rumour, I believe.' I waited. No one met my eye or was brave enough to speak. 'Come now, I won't bite,' I assured them. 'Or, if I do, there are plenty here who could dress the wound.' This at least drew a little laughter.

A nurse with pretty hair the colour of pale heather honey raised her hand. I nodded at her. 'Is it true, Sister, that you have met the great Florence Nightingale?' she asked.

'What is your name?'

'Rose, Sister. Rose Farley.'

'Well, Nurse Farley, I'm sorry to say I have never had that honour. I did, however, travel to the continent and serve as a war nurse shortly after her time in the Crimea. I went to Bulgaria, where I nursed in the Russian-Turkish war. Miss Nightingale's methods were already in evidence there, and the use of them saved lives, of that there is no doubt.'

'What was it like?' Nurse Farley went on. 'Being near to the battle and nursing those poor soldiers, I mean, were you close enough to hear the cannon?'

'Indeed we were.'

'I should have been terrified!' she said, and others muttered their agreement.

'There was not time for terror,' I told her. 'When you are nursing in such circumstances each moment is reduced to the wounded soldier in front of you. His pain, his suffering, and what you can do about it. Beyond that, there is no room for one's own fear.' I stepped out from behind my desk and walked in front of the nurses as I spoke. 'You are aware of the dangers, of course. That awareness lingers in your mind, and perhaps it is what keeps you safe. You are reminded with every limbless patient, every youthful face imploring you for help, just how violent and terrible a place you have come to. The hospitals themselves are beyond the reach of the cannon, but you hear them still, they are so incredibly loud. The thunder of the artillery becomes as normal to you as the sound of a busy street. The stink of cordite as familiar as the aroma of baking bread or the smell of a farmyard. What before you could not comprehend, becomes the rhythm by which you live your life. And if you are asked to go forward to a field hospital, onto the battlefield itself at times to help the fallen, then you can feel the heat of those explosions, the blast of the guns, and of course, the pitiful cries of the men. It is their voices you hear the most. It is for them that you are there. Though the mud drag at your feet, though chaos rain about your head, you seek them out, you take them God's word, and your skill as a nurse, and you do what you can.'

They were listening in quite a different way then, their minds whirling with the notion of finding themselves in such a place.

I stopped in front of Nurse Farley. Her clear blue eyes met mine, and I saw that she was moved by what she had heard.

'To be a war nurse is a noble calling,' I told her. 'But in the end, it is the hand you hold in yours as you do your work that matters. Not the circumstances or surroundings in which you hold it.'

My first meeting with the Tsarina was, I only later understood, typical of her thoughtfulness. She could have received me, as Queen Victoria had done, in a state room, seated while I stood, our introduction coldly formal, her aide taking notes, the distance between us maintained and underlined by every aspect of the meeting. But she did not. Instead she chose to have me shown into one of her favourite rooms in the Winter Palace. It could not have been called small, by any measure, but it was modest compared to others in that voluptuous building. I stood waiting for her, my own sombre, simple garments a foil for the ornate beauty and exquisite detail of the room. The windows faced south, and the late spring sunshine fell through them, setting the exotic rug aglow, making the gilt worked into the edges of the elegant furniture gleam and shine. The walls were covered in silk wallpaper depicting birds of bright plumage, green and blue, singing from leafy boughs. The ceiling, high, high above, was worked with more gold, its chalky whiteness like nothing so much as the pristine icing of a wedding cake. I made myself quite dizzy gazing upwards, so that when Maria Feodorovna entered the room my head swam as I dipped an unsteady curtsey.

She held out her hand, her eyes warm with a smile.

'Nurse Marsden!' she exclaimed, her voice sweet, even a little girlish, as if discovering me where I was meant to be was the most pleasant of surprises. 'I am so very pleased that you have come to me,' she went on, 'and that you have given me the opportunity to be a part of your tremendous mission.' Her English was excellent, softly accented with the music of the Russian language. I knew she would more usually have conducted such meetings in French, and was grateful not to be put at such a disadvantage. It would have been a stilted conversation indeed, had we to rely on my poor skills as a linguist.

I reached tentatively for her outstretched fingers, uncertain as to the protocol regarding touching the Empress of Russia, but I need not have concerned myself. The Tsarina clutched my hand in hers and gestured for me to rise, before leading me to a little table and chairs by the window. She took the seat facing the sun, and indicated I should sit opposite her. Even in this small gesture she showed her kindness; for with my back to the sunlight my own awkwardness was not highlighted. Instead I could look upon her – and she was surely accustomed to the gaze of others – and remain comfortably in shadow.

A liveried servant, his spotless hose and braided jacket matching the decor of the room, held the door open for two maids, who scurried in with trays of tea things, followed by a further manservant whose job it was to carry aloft upon a gilded tray an intricately fashioned silver samovar. These things were set on the table between us with no small ceremony. The Tsarina quickly waved the servants away, content to serve me herself!

As she poured hot tea into glass and silver cups she questioned me about my proposed journey. Even now, thinking of it, I recall how that simple action prompted another memory, though not a pleasant one. I had been watching my mother pour tea as we sat in the small living room of our home in New Zealand. Mama was still frail with grief, and her hand shook as she held the teapot. There came a knock at the door and, the maid being out, I went to answer it.

On the doorstep I found a smartly dressed young man of wiry

build. He had about him a restless energy and a wariness in his eyes. He raised his hat, though the polite gesture clearly cost him.

'Miss Marsden?' he asked. 'Miss Kate Marsden?' He did not wait for me to respond before continuing. 'Desmond Mackintosh of the *New Zealand Times*.'

He took out a notebook and pencil. I resisted the desire to close the door upon him.

'What can I do for you, Mr Mackintosh?'

'I am writing a piece regarding your proposed work for the lepers.'

'My plans are as yet unformed, though my intention is a mission to India, or possibly the outcasts in Siberia.'

'Quite so. You are acquainted with my cousin, I believe. Miss Jessy Brodie?'

This put me on my guard. I withdrew from the threshold a little, and as I did so I noticed that the doorstep was cracked and less than safe. A legacy, perhaps, of the earthquakes to which the country is subjected. I felt then that the very ground on which I stood, in that place and in my life, might not be stable.

I responded to his query. 'Jessy and I share a passion to do work that will help those abandoned by their own communities through the scourge of leprosy.'

'And she has been very generous in her support, has she not?' His tone was sharp.

'It is necessary to raise funds if we are to progress our plans at all.'

'My sources tell me you claim to have monies promised by wealthy philanthropists, rich businessmen, even royalty. The truth is you have no benefactors, nor any funds available, save those you take from vulnerable women. Women you exercise an unholy hold over. Women you manipulate, caring nothing for their reputations or their financial security, as long as you get what you want. Is that not the truth of it, Miss Marsden?'

'Nurse Marsden? A little sugar?'

And there I was again, in the Winter Palace, with the person who understood my mission more clearly than anyone else ever had. She handed me the glass cup. 'You aim to travel far to the east, I understand. To Yakutsk?'

'And beyond, Your Imperial Majesty. That is to say, beyond the city itself, further into the province.' I sipped the tea, breathing in the aromatic steam which helped both clear my thoughts and soothe my taut nerves.

'How I envy you the freedom to travel to such a magical place, to experience such magnificent wilderness.' Her comment made me smile. Seeing this, she asked, 'You're laughing at me. Do you think me insincere?'

'Oh no, Majesty! It is simply that my mother would be astonished to hear I have the envy of an empress!'

She laughed lightly at this. 'Katerina – may I call you that? – what sights you will see! Such adventures! And I understand you are to write a chronicle of your expedition.'

'As a means to raise funds for the hospital we hope to build, yes.'

'I am certain it will be a marvellous book.' She was thoughtful for a moment and then continued. 'Such a pitiless disease, by all accounts, anything that can alleviate the suffering of those afflicted by it is to be welcomed.'

'It is heartening to hear such sentiments from you, Your Majesty. Were you to lend your support to my endeavour, well, the effect would be immeasurable.'

'The people you encounter on your journey will be impressed by you, Nurse Marsden. By your courage and your charity.'

'I am sustained by God's love, Majesty. It is He who sends me where I am to go.'

'But, tell me, why Siberia? I know that you have nursed the sick and the wounded in many places around the world. And alas, there are many countries besides our own who have lepers among them. What is it that compels you to travel to a place so little known, and so inaccessible?'

I hesitated. It is not a simple thing, to tell of a miracle.

Surely you were afraid, out there, so far from civilisation, alone with only guides and soldiers, horsemen, peasants. Any woman would have been afraid at times.

Why would any of those who had agreed to help me do me harm?

You were beyond the reach of propriety, of law.

If you think that you do not understand people. The men who acted as my guides did so willingly. They were paid for their services. We treated one another with respect. Why do you imagine them to be without morality? Without restraint?

But who would have known, if they had behaved... inappropriately? It would have been their word against yours.

Their word? We did not have so much as a common language. For many months I was without a translator. We travelled in a spirit of fellowship. Once somebody agreed to help me they took upon themselves a care for what it was I was trying to do. We overcame the obstacles of different languages, of my being a woman, of our differing cultures. These things were incidental, matters to be dealt with simply and quickly. Our journey was arduous, the terrain and weather extremely testing. Why would we do anything to make our circumstances more difficult?

Men can be... opportunists, can they not? And some were drinkers, you said as much in your journal.

A man may drink without losing all sense of what is right and what is wrong.

Some may.

I promise you, though they may not have been born such, each and every one of those who accompanied me on my journey behaved as a gentleman, beyond reproach.

Don't you think that strange?

I do not.

Could it be they had very singular reasons for taking so little interest in the fact that there was a lone woman among them?

I do not understand the point you are trying, rather rudely if I may say so, to make.

Truly? Do you truly not understand?

My first ball at the Winter Palace was an experience to match any in my life for dazzling spectacle, and was as strange to me as any custom I later encountered on the far side of the wilderness. Everything about the building, and in particular the ballroom, seemed designed expressly to make one feel insignificant. The scale was grander than could ever be necessary, wilfully so, one might say. Up until my visit to St Petersburg I had believed all such splendour reserved for the glory of God as demonstrated in the construction of cathedrals. I confess I was uncomfortable within the palace when I brought this comparison to mind. Did the Tsar who ordered its design set himself so high? Was I in some way acknowledging this lofty status by being there? Of course, I was. There was no escaping the fact. I satisfied my conscience by reminding myself of the reason that had taken me to such a place. The ball was to find sponsors for my mission, to raise money for the cause of the lepers in Yakutsk and establish a hospital and colony for them. All around me were men and women of wealth and influence, summoned by the Tsarina herself for my benefit. I must not quail. Though I felt near overwhelmed by the press of people, by the sophistication of the occasion, by the company of such society, I must be bold, I must hold fast to my purpose. At the far end of the ballroom the orchestra were taking their seats. Soon there would be music and dancing. Would I be compelled to dance also?

'Katerina? Katerina?' The Tsarina's voice reached me through the hubbub. I turned to see her making her way through the throng with ease as her adoring subjects bowed, curtseyed, or stepped back in haste to allow their Empress to pass. She was wearing a gown of cream, encrusted with pearls and gold stitching. The cut of it was glamorous yet decorous, and the colour and fabric showed off the lustre of her skin to best advantage. Her dark hair was piled high upon her head and crowned with a tiara of diamonds that caught the light as she moved. She wore a matching necklace and earrings. On many, such ostentatious jewels would have seemed vulgar, but on Maria Feodorovna they appeared somehow right. Somehow fitting. As if they were an outward manifestation of her shining soul.

'Here you are!' she exclaimed, taking both my hands in hers. Through the softness of her gloves I could feel her delicate fingers, but her grip was firm. 'Come, there is someone longing to meet you.' She led me away to the far side of the room. How my heart raced to be seen traversing the ballroom hand in hand with the Tsarina. What must people have made of this plain nobody in the simple gown who so took the Empress's attention? As we progressed she nodded and smiled and exchanged cheerful words with this baron and that duchess, effortlessly and expertly. At last we reached an unassuming man, not mature in years, and yet without the bloom of youth upon him, tall, neatly turned out, and, judging by the high colour of his face, as uncomfortable as was I in such a place.

The Empress beamed at him. 'Nurse Marsden, allow me to present Count Andrea Dimitri Kristov. He has travelled all the way from Vladivostok to be here today, so enamoured is he of your cause.'

But when I looked at the count, when I looked at him looking at Maria Feodorovna, I knew that it was not a passion for my mission that had seen him drag himself halfway across Russia; it was his passion for the Tsarina. Indeed he regarded her with such puppy-like adoration I was embarrassed for him. For both of them. The Tsarina, naturally accustomed to such uncloaked expressions of devotion, contrived not to notice at all. It struck me then that I must not shrink from the business of talking of my plans. There was nothing to be gained from being reticent, and perhaps much to be lost.

'I am heartened, Count,' I said, offering him my hand, 'that you have made time to come here and learn of my mission. The Empress tells me there are many philanthropists such as yourself in Russia.'

He was obliged then, to turn his attention to me. He bent low over my hand.

'Nurse Marsden, when the Tsarina told me of your intentions, well, I could not stay away. Such a laudable cause. Such bravery on your part, to undertake a journey of the scale and difficulty yours will inevitably be.'

'I cannot allow geography to be a bar to my work, Count.'

'Indeed, but even so, I cannot help but be concerned for your safety. For a woman to travel over such wilderness...'

'Do you think me too frail, Count? Do I appear frail to you?'

He blustered. 'Why no, that is to say...surely you will allow the route is long and hazardous?'

'I do not believe my sex to be a hindrance, nor people's objection to it to be the greatest obstacle I will face,' I told him. I noticed that our conversation had begun to draw the attention of others. Of course many stood close to be near to the Tsarina, but now still more were turning, pausing in their own conversations to listen to ours. 'Where God sends me I must go,' I said. 'Those afflicted with leprosy suffer terribly; surely it is up to those of us blessed with good health to do what we can? The afflicted must not be left beyond the comfort of Christian charity.'

At this Count Kristov's expression hardened and I sensed he had taken my remark as a slight, if not against him personally, then against his fellow Russians.

'We are not all at liberty to devote our lives to a cause, Nurse Marsden, however worthy. You must allow that the Russian people are godly, and as caring for their fellow man as any you will meet elsewhere in the world.'

The Tsarina smiled. 'Dimitri, don't be so bristly. Nobody is suggesting you climb aboard a dog sled.'

While others laughed politely, the count didn't know whether to enjoy the Tsarina's gentle teasing or defend himself. His Empress saved him.

'We all have our part to play in God's work,' she went on, addressing those standing near as well as Count Kristov. 'We are blessed to have such a fearless champion as Nurse Marsden. We should be grateful that because of her we are not required to endure the hardships and dangers of a long journey across wild county. Instead we can offer her our support. I know many of you came here tonight to do just that.'

There was a general murmur of assent. A lady with ostrich feathers in her hair spoke up.

'Nurse Marsden, are you not afraid to travel so far alone?' she asked.

'I shall not be alone. I shall have my friend Ada Field with me, who speaks excellent Russian. And of course I shall have guides and men hired to assist in transporting our supplies.'

The gentlewoman shook her head. 'But you will not have a husband with you,' she pointed out.

'Alas, not having one of my own, that would be difficult.' I smiled and then added, 'Unless of course I could find someone willing to lend me theirs.'

There was a burst of laughter from the gathering. The woman with the feathers flicked her fan in the direction of a tall, pale man. 'Oh, Madame Marsden, take mine, do!' she laughed. Her husband took the joke happily.

'I'll go!' he cried. 'And I'll shoot a bear for you, Natalia, how would you like that?'

Beside him a bespectacled man piped up. 'Well, with Pierre to see to the bears, that only leaves ten thousand miles of snow and forest, packs of wolves, frozen rivers... not to mention the damn Cossacks!'

'Hey!' objected a Cossack to his left. 'I'd like to see you in snow shoes, Ivan.'

I sought to capitalise on this good-humoured banter.

'I will happily take whomever is moved to come with me, but this will be no hunting trip,' I warned. 'There will be no time for sport or recreation. Yes, the men with me will be armed against bears and wolves, but for our protection only. I myself will carry a pistol.'

The Tsarina gasped. 'Oh, Katerina,' she said, slipping into that dear pet name she had chosen for me, and by doing so granting me high status indeed in the eyes of those present, 'I have such a picture of you in my mind now!'

The count objected. 'A woman with a pistol in charge of a gaggle of wild men in a desolate part of the country? Ha! Madame, you will be telling us next you plan to wear breeches.'

I shrugged and met his eye. 'How else am I to ride astride?' When there were gasps at this I went on. 'To attempt to ride spirited

Siberian ponies side-saddle for two thousand miles through dense *taiga* would be folly indeed. Yes, I shall appear outlandish, ungainly, no doubt, in my curious garb, but I care not about my appearance. And yes, I shall carry a gun at my hip, for if I am charged by a bear or challenged by a wolf I will not wait for a man to come to my rescue. Those niceties as protect us in comfortable society are not to be relied upon in such a place. I will not be taken, like a package, to meet those I propose to save. How will they look upon the instrument of God's will if she is delivered to them like a sack of potatoes, helpless, unable even to care for herself?' The frivolous nature of the moment had altered subtly, and I knew now that I had gained their interest and attention. 'For finding the lepers will be only the beginning. I must convince them that I am able to help them. Just as I must persuade the people who have cast them out that I am to be trusted. I must earn that trust.'

Another woman stepped forward to study me closely. 'Tell me, Nurse Marsden, how will you do that? You cannot speak Russian, nor, I suppose, the languages of those in such faraway places. You are a woman from another country, not known to anyone. How will you bring them to your way of thinking? After all, nobody likes to be told how to look after their own, do they?'

'You make such good points, madam,' I told her, 'I am tempted to ask you to accompany me as my spokeswoman. In fact, as you might imagine, I have given this matter a great deal of thought. Of course I shall require the services of Ada as translator, but beyond that, I believe that everywhere the word of God is spoken. I truly believe that people will see that what I am trying to do is to help them. I wish not only to rescue those outcast lepers who suffer in such terrible circumstances, but to show their families, their communities, that there is another way. I aim to locate a place where a hospital may be built for all sufferers of the disease. There will be permanent homes there for them, as well as a church, of course. This is my vision. And with the help of people such as yourselves, and with the blessing of the Tsarina, and with God's guidance, this is what I shall bring about!'

'Brava!' cried the woman with the feathers, clapping her gloved hands, and her husband took up the cry. Soon there was a clamour of good wishes and hurrahs, and all were caught up in the excitement of that golden, hopeful wish I would clasp to my heart across half the length of Russia.

At that moment, the orchestra struck up a lively waltz. A collective cry of delight went up and people eagerly took their partners. Count Kristov invited me to dance and I happily agreed.

'Miss Marsden? Are you awake?'

The nurse who brings my breakfast on a heavy tray does not wait for an answer. She swiftly and efficiently puts the tray down, helps me to sit up, rearranging my pillows so that I do not tip out of bed, and then places the breakfast before me.

'Would you like me to do that for you?' she asks as I clutch at my spoon.

'Thank you, no. Porridge is something I can still manage,' I tell her.

She notices the sweet peas in their vase beside my bed.

'Oh, how lovely,' she says, enjoying their perfume. 'Did Miss Norris bring them in for you?'

'She may have.' In truth I cannot recall who brought them, or indeed when they were brought. I stare at them and try to bring the moment to mind, but all that will come is 'pink' 'blue' and 'smell'. 'They are not yellow,' I say at last. 'The other flower was yellow.'

'Other flower?' she asks absentmindedly as she holds my wrist to measure my feeble pulse.

'The one I went to find. It was yellow.' I want to tell her more but forming the words aloud is so very difficult. I do remember that flower. It had no smell, or at least, no perfume. Rather a plain little thing. I can see it clearly in my mind's eye. I close my eyes for a better view. Small, woody stemmed, an unremarkable thing. And yet I had set so much store by it. As many others had done before me.

All nurses quickly become accustomed to working long hours, and the work is fatiguing. A nurse who is employed near the battlefield, however, cannot reckon upon schedules and times marked down for rest. War will not so conveniently shape itself to one's ideal work pattern, so that at the end of a twelve-hour shift on the post-operative ward I found myself called upon to assist in the surgical ward due to a failed attack that had left many wounded. By the time I reached the building that served as the nurses' quarters my only thought was of sleep. It is a curious thing to discover then that a person can pass beyond extreme tiredness into a sort of somnambulist state, where both body and mind are too restless and weary to cease their activities. On a muggy night in Constantinople I was in just such a condition, so that instead of going into the low building that housed the dormitory I sat upon the step outside. I did not look at anything around me, nor did any thought occupy my brain. I simply sat, as orderlies, nurses, soldiers and doctors hurried past.

It was as I remained seated there that Dr Calvino emerged from the ward door opposite to take the air. The young doctor, Italian by birth, had travelled extensively, and had the look of a man who would be at home wherever he was. He stretched his tired arms to the sides and rolled his head to release the tension in his neck. Next he shrugged his shoulders once, twice, three times. Finally he raised his arms high, interlocking his fingers, stretching until small popping noises could be heard. There was not a trace of self-consciousness about him as he went through his little routine. He took several deep, slow breaths and then walked over to me.

'May I join you, Nurse Marsden?' he asked, indicating the space beside me. When I nodded he lowered himself heavily onto the stone step. For a moment we sat together in silence, watching and yet not watching the business of those around us. 'A fine spot you have here,' he said.

'I was on my way to bed.'

'Ah, bed,' he gave a dry laugh. 'I have taken to using the chair in my surgery,' here he waved an arm in the direction of the ramshackle building to our left. 'I find it easier to get up from an uncomfortable chair than a soft bed. Not that I have spent much time sleeping since the latest skirmishes. I think the enemy believes they will defeat us by depriving our army of the chance to either sleep or eat.'

'An effective tactic,' I replied.

He nodded and was quiet again for a while.

I was on the point of getting to my feet when he asked, 'Have you seen the lepers brought in yesterday? They have been put in the tent behind the morgue.'

'I have seen them, yes. I spent some time applying fresh dressings to their sores and wounds. I was told they were found during the search of a nearby village.'

'Some of the worst cases I've seen.'

'You are familiar with the disease?'

'Oh yes, I've seen it all over. Leprosy is not a respecter of borders.' He shook his head. 'It is a pitiless thing. So disfiguring, so ugly, so relentless. There is a man in there with neither feet nor hands, and his wife has been blind for two years. The others with them are covered in sores, as are they. It is hard to look upon them, poor creatures.'

27

I bridled at this description. It pained me to hear innocent sufferers reduced to something less than human. 'They are all God's children,' I reminded him.

He looked at me coldly. 'Then God is a bad father.'

'He will not abandon them.'

'Do you not think He has done so already? Where was God when the old man lost his hands? Where was He when darkness fell upon that woman forever?'

I did not allow myself to enter into an argument, for I knew Dr Calvino to be a fine surgeon and a caring man. He was tired beyond reason, and nothing brings a medical person closer to despair than being faced with a patient whose condition confounds him.

'It is not uncommon to have one's faith tested in testing circumstances,' I said.

'Tested?' He shook his head again. 'Rightly or wrongly, Nurse Marsden, I put my faith in science now. It will be medicine that rids the world of leprosy one day, not God.'

It was my turn to look at him. I had only recently been called upon to nurse lepers, and I was appalled at their suffering and the lack of an effective treatment. 'Do you believe there is a cure?' I asked the doctor.

'Of course there is. Nature does not supply the poison without its antidote, nurse, you must know that. Unfortunately, nature has also seen fit to leave it to us to find the thing for ourselves.' He leaned close to me, suddenly intense and animated. 'There was a soldier here a few weeks ago, a Russian grenadier, whose family came originally from Siberia. He told me where but I do not recall the name of the place, it was somewhere far from anywhere else. The type of place nobody knows of unless they are born there. Anyway, he told me that the shamans there, they grow a plant, a flower, he said, and this flower, it has the power to heal a leper.' He slapped his thighs and leaned back. 'Imagine that, Nurse Marsden. Something beautiful that can defeat all the ugliness in that tent over there.' He stood up then, rubbing the small of his back as he did so. 'It is a thing to dream about, is it not? If only we had the time to dream,' he added with a wry smile.

At last we were in the final stages of preparation for our journey. Our time in Moscow had been one of such sociability, as I attempted to raise awareness of my mission, that it was hard to imagine we would soon be in the wilderness and might not hear a word of English spoken for many months. My dear and stalwart young friend, Ada Field, was every bit as excited as myself as the moment of our departure drew near. Indeed, amid all the perils and travails and sickness and hardships of those two years, the short time spent amassing supplies for the journey was a merry interval. As new friends and supporters rallied to the cause, there was an atmosphere of almost festive anticipation, much like the preparations for a wedding!

And as with a wedding, food occupied our minds a great deal. The apartments from which we were to soon depart became filled to bursting with our provisions and necessities. Boxes, crates and cases stood stacked in every available space. There were suggestions from all sides as to what would not spoil and what would provide nourishment and flavour, with many mentions of bottled fruit and potted meats. At last we settled upon tinned fish, tea, some bread (mostly of the black variety) and biscuits. The happiest supplement to this I had brought with me from England – fifty pounds of plum pudding. Always a favourite of mine, it will keep beautifully in cold weather, and I hoped it would provide a welcome lift, as well as perhaps a much needed taste of home. Besides food, there was also a good supply of candles and wicks. More important perhaps than these were the clothes I had ordered, after much deliberation. It was as I dressed myself in these that Ada, who had been out to collect yet another parcel from the postal depot, returned.

'Goodness, Kate! Whatever are you wearing?' she asked, setting down the packages, a little out of breath. I was struck by how delicate she was then and experienced a pang of worry. Was I wrong to have chosen such a slight young thing to accompany me on my arduous mission? Should I have selected a more robust person? But then, there were not many willing to take on the job of interpreter on such a journey. She picked up one of the foundation garments. 'And what can this be?'

'My dear Ada, that is an essential part of our winter wear. The Siberian tundra will test us in many ways. At least the cold we can do something about. Here, I have a set for you,' I told her. She gasped at the sight of the unfeminine combinations which came only in an unflattering shade of oatmeal. 'Come along,' I threw them to her. 'A dress rehearsal is required!'

We proceeded to clothe ourselves in the entire outfit that would be our protection against the unforgiving elements we would face in the first months of our journey. I had spent a great deal of time selecting what we would need. The resulting ensemble comprised of a layer of Jaeger undergarments, on top of which was a loose type of body lined with flannel; gentlemen's hunting stockings; Russian felt boots; an eider-down ulster the sleeves of which reached to cover the hands, and the fur collar of which reached up to protect the head. Over this came a sheepskin, its own hood covering the fur one, and extending down to one's feet. The whole was topped off with a *dacha*, which is a heavy garment of reindeer skin. We added balaclavas to the ensemble, the heat of the room insufferable in the things. The tiring effort of dressing ourselves in such bulky and outlandish clothes brought on a bout of giggling which only resulted in rendering us weaker. By the time we stopped to consider our reflections in the looking glass we were a red-faced pair indeed. I confess I scarcely recognised the wrapped and swaddled creatures who stared back at us, so grown in size and bulky in shape were they, with faces all but obscured save the eyes. Ada could contain her mirth no longer and gave way to unrestrained laughter. I, too, fell to laughing so heartily that we were both relieved when the maid appeared and we could implore her to help us out of our suffocating garb.

It is easy to imagine we were over-clad, but experience was to show that we wore not a stitch of clothing for which we would not ultimately be deeply grateful.

It was in this spirit of gratitude that I went to the Tsarina's private chapel in her Moscow home. Her royal residence there could not match the splendour of the Winter Palace, but still it had many a grand place of worship. It was to her own preferred chapel, however, that she directed me during my stay, and I found such solace there. The traditions of the Orthodox church determined that it still be an opulent space, however modest in proportion. There was much by way of gilding, and paint of such hues as to seem to have their own light, even beneath the soft flicker of candles and scant daylight through the heavily decorated windows. I was not interested in such adornments, however. I wanted only a quiet place to pray, to talk to God, to offer Him my humble thanks for bringing me to the start of my mission so well supported and set up. He had answered my pleas for help, and now I could set about His work. As I knelt on the cold flagstones I kept my eyes tight shut against the pretty distractions of the chapel and thought only of Him. There I stayed for over an hour until the chill began to work to my bones and my knees could kneel not another moment.

By the time the porters had carted all our supplies onto the correct platform it was almost time for our train to depart. The biting cold of the Moscow winter was lessened somewhat by the heat of the great engine as it drew its fiery breath in the confines of the station.

'No!' I admonished a porter, 'I shall keep the valise with me. And the hamper also. The rest must be loaded in the luggage compartment, but I will not part with my valise. Where can Ada have got to?'

I scanned the platform, searching the throng of travellers and loved ones who were embarking or saying their farewells. At last I spotted Ada, running, one hand holding her hat to her head, the other excitedly waving a newspaper.

'Ada! Make haste.'

'Oh, Kate...' The girl was out of breath as she folded the pages of the paper to show me an article. 'Look, do! You are famous, Kate. Everyone knows of your mission now, see?'

There was a small piece on the bottom right hand corner of the second page, showing a poor picture of myself, which was not of interest to me. More important was the headline, which being in Russian, I could not decipher.

'What does it say, Ada?'

'*Nurse's Mission to Save Siberian Lepers!* Let me read it to you.'

'Once we are aboard. Come, it would be a sorry start to our great journey to be left upon the platform,' I said, ushering her onto the steps of the train. In truth, I could not bear to have her read the article then. I felt the need to be under way, to wait until there was no turning back before hearing what the Moscow journalists had seen fit to say about me. For I had suffered at the hands of newspapermen before. It had begun in New Zealand. I feared even then I would never be free of their scorn and hounding.

Adventuress! The pages of the *New Zealand Times* had trembled in my hands as I read the damning headline. Such vitriol. Such venom directed at me but finding expression in the most public of ways.

'Kate,' my mother fidgeted on the chaise behind me, 'what takes your attention? Can there be anything of note to read in such a paper? I am told it contains little more than salacious gossip and wild storytelling.'

I had flattened my copy of the newspaper onto the table in front of me, the better to let the light from the window fall upon it, and to prevent my mother noticing how my hands shook. I ran my palm over the page, as if I might rub out those words which condemned me.

The True Nature of Pious Kate Exposed! went the story, penned by one Desmond Mackintosh. That name was already familiar to me, though I did not know then how far and how relentlessly the journalist was to dog my footsteps.

"At last the 'Good Kate Marsden' has revealed herself to be what this writer has always suspected: a self-serving creature, devoid of scruples, stony of heart, and with nothing more nor less in her sights than fame and fortune! She would not have it, of course, that her intentions are anything but of the highest altruistic sort. That she seeks only to do good works and help those unfortunates who suffer. She would like us to believe this, oh yes! Yet when I stood before her and questioned her directly a direct answer was what she would not supply. How did she plan to finance her 'mission' to save 'her lepers' (!) in some far flung place? Whose purse would she raid? Where were her philanthropical backers? Though she gave no reply to these challenges I knew too well, for has she not already emptied the bank account of my own cousin, a gentle woman and fine nurse known for her genuine selflessness and good works? This, I can attest, is fact, and a cold one at that. I went further, how was it, I asked, that the Godly Miss Marsden

had profited so handsomely from her own recent 'accident'? This fall at her place of work had resulted in a handsome payout by her employers and not one but two insurance claims! The brazen woman shouted me down, questioning my facts, and taking herself out of my reach so that I might not press her further upon the matter...

'Kate,' my mother would not be ignored, 'have you no better use for your time?'

I closed the newspaper, folding it tight and small so that I might more easily remove it from the room without drawing her further attention to it. 'Forgive me, Mama.' I got to my feet. 'I shall fetch us tea. The day is not yet too hot, shall we take it in the garden?'

I succeeded in distracting my mother and she was content to chatter on about inconsequential matters as I helped her outside and settled her in a shady seat beneath the *pohutukawa* tree, its red blooms glowing where the sun touched them. All the while my own mind was galloping forwards. I could not stay longer in New Zealand, that much was clear to me then. This man would not let me be. I might have seen his intention to ruin me at our very first meeting, for it was clear then he did not approve of my friendship with Jessy. How it must have galled him to see her take us into her home. I did not then believe, nor have I since, that he acted out of a sense of protection towards his cousin. Jessy was a shy creature, but perfectly able to know her own mind. No, his disapproval of me was deep-rooted, and that twisting plant of spite and loathing twined through him, heart and soul. Why do men so despise women when they cannot be as they would wish? What does it profit them to crush another person so needlessly and vindictively?

Whatever his true motives, the effect would be the same. He would not stop until he had my reputation in shreds, my hope of future employment dashed, my association with the St John's Ambulance dismantled, and no doubt my tenuous position in society taken from me. What would become of us then? What of Mama? What of Rose? Oh, Rose!

If I had harboured any notion of sledging being a gentle, effortless mode of travel, where one is borne across the smooth snow on swiftly gliding runners, pulled by horses with bells upon their harness, I was quickly disabused of it. The roads from Zlatoust – where we had disembarked from the train – were rugged and broken up due to the heavy traffic making its way to the Siberian February fair. Such was their condition that we progressed as if on a stormy sea, dipping and leaping through and over the troughs and ridges – bump, jolt, bump, jolt. Ada and I were lain atop our luggage in the 'hold' of the sledge, so encased in our heavy clothing as to be unable to properly bend or move into more comfortable positions. We were reduced to helpless cargo. So it was that we were thrown against the sides and roof of our cramped compartment. If my head was not hitting one solid surface it was hitting another. We were violently thrown forwards as the conveyance dived into a furrow, and then flung backwards as it lurched out again. Imagine our tortuous journey continued in such a way, hour upon hour, for miles in their thousands. We were bruised and battered, stiff and sore, our bodies and tempers both tested to their limits.

In addition there was the noise to contend with, as our driver saw it as an essential part of his work to shout and curse at his horses as he cracked his whip, urging them on to ever more reckless speeds. We would tear through villages, scattering unwary pedestrians as we raced by. When longed-for night came, still we travelled on. At one point I recall seeing the lights of houses set back from the road.

'Driver!' I called, desperation raising my voice sufficiently for him to be able to hear it. 'Ada, tell him we should stop awhile. We could take a short break and find refreshment in one of those houses. Tell him, Ada, please.'

Ada did as I asked, leaning forward with difficulty, raising her voice as best she could to translate my query and put it to the driver, struggling to hear his response as we were jostled and buffeted.

She sank back into the makeshift seating.

'There are no houses,' she informed me.

'But the lights...?' I gestured in the direction of the window.

Ada met my questioning look. Her voice was shaky as she replied.

'Sometimes, when the moon is bright, it can be seen to catch the eyes of the wolves and shine in just such a way.'

As if to underline her point there came then the unmistakeable note of a wolf signalling to his pack.

I looked again through the narrow window and could see that the lights I had mistakenly taken for indications of safety and habitation were in fact moving, following the tarantass, increasing their speed in a determined pursuit.

I, too, settled deep into the bedding on which we lay. I indicated the driver above and said to Ada, 'Be so good as to instruct the driver to go a little faster, would you?'

As we emerged through the doorway of St Thomas's church the worshippers of the Nelson area stepped into sharp sunshine, causing bonnets to be dipped and hats tilted against its glare. The warmth of the day was already bringing forth the scent of macrocarpa and spring bulbs. The path was gritty beneath our feet but was not yet the crumble of earth and dust it would become as the year progressed. My mother held my arm and I guided her down the porch step. She had aged visibly since Annie's passing, and no amount of New Zealand sunshine would give her back the years that losing yet another daughter had cost her.

'I have such a thirst,' she told me. 'Hymns have a way of drying the throat, I find.'

'But such lively singing,' I said, smiling over at Nell who walked on my mother's other side. 'A joy to hear, a delight to partake of, do you not think so, Nell?'

Nell nodded, her face radiant after an hour's worship, the blue of her gown and bonnet a shade that suited her so well that I thought for the first time that there was, after all, a prettiness about her, if only she knew how to bring it out.

'Uplifting,' she agreed, holding my gaze a fraction longer than was necessary and then blushing at having done so. She cast her eyes down suddenly, as if her feet were of the utmost interest to her. I was on the point of teasing her a little when I heard my name called and turning discovered the odious Desmond Mackintosh approaching, notebook in hand.

'Mr Mackintosh,' I affected a casual tone, though his presence never failed to irk me. 'Do not journalists observe the sabbath?'

'My profession compels me to go where I must, when I must, in order to seek the truth,' he loftily informed me.

'Ah, then here you are certainly in the right place,' I replied, and made as if to walk on. The man barred my path. I frowned at him. My mother looked confused, as did Nell.

'It is from you I must have it, Miss Marsden. If you would only answer my questions, put your side of the story...'

'I refuse to see myself as part of a *story*.'

'I insist that you are. And it is one I aim to tell, with or without your cooperation. Would you not rather defend yourself?'

'Such a question suggests I have done something reprehensible,

Mr Mackintosh, and yet here I am respecting the Lord's day, and here you are defiling it with your slander.'

'Kate,' my mother would be quiet no longer, 'who is this? What business does he have with you?'

'None at all, Mama. Nell, would you be so kind as to take my mother to the carriage? I will follow on directly.'

My mother began to protest, but Nell, seeing my determination, took her arm, and led her away. I strode off the path and across the churchyard, out of the reach of the straining ears of town gossips, the newspaper man trotting behind me. I knew we presented an unseemly and suspicious picture, but what was to be done about that?

I came to a halt at an elaborate grave topped with a stone angel, which I made as if to study to confuse any who might be observing us.

'This constant hounding will gain you nothing,' I told my persecutor. 'I have no wish to answer your questions.'

'You would have me write the story without chance of redress?'

'I would have you give it up altogether.'

He shook his head, a nasty smile doing nothing to improve his unimpressive features. 'Oh I shan't do that! I shall show you for what you are, show your true colours.'

I did not respond to this but waited to see what it was he thought he knew of me that could be so damning. I noticed the face of the angel had been damaged by weather so that there was a hole beneath one eye. I reached out and touched the ruined cheek. The stone felt rough and fragile under my fingertips.

Mackintosh, like most men of my acquaintance, enjoyed the sound of his own voice and the shape of his own reasoning. 'I will tell how you are ruthless, how you exploit friendships, playing up your famous history as a medalled war nurse, cajoling and bullying to get what you want, caring not whom you hurt.'

I refused to be provoked into a response, even though I seethed with indignation. He continued to the point I knew he had been working towards.

'Innocent, good-hearted people such as my own cousin.'

'Ah, dear Jessy. Such a good friend.'

'A friend you see fit to take advantage of. You avail yourself of her house, her money...'

'Both freely given, as she will tell you.'

'Given on the promise of what, will you tell me that, Nurse Marsden?'

I looked at him then. Saw his mean-minded expression. Saw that he was a man conflicted, for he could not bring me down without also risking his cousin's reputation. And he and I both knew it. When I still stayed silent he could stand it no longer, his temper, and his own nature, revealed as he hissed, 'Your kind! I will expose you. The world will know you for what you are!' He spoke with such suppressed force that his pencil snapped in his hand. He flung the splinters to the ground, turned on his heel, and stormed from the churchyard. I waited until I was certain I had regained my own composure completely before leaving to join Nell and my mother. With every step I told myself *He knows nothing. He cannot do me harm.* And yet I feared he would not stop until he could find a way.

There are days now when I wonder if it were not some other person who made that great trek. My frailty now, my diminished strength of will even, do not seem to belong to that bold, fearless creature who strode across the frozen snow of the Yakutsk province, or rode through the *taiga* for hours on end. Perhaps, after all, my traducers have the truth of it when they say I imagined and invented more than I actually accomplished. Perhaps my mind was as jumbled then as it is now. How can I know?

You did go, Kate. You trod every step of those miles, rode every twisting path.

You are certain, at least.

The greatest part of you was always your determination, and you had set your mind to finding those lepers in their icy tombs and forest gaols. No one could have stopped you.

Many tried. And when they could not, they sought to pour scorn upon my ventures.

Even when the hospital was built?

Even then.

The house of my childhood in Edmonton was ordinary, as indeed was my family. For it was not out of the ordinary to lose siblings to disease. Nor to lose a parent. The emotional impact of suffering the loss of a brother or sister is great, and leaves a sadness to carry though life. It cannot compare, of course, in practical terms, with the death of one's father. I find I can no longer summon his face in my memory, though I do remember his voice, for it was very deep, and had about it a rich timbre. He was a man of even temper, yet that voice would carry through the house. And then, one day, it fell silent. We were not a wealthy family, and yet we did not live in penury. A middle class existence such as ours brought with it its own expectations and demands. We were educated, boys and girls alike, though not at a school that would have elevated us in society. There was not money enough for that, nor for a private tutor. Our house was comfortable, but not grand. Even so, we had a cook, a maid, a nanny, a groom for the horses – for we had our own modest carriage – and a gardener. When my father died, all these things had to be kept up, and yet we were deprived of the means of paying for them.

My mother wore her widowhood as a badge of honour, and saw it as a condition she shared with our queen, and therefore something to be born proudly and stoically. Poverty, on the other hand, or even the contemplation of it, was too much for her mind to absorb. How could we not live as we always had? How could we dispense with a maid? And indeed, we had a duty to the girl, did we not? We could not simply turn her out. Mama's manner of facing up to our impending poverty was to berate all of us at home, loudly and often, reminding us that if we were not contributing to the household expenses we were a burden upon them. I was fourteen at the time my father died. I quickly learned that my childhood had ended that day. The youngest of eight, two of my siblings had already succumbed to consumption. Our new circumstances dictated that William, Annie, Joseph and Eleanor all leave home to make their own way in the world, so there were only two of us left with Mama. Annie sought to install herself into society, such as it was, in New Zealand. There being so much competition for a good husband at home, and none of us blessed with an abundance of prettiness, she considered the distance worth travelling. We lacked the connections in India so Annie had taken up an offer of accommodation on the far side of the world with a family friend in the hope of it leading to work or marriage. Such was the breadth of our choices. For me there was only one path to follow. I do not recall it ever being decided that I should become a nurse; it was simply all and ever that was meant for me.

Rose Farley was a natural nurse, if such a thing can be. She had a manner with the patients that put them at their ease. She was not, it must be said, the most skilled at the many tasks asked of her. Indeed some of her dressings were so badly applied that they had to be redone. But her ability to raise the spirits of the most frail patient was invaluable. It was not something that could be taught, and I believe it was, in itself, both a balm and a tonic to those who received it.

On one occasion I spied her sitting on the bed of an elderly patient. I was on the point of remonstrating with her for such unprofessional behaviour, but as I approached them I heard laughter. The two were sharing a joke, and I think it was the only time I saw real joy on that man's face in all the time he was under our care. When she saw me the young nurse jumped quickly to her feet.

'Sorry, Sister, I was just...'

I tried to look disapproving, but I know my expression must have given me away, for she smiled at me then, realising she was not in trouble after all. 'I'm sure you have duties to attend to, Nurse Farley.'

'Yes, Sister.'

'Hurry along now.'

She did so willingly, but not without a backward glance and a wink at the patient. A wink! She was fortunate not to have been observed by my predecessor, who would certainly have reprimanded her.

Later that same day I called her into my office. I remember her standing in front of my desk, her hands clasped behind her back. There was so much youthful energy about her, and a smile always tugging at the corners of her mouth.

'You are popular with the patients, Nurse Farley,' I told her, 'but do not allow that popularity to go to your head.'

'No, Sister.'

'There are other nurses here, less experienced than yourself, who are, quite frankly, more skilled than you. Do not set yourself up above them.'

'I wouldn't dream of it, Sister.'

'There is much you could learn from Nurse Wilson, for example. She is adept at administering injections, and her bandaging is first rate. You might take the time to observe her.'

'I will, Sister.'

She stood waiting a little restlessly, for it was the end of her shift, and she must have been eager to leave. She was a pretty girl, slender, with long limbs. I wondered, suddenly, where she went when she left the hospital. How did she fill her free time? I knew she lived in the nurses' quarters behind the hospital, but beyond that I knew nothing of her life. All at once I had a fierce curiosity, one that surprised me. I found myself asking, 'Do you enjoy your work here, Nurse Farley?'

'Yes, Sister, very much.'

'Your family is not from Wellington, I understand.'

'From Knatsford. Up north. It's not much of a place really. I prefer the city. That's why I chose to come to the Wellington Hospital.'

'You were tired of provincial life?'

'I wanted to travel, to see something more of the world. My father used to tease me, calling me Rambling Rose! He knew I longed to go somewhere, *anywhere* besides stuffy little Knatsford.' She hesitated and then looked at me curiously, 'Like you, Sister. You have been to so many exciting places, have you not? Turkey, India, Africa, the names alone sound tremendous. I can only imagine visiting such places. You've nursed in wars, right in the midst of battle...! What adventures you must have had.'

She smiled at me then, another of those joyful, bright smiles. In that instant I could not see her as a nurse, nor myself as her superior. I saw her only as a girl, full of wonder at life and what it had to offer her. I felt my composure fracture, and feared that in that moment she could see past my professional facade, through the veneer of the face I presented to the world, and into my heart's desires.

43

I stood up abruptly. 'War and nursing are not about adventures, nurse, as you will one day come to understand when you are sufficiently mature in your thinking.'

She dropped her gaze, the rebuke causing her to shrink from me in a minute altering of her stance. It was such a small change, but a telling one, and I hated myself for bringing it about.

'You may go, Nurse Farley.'

I stood watching her leave the room, and for some time after she had gone I simply stared at the closed door, waiting for my heart to return to a calmer, more sensible rhythm.

I remember the snow was black. The night sky was full of cloud, absent of the slightest hint of starlight, and yet the land beneath it appeared darker. It was a flat, matt blackness, and I had the sensation that if I were to fall forwards I would disappear into its fathomless depths.

Our guide indicated that we were to wait. The young Russian soldier, Vladimir, who had been sent to assist us, explained to Ada that the thaw was beginning, and so the ice would have to be tested before we dare travel across the frozen lake. It was past noon, and we had already endured several hours of bruising, jolting travel in the covered sledge. The horses stood and champed at their bits, their necks flecked with foam.

'Should we get out?' Ada asked me, leaning forwards to peer from the side of the sledge.

'Let us see what is decided,' I said.

In truth, the struggle of extricating ourselves from our conveyance in our heavy garments, and the necessary manhandling that would entail, was not a prospect I relished. I had no wish to put us through it pointlessly. I shuffled forwards so that I might watch the inspection of our proposed route. We were a party of fifteen, comprising our guides and porters, our loyal soldier, and ourselves. There were three heavy sledges. Our own was pulled by three bony horses who shared a bad temper that the driver wrestled with every mile. They had begun the day feisty and hard to manage, but the hours had quietened them, so that now they rested, heads low, glad of the break in their work. Through the sweat-steam that rose from their flanks I saw two of the guides walk onto the surface of the lake. Their method of testing appeared to me somewhat simplistic and extremely risky. They had no stick with which to probe or prod, but merely relied upon the reaction of the ice to their own weight. When they found an area they thought suspect, they jumped up and down a little to see if cracks would form!

'What is happening?' Ada wanted to know. 'If we sit here any longer my feet will surely freeze.' She started wriggling her legs as best she could whilst reclining in an effort to encourage circulation.

The guides shouted back to their fellows. There was much gesticulating and muttering. The soldier listened to what was being said and then returned to the sledge. As he relayed the information to Ada I watched the tension build in her expression.

'It seems the way forward is useable,' she explained to me, 'but only with care. We must disembark in order to lighten the load. They will also distribute some of the supplies from the sledges among the riding horses, and we are all to walk.'

'Walk? Are you certain?' I looked again at the expanse of lake ahead. The faint line of the nearside shore disappeared into the whiteness of the horizon, and I could neither see nor imagine an end to it. 'Ask him how long we will be on the lake. How many miles is it?'

Ada conversed further in Russian and was then able to tell me, 'He believes seven, perhaps eight. After that we take up another road on land and will be able to use the sledges again.'

'But our progress will be woefully slow. There can be no more than two hours of daylight left to us.'

'Apparently they consider the lake an easy path to navigate in the dark,' she said.

We fell silent, both of us keeping our fears to ourselves. At last I felt I must speak to reassure her.

'They are experienced guides, Ada. They would not press on unless they considered it safe to do so.'

'Vladimir tells me there is no other route,' she said. 'Or at least, only one that would involve retracing our steps for many miles. We would lose a great deal of time. They are determined to cross the lake, he says, whatever the risks.'

'Then we must join them in their determination.'

'Do you trust them, Kate? Truly?' There was such naked fear in her voice that I felt at once the burden of guilt, for it was I who had brought her to this dangerous place. Had she ever properly understood what she might face by accompanying me on my mission? Had I played down the risks?

I patted her thickly gloved hand with my own. 'God has sent us these men. He is with us, Ada.'

Vladimir and two of the guides assisted us in clambering out of the sledge. The afternoon was at least devoid of wind, so that we were not assailed by the frigid blasts that had swept us eastwards and northwards for so many days. There was, however, something deeply unsettling about such stillness. It may have been only that we were unaccustomed to it, but it was as if we were in the midst of an eery calm. The snow lying on the ground and clinging to the pine trees that fringed the lake near us subdued all sound and deadened the air somehow. Our breath puffed in front of us, the wetness of it freezing onto the scarves that we pulled across our faces.

The men worked for an interminable time unpacking and repacking the sledges and horses until the supplies were distributed to their satisfaction. At last the signal was given to move forwards. Our two fearless pathfinders went ahead, a gap was then left, with two more guides leading their horses, Vladimir, Ada and myself, then the first sledge, another gap, and so on. We were strung out over what was considered to be a safe distance, these gaps spreading the weight we were to inflict upon the ice. We all knew, though none of us said so, that this was also a tactic designed to minimise losses should the ice break.

For we two women the march was made more difficult because of our clothing. We had dressed for another journey in the sledge, wrapped against inactivity in the severe cold. We had anticipated hours of being conveyed over and through snow drifts, into and out of troughs and ditches, being battered and bashed as we were thrown this way and that. We had not envisaged walking, and our garments allowed us little freedom of movement. We waddled inelegantly, each step an effort. I saw Ada struggling as she held onto Vladimir's arm.

'It is a joy to be out of the sledge, do you not agree?' I asked her, my words mumbled through my scarf.

Ada puffed as she spoke, 'For now, it is, though I suspect I shall be glad to crawl back into it after seven miles of this!'

She left unspoken the fact that a distance that might ordinarily take two hours was sure to take more than double that in such circumstances as we found ourselves. How endless such time would seem with each step fraught with fear, our bodies poised to evade sudden calamity. How long, how far, could we hold ourselves in such readiness?

'At least we are warm,' I pointed out, though in truth the clammy warmth of exertion was not a pleasant trade even for the chilly inactivity of riding in the sledge.

We trudged on, every now and again halting in response to a raised hand from our lead guide. A tense few moments would pass and then we would continue. This was the pattern for over an hour, and as dusk descended we were still a fair way from the point where we could reach the far shore of the lake.

Suddenly, there came shouts from behind us. Turning, I saw the porters behind our sledge waving their arms and yelling to one another.

'What is it, Ada? What are they saying?'

Before she had time to respond I had my answer. The sound of ice cracking, as loud as a fork of summer lightning, cut through the thick air. A fissure appeared in the ice between our sledge and the men behind it. Everyone in the party stopped, standing motionless, fearing the least movement would provoke a catastrophe. I could clearly make out the jagged line of the break now. It zig-zagged for several yards, almost touching the feet of one of the porters, who held his horse's bridle and spoke soothing words to the animal while its nostrils flared.

The moment was but a hiatus.

The following second, all was noise and commotion and movement and panic. Two of the guides nearest the break turned and ran, one towards the shore, the other further out onto the lake. The driver leading our team of horses dragged them forwards at a frantic trot, so that we were compelled to stagger aside to let him and the sledge pass. Such a sudden movement caused me to fall, so that I lay helpless upon the ice. One of the riding horses gave way to its terror and bolted, two men running after it. I heard Ada scream as the fracture in the surface upon which we all now clung flimsily to life widened, black water lapping onto its edges. Those at the rear of the line fled back the way we had come. The riderless horse tore away so quickly that its pursuers had to give up and concentrate on saving themselves.

'Kate!' Ada called to me as she and Vladimir staggered to remain upright.

I tried to answer, but I had not the breath for shouting. I put all my strength into righting myself and forcing myself to get up. I was on my knees when I saw that the split in the ice now had a twin, and that both were travelling towards me.

I was aware of my name being shouted, and of curses and entreaties in several languages ringing through the heavy day. I knew I must run or be lost to the depths of the lake, and yet my legs would not move. As I looked up I saw one of the guides backing away from the encroaching water, his feet slipping, so that he must surely be moments away from disappearing into that dark death. His frightened horse would not move without him, so he was able to grab its mane and pull himself up, swinging himself onto its back. In a heartbeat the animal swung around and scrambled for the shore.

I am unclear about what happened next, but I know that I felt strong arms about me, and that those arms lifted me upwards, and that I was borne away from danger. When all was calm once more, and everyone accounted for, I was sitting at the very edge of the lake close to our starting point. I looked about for the person who had risked his own life to save mine.

'I must thank him, Ada,' I insisted. 'You must translate for me, be very clear. He must know how grateful I am.'

'But Kate,' she said softly, placing a trembling hand on my arm. 'No one helped you. There was not time. You could not be reached. You escaped harm by your actions alone.'

On hearing this I was, at first, astonished, but then I understood, and my heart was filled with joy and gratitude.

'Oh Ada,' I said, 'do you not know by now that I am never alone?'

What was it like? When you found the first outcasts in those desolate forests, what did you feel?

What could one feel but pity?

You felt more.

It was heartbreaking, to see such suffering, of course it was. And yet I was pleased to find them, to finally have arrived at the reason for my journey. Now my work could truly begin.

Always the work, always practical Nurse Marsden. Doing what needed to be done. Doing what no one else would do. But what did you feel?

I have answered your question.

No, you have not. Not completely. You have sidestepped, away from the personal and into the safely practical.

I have told you, I felt pity for them.

You felt rage! Fury! Anger beyond thought, beyond reason! Hate surged through you and threatened to burn you up. Hate for the ones who weren't there for you to scream at: the people who had sent those pitiful, ruined men, women and children into the woods to endure their torment in the harshest and loneliest of places.

I knew why they had acted as they did. I understood.

You would have struck them! If one of those responsible for such cruelty had stood before you at that moment, when you discovered the dead and the dying, the abandoned and the unloved, you would have struck them, and screamed at them, and condemned them for what they had done!

My mission was not to apportion blame. Not to judge. My mission was to offer assistance.

But someone was to blame. Someone had taken the decision to banish them. Someone had sent them out there to die a slow, lonely death. In the choking cold, among the towering, rough bark, with wolf noises, and bear smells, haunted by hunger, dogged by despair. Someone did that to them.

What was done was done out of ignorance. Part of my work was to inform, to enlighten, where possible to remove fear.

Were you afraid?

Of the disease? No. I knew how to protect myself. But there were times on the journey when I knew what it was to be afraid. In those moments I would remind myself that I was in God's care. He had a purpose for me. I put myself in His hands.

And the Lepers put themselves in yours. That must have made you feel important. Powerful, even.

They were in no position to refuse help if it were offered. They would have taken that help from anyone.

⊛

The Russian-Turkish war had been causing misery for some time before I obtained my posting to serve as a nurse in the Bulgarian hinterland. I was young, and although eager and determined, I had not travelled, and so had no experience of the world beyond England and the hospitals there. So it was that I was thrown into the brutal truth of war. I saw at first hand its disregard for life. Its random cruelty. Its insatiable hunger for suffering.

Along with my fellow sisters sent from the Deaconesses' Institute at Twickenham, I went via Sistova to the distant location of Varin. My post there was initially at a military lazaretto, managing cases mainly of typhus. Indeed we sisters spent a deal of the time nursing each other, as two of my fellows fell to the disease, and another was in a poor state after having her face badly bitten by rats whilst she slept.

However, such was the ferocity of the conflict that I was soon moved on to a field hospital. Here we nurses had to make do with what meagre supplies and facilities we were given with which to tend the soldiers. Their wounds were terrible, caused as they were by swinging blades, rifles and heavy artillery. Those who were not lost to the trauma of amputations and exsanguination from their injuries were often to succumb to the creeping death of gangrene only a few days later. Despite the horrors and the pitiful plight of the brave soldiers, I acquitted myself passably well, so that my superiors took note of my cool head and ability to act swiftly and without melodramatics. It was because of these talents – for which I take no personal credit, but accept them as God-given – that I was selected to go forward to help the fallen troops further out on the field of battle.

It is an onslaught to all the senses to be amidst the fighting proper, though I was still sufficiently removed from the firing so as not to become a target myself. The big guns thundered, louder than the storming heavens, yet even so it was possible to hear the screams and cries of the men as they were blasted or cut. I moved quickly from one casualty to the next, applying rudimentary treatments to stem the flow of blood, to aid breathing, or simply to hold the hand of a dying boy. There was no time for anguish or sentiment of my own. I had work to do, and I thanked God for giving me the courage to do it.

I recall being with Sister Janet, and that we moved beyond the main grouping of the stricken, checking on the periphery of the battlefield, to which many had crawled in an attempt to protect themselves from further injury, or perhaps to find a quieter place – where quiet is merely the absence of mortar fire – in order to find a more final and permanent peace. Our search took us to a small barn, long abandoned by any farmer. Sensing movement inside we went in, and what we found there was to shape the rest of my life.

Two men crouched in fear of their lives, but it was not the war that would send them from this world. These were victims of leprosy, and the first that I had ever encountered. Their condition was so extreme and so shocking that I forgot for a moment the ghastliness of battle wounds, and was moved and horrified at the extent of their suffering. One of the men was so disfigured by the disease as to be scarcely recognisable as human. Both were in a state of weakness and despair, blind, sore-ridden, starving. One's only reaction upon seeing them was to recoil, and even as I did so I was full of loathing for my selfishness. I knew then, in that moment so filled with death and decay, that these were the people in the world most needy and abandoned, whom I felt at once a powerful calling to assist with my whole being and my whole life. I had seen sufficient disease and suffering to know that there were many who could claim to be in as much agony and fear, but I knew that most of these existed within the reach of philanthropic Christian societies to which they could turn. Those afflicted with leprosy, I reasoned, suffered the dual curses of disease and banishment. They were outcast from their communities, their homes, their lives, and put beyond the boundary of such assistance as others might reasonably hope for. They were cut off from their fellow Christians, and yet they were indisputably Christ's lepers. I then and there dedicated myself to finding lepers, wherever they might be on this earth, and devoting myself to helping them.

When I turned to my medical training and the collected knowledge on the disease the words 'No remedy – no relief!' were all that could be found. How they came to haunt me! Time and again I wished that our Lord's Healer were with us again so that he might utter the gentle command 'Be thou clean.'

Much later, I had the honour of going with my fellow sisters to St Petersburg to accept the award of the Russian Red Cross for my services during that war. I wore my medal with great pride, but beneath it, nearer my heart, I kept the memory of those first two lepers who had altered the direction of my own life so irrevocably.

'Miss Marsden? The doctor is here to see you.'

The nurse's voice stirs me from my slumber. I am easily woken, though in truth these days the greater part of my waking hours have taken on the quality of a dream, so that at times it is hard to tell when I am asleep. Now I can see the smiling face of the young nurse who tends me with such care. I see a little of myself in her eager, gentle features. But that was me a long, long time ago. That person of vigour and purpose has been replaced by another whose body now struggles to move at all.

'Let's have you sitting up, shall we?' the nurse suggests, slipping her arm around my shoulders and adjusting my pillows.

At the foot of my bed stands a tall man in a dark suit. His face is not familiar to me. I think he is new here. I forget names, but not faces. This one has an abundant moustache and bright blue eyes.

'And how do we find you this morning, Miss Marsden?' he asks, glancing down to consult the notes that are in his hand. 'Are you sleeping well?' He turns to the nurse, unwilling or unable to wait for me to speak for myself. 'Is sleeping causing any difficulties?' he asks her. 'We can increase the night-time medication...'

'I sleep well enough,' I manage to tell him. He looks at me with mild surprise, as if it is a novelty to be spoken to by a patient. Indeed he regards me with such a curious stare that I wonder if my words came out as I intended. Had they instead been delivered as a jumble? I try again. 'I sleep well enough, Doctor. Thank you for your concern.'

'Excellent! And the pain remains manageable?'

'Quite so.'

He nods and then adopts an expression of particularly earnest concern. 'And how are you in yourself?'

Such an irritating line of questioning. I am not so addled as to be unaware of its meaning. With difficulty I shift to sit a little more upright. 'This hospital is no longer an asylum for lunatics...'

'For such patients we now prefer the term "feeble minded".'

'But you treat them just the same. I assure you, Doctor, while my frame may be feeble, I am of sound mind.' I meet his gaze. 'Whatever you might have heard to the contrary.'

The nurse smiles at me but addresses the doctor. 'Miss Marsden's wits are perfectly sharp,' she tells him. 'She is even setting her thoughts down in a book.'

'Really? Is that so?' Now he is intrigued. 'I understand you already have several writing credits to your name.'

'All written a very long time ago,' I say. 'And some things...are missing. There are things yet to be said. And to be put right.' Suddenly I feel the weight of the past settle upon my shoulders once again.

The young nurse is sensitive to the smallest alterations in her charges and squeezes my hand. 'Miss Marsden tires easily,' she explains.

'We shall leave you to rest,' the doctor announces, and waves cheerily as he moves away from the bed. Even now he is studying the next set of notes, his mind racing on to the next case, my own details dismissed as uninteresting.

'But how are we to live, Kate?' My mother put the question baldly, and not for the first time.

'Mama, do not concern yourself...'

She flapped a hand at me in irritation. 'Do not treat me as though I were a fool. Old I may be, but I am perfectly able to discuss the matter of money, and discuss it we must. You are too fond of wait-and-see, Kate. Too ready to look away from the problem.'

'Truly, Mama, there is no problem. I have my work at the hospital. My job there is secure.'

'We cannot live on the wages of a nurse.'

'I am Superintendent, the most senior position a nurse can hold...'

'Senior, not senior, what does it matter? A nurse's income, of whatever variety, is not sufficient. There are bills to be paid, Kate, this house must be kept up, the maid paid, and the cook, the roof repaired... We have neither of us so much as visited a dressmaker since we arrived in Wellington.'

'I have more than enough dresses, Mama, and those you have are still quite presentable.'

'I have patched and mended until there is more patching and mending than there is dress!' She raised her hands and then let them fall in exasperation. 'It is all very well for you, Kate. You have your work at the hospital. You are occupied. I am in a city where I know no one. How am I to establish us here, how am I to find a place for us in society if we have not the funds to accept an invitation, much less entertain?'

'I have no interest in society, Mama.'

'Well it would be to our benefit were you to develop one. A good marriage is your best hope of financial security, there is no point pretending otherwise.'

'Oh, Mama, please.'

'Why, Kate? Why must you so set yourself against the idea of becoming a wife? I simply do not understand it.'

'I am very busy at the hospital.'

'Nonsense, it has always been the same. I believe you chose nursing specifically to avoid marriage.'

'Nursing is my vocation.'

'And a vocation is a luxury we can ill afford. After your father died, God rest his soul, I gave my all to raise you and your brothers and sisters. It was no easy task on such little money as we had.'

'I know, Mama, and I am grateful.'

'Well you don't seem it. It would be better for both of us if that gratitude manifested itself in a desire to find a husband.'

I sighed. Money and marriage. Two sticks with which my mother beat me with wearisome frequency. On the subject of marriage I would not be swayed. Could not be. It was not difficult to sidestep the matter, as Wellington was a small city, with an even smaller supply of eligible bachelors, and few of those had any wish to marry me. Why should they? Our lack of money was harder to ignore. Mother was right, we were living beyond our means, and something would have to be done about it.

The black bread, the foundation of our rations, had turned to dry stone. It crumbled to a powder, to which was added sour milk and water. This grey mixture was stirred over the flames of the fire until it resembled a blackish gruel, which we ate hungrily.

The first time I found myself alone with Rose came about purely by chance. It was the end of a long, hot April, and a picnic had been planned for the nurses under my care. This one day holiday had been eagerly anticipated by the young women, and I had permitted them to organise the outing of their choice. A great deal of preparation had gone into the little event. We had obtained permission to have use of the carriage and pair belonging to Dr Richardson, who was, at that time, away on sabbatical in Auckland. There were to be the four of us, and we were to do without a driver to spare the horses and allow more space in the little carriage. Two days before the holiday, however, Nurse Wilson had succumbed to a heavy head cold, and the night before the date Nurse Carlisle caught it too. I suggested we postpone the picnic, but both poorly girls were adamant we should not miss our treat, and so on a bright Monday morning Rose took the reins and we drove out of the city and headed for the green hills to the west.

It was a joy to leave the bustle of the noisy, dirty streets behind, and to shake off the cares of work, if only for a few hours. Rose proved to be a competent horsewoman, a skill she had learned on her family farm, she told me. What was she thinking, I wondered, as we drove deeper into the verdant countryside? Were the thoughts that dwelt unspoken in her mind as anxious and breathless as my own? I was always a confident woman, a person who could present herself well, without concern, and felt myself capable of responding sensibly and correctly to any situation that might arise. But in Rose's company I was given to nervousness. When we worked together there at least existed the protective distance of our stations, our positions as junior nurse and her superior. Protocol and professionalism, the needs of our patients and the requirements of our employment guided and constrained us. In that little carriage, however, wearing our holiday clothes, removed from the context of the hospital, I felt our roles reversed: she was the capable, calm person, while I was the timid creature.

It took two hours of driving before we turned off the narrow road that wound beyond the small farm belonging to one of the orderlies' parents. The track took us past pretty meadows and woodlands and then to a small, secluded area of pasture beside a river. Rose had visited the place before, and grinned at me, enjoying my obvious delight.

'Isn't it lovely?' she asked, persuading the horses to a halt.

'Yes, quite lovely,' I agreed solemnly, finding that I did not wish to reveal precisely how happy I was to be in such a place with her.

Rose laughed loudly. 'Come on,' she said, jumping down lightly from the driver's seat, 'let's set the horses to grazing and then we can eat. I'm famished.'

She was at ease with the animals and quickly had them out of their harness and turned loose onto the lush grass. I spread the blanket beneath the shade of a chestnut tree on a patch of ground close to the water's edge, though slightly raised from it. It was the perfect spot on which to sit and gaze at the sparkling river. I lifted the hamper from the cart and began setting out the cloth, plates, and food. Rose sat beside me, giving a small squeal of delight at the sight of the feast.

'All this for us? Poor Phyllis, poor Suzette.'

'Perhaps we should have left some more of the food behind.'

'Nonsense, they didn't want our day to be ruined too. Ooh, look at that chicken pie! I swear I could eat the whole thing.'

She was always a creature of appetites and of impulsive behaviour. Without a hint of self-consciousness she cut herself an enormous slice of pie and began eating it, the crumbs falling where they would. 'Mmm! That's delicious. You must try some. Here.'

Before I had a chance to protest she held the pie to my lips and I found myself biting into it.

'Isn't it good?' she asked.

'Wonderful,' I agreed, nodding.

'This was such a splendid idea. I am not going to think about the hospital, not about bandages or bedpans or beds or anything, not for one second today. And neither must you, do you promise?'

'I had not thought to...'

'Oh go on, Sister Marsden, *promise*.'

She cocked her head, waiting for my reply.

'Very well,' I said. 'I promise.'

'Excellent. But then, I can't call you Sister and you can't call me Nurse, else the whole thing will be spoiled. So, what shall I call you?'

'Well, my name is Kate, but I'm not sure...'

'Just for today. Oh *please*. The second we arrive back in Wellington I shall be yes Sister, no Sister, just as before. But for today, while we are here, may I call you Kate?'

The pleasure I felt at hearing her say my name shocked me. Had I distanced myself from such simple friendship so very much? 'Yes,' I said at last, 'if you wish. You may call me Kate. Just here. Just today.'

She beamed at me and began tugging at the laces of her boots. 'And you must call me Rose. I know my proper name is Rosamund, but nobody actually calls me that. Come on, it's so hot and that water looks divinely cool. I simply have to paddle, and I can't do it on my own with you sitting here on your own. Come along!'

First I was condemned for embarking upon such an expedition because I was a woman. Such exploration, such endeavour, was the preserve of men, and they did not care to have a woman trespass upon their territory, however far and forgotten it might be. It was not right for a woman to disport herself in such a way, wearing men's clothes, carrying a man's gun, venturing where only brave men should dare to go. It was not womanly. I accepted their approbation without comment, for it was not my purpose to change anyone's mind on this matter. So, when they said it was not seemly, it was not ladylike, I did not speak up. But, when they said it was not the way God intended women to behave... well! Then I could not stay silent. Who were they to tell me God's purpose? Who were they to know, better than I, what He wished of me? It was to do God's work that I made that journey. It was to do His bidding that I suffered to be spurned as a leper myself. I could not have done it without Him. Let them call me what they would, they could not part me from Him. And God knows how the defeated will stop at nothing to turn the tables, for then they called me such names, accused me of such things, flung such slanderous allegations at me, all in an effort to see me brought low. Was it for jealousy? Was it for upsetting the order of things? In the end, after all, I neither know nor care. God knows the truth of it. God knows me. That is enough.

I have no clear recollection of meeting Jessy Brodie. What does that tell me about how I regarded her, I wonder? Is it that I was careless of her friendship, or is it that my regret at how it ended puts distance between my thoughts and the facts of the matter? I know that when I met her in Wellington her kindness, her usefulness, I will not deny it, seemed God-sent. Why would I refuse her help, then? How ungrateful, how foolish it would have been to turn away such much needed assistance.

What was the hardest thing for those unfortunates to bear? What do you think caused them the most suffering?

It is a cruel disease but not, in itself, most of the time in the earlier stages, a particularly painful one. Pain comes from secondary problems arising from problems with the eyes, affliction with sores, and the lack of sensation in the extremities. If a person is unable to feel the tips of his fingers he will, unavoidably, sustain injuries. He is insensible to the blow of a hammer, or the heat of a flame. His fingers become damaged, and healing is often impeded by infection. This was something I knew could be improved upon. I could teach the afflicted, and those caring for them, how best to treat such wounds so that fingers, toes, sometimes hands and feet entirely, might not be lost.

Such debilitations must indeed be hard to endure.

They worsened an already life-threatening situation. Imagine attempting to live in the wild *taiga* far from medical care, or indeed support of any kind, lacking proper nutrition, battling against extreme cold in winter and stifling heat and insects in the summer months. Such an existence would test the fittest of people. A person afflicted with leprosy had already to cope with the discomfort of sores, possibly failing eyesight, a generally weakened state. They were not in the best of conditions to manage the privations visited upon them by their banishment. To lose toes, hands... to become crippled... the task of survival is made impossibly difficult.

And what of their mental anguish?

There is no doubt that their minds were greatly affected by their situation.

By being made outcasts?

Enforced solitude, often separation from loved ones... such things are hard to bear.

As is being seen as unfit for society.

People shun what they fear, and they fear what they do not understand.

And that is something you know about, is it not? Being shunned. Being rejected, ostracised, dismissed as unacceptable.

Not everyone felt so.

Cast out into a social wilderness.

My situation could hardly be compared...

Being branded a liar.

We stood up to our knees in the little river, giggling like schoolgirls. The water was blissfully cold. Our bonnets gave a modicum of shade from the fierce Antipodean sun, but I could already feel it burning through the muslin of my summer dress.

'Oh, Kate, isn't this glorious?' Rose laughed, her face bright with the fun of the moment. 'I wish we could do this every weekend. Can you imagine? We'd escape from the hospital and bring our poor tired feet up here and take off our boots and run into the river and feel like this every week!'

'And what would happen to our patients while we were busy paddling?' I asked her.

'There are other nurses, you know. Go on, admit it, you love the idea. It would be our secret place. Other people would just spoil it, don't you think? We'd be just we two, like this.' She beamed at me.

I wanted to tell her that I could think of nothing I should like better. That I found her company delightful. That I would be content to simply stand and watch her just as she was at that moment, face aglow, smiling, happy. Just we two. But I was afraid.

'Let's eat,' I said. 'You must be hungry after that long drive.'

I turned away from her and waded through the fast flowing water and out onto the river bank, and all the while I felt her watching me, felt her eyes upon me as I went.

❦

At last we pulled up at the post-station. Our driver took time to drain the few remaining drops of vodka from his flask before slipping down from the sledge. The horses were foam-flecked and puffing and needed no tying, being greatly relieved to stand idle.

Ada and I were manhandled from the sledge in the inelegant manner to which we had quickly become accustomed. The road, if such the rutted path of deep snow could be called, was at its most poached here, where other weary travellers had passed before us. In our unhelpful swaddling, we two struggled the short distance from our conveyance to the 'hotel' door, scarce caring what manner of building we were being taken to, so great was our desire to be anywhere other than the torture box in which we had been buffeted and bruised for so many miles.

It was not until that door creaked opened and we staggered inside that the true nature of our accommodation was revealed to us. It made itself clear first by its stink. I say to all who would venture after us upon this route, when entering any post-station for the first time, be sure to clamp your pocket-handkerchief to your nostrils, for you will not stand it otherwise. Indeed when that first gust of foetid air reached our nostrils we reeled backwards, until we remembered the cold outside, and our gnawing hunger, and we were compelled to go forwards once more.

The 'menu' certainly suited our own tastes, as it was comprised entirely of what we had brought with us; those items that had not been lost off the sledge during its rough journey thus far. We were to feast on black tea – thanking God that the sugar had been spared – tinned fish, and black bread so tough it could only be rendered edible by slow dunking. It was well that we kept in mind how fortunate we were not to be disturbed by any waiters!

Our bed was the middle of the floor in this salubrious establishment, and consisted of a pile of sheepskins, none of them the cleanest we had seen. Indeed, we did not want for company at all, as the bedding and walls wriggled and jumped with vermin in great numbers. To further expel any possible loneliness, we were to welcome other travellers through the night who pitched up, snow-covered and weary, to share our very bed! The warmth of this place of comfort was welcome at first, but by morning we had both sworn we would never again set foot inside such an airless hole. But we were early in our journey, and ignorant of the way things would be, so that even the very next night we would find ourselves gratefully falling into that grim hovel's twin.

And when we did so, my ungrateful heart pained me, for had not God sent me on this journey? Who was I to complain at what conditions I must endure? Guilt, my shadow, near overwhelmed me. I explained to Ada that I must, as a matter of urgency, attend church.

'But Kate, where are we to find one?' she asked, raising her arm and then letting it drop in a gesture of hopelessness that seemed to take in both our mean accommodation and the dark wilderness without.

I paced, fretting. 'This is a God-fearing country, however dispersed and poor its people,' I told her. 'There will be places of worship. There must be.'

When I made as if to open the door onto the snowy night Ada gave a cry.

'Kate, for pity's sake!'

I heard the exhaustion in her voice and reluctantly acceded to it. 'Very well,' I agreed, 'I shall make do with my humble prayers in this place. For tonight. But from here we shall instruct our guides to seek out church or chapel wherever they may along our route. I am about God's purpose, Ada. I will not pass by His house; not miss the chance to offer him our thanks at any opportunity, do you see? Do you see that I must?' I asked.

I must have shown desperation in my expression then, for she took both my hands in hers.

'I see, Kate,' she said gently. 'I see.'

I recall being in the kitchen of our house in Wellington. We were pickling onions to preserve them, Mama and I. There was a maid, too. I forget her name, but I can still smell those small, sweet onions as they simmered. There came a knock at the door and I sent her to answer it. She came back and handed me a business card.

'A Mr James, Ma'am,' she told me. 'Says he's selling insurance.'

I read the details on his card as she spoke. 'What manner of insurance?' I asked.

'He didn't specify, Ma'am.'

My mother tutted loudly. 'We have neither money for nor need of his services. Send him away.'

'No,' I said, drying my hands. 'I shall see him. Show him into the drawing room.'

I went to take my place at the little table in the window, my mind filled with possibilities. I told myself if God opened a door for us, we would be wrong not to at least peek through it.

It was in Ekaterinburg that Ada and I met up with Mr Yates and Mr Wardropper, English friends indeed, as well as the agent of the British and Foreign Bible Society. I am much indebted to these fine gentlemen for their help. It was they who suggested that we should go to Irbit for the annual fair. The hope was that a merchant of some renown who travelled from Yakutsk might be there, and might have information regarding the lepers of that region. In addition, it was possible he could know something of the precious plant that I was in search of.

So it was that we made the arduous journey – one of over a hundred miles – by sledge, again submitting to the tribulations of this mode of travel. The snow was deep and often rutted and drifted, so that our progress was both slow and difficult. At times the driver was forced to halt, climb down, and peer into the next hole to see how deep it was. I anticipated us all ending in a chaotic confusion at any moment. Both we passengers were severely shaken and bruised by the many miles of bumping down holes and up holes and jolting over great frozen mounds of snow that littered the road, leaving us wearied and dazed.

We found accommodation of the regular kind for these parts. There was a hotel, and in it a room, but no proper bed, save for a naked bedstead, and a few aged sticks of furniture besides, and no fire in the hearth. Ada and I were already prepared to take whatever we were given by way of lodgings, for there was little point in searching for alternatives. When a room was offered it was, more often than not, the only room to be had, and so we resolved to make the best of it. It was, however, hard not to let one's spirits be affected by the grim nature of the lodgings. Ada's shoulders sagged as she took off her hat and let it fall to the comfortless bed.

'The Winter Fair is quite the highlight of the social year, by all accounts,' I told her. 'We were fortunate to obtain a room at all. We must brush up as best we can, put on our brightest smiles, and join the celebrations.'

'I fear I have not the strength left in me to celebrate anything,' she said.

I placed my hands on her shoulders.

'Courage, my dear. We have come such a great distance in our quest. We must not falter now.'

'Do you truly believe these traders will know where the plant is to be found?'

'I am certain of it! What is more, the merchants are sure to have information regarding the whereabouts of more outcasts. Come now, let us seek out food and cheer.'

We did our best to run a comb through our hair and brush off our garments. In truth it was hard to make anything more than the most minute of improvements in our appearance, but in attempting to do so I felt we marked the step from workaday to festive. In any event, it was better to be moving than to huddle in the chill of our room, for the temperature showed no signs of rising, and the windows were glazed with a coating of ice.

Outside, the fair was well under way, stallholders, fairgoers, merchants and travellers of all varieties having been up early to claim a good pitch or seek out the most appealing bargains. Ox carts and pony wagons were driven at crawling speed through the melée, laden with rugs and baskets. I even saw camels, looking as out of place as we were in the snow-packed streets! I was astonished at the variety of faces and physiques that went about the town square. There were Russian peasants and businessmen, some accompanied by wives in their brightest headscarves, but for the most part women were absent. There were several shamans sporting scarlet coats adorned with ribbons and bells, each apparently trying to outdo the other, like rare birds of gaudy plumage. Among these familiar Slavic faces were more markedly Asian ones, with skin the colour of mahogany, eyes angled and almond-shaped, and smiles as wide as the Lena. I saw a group of men who stood head and shoulders above the rest, their shoulders swathed in wolf fur, their beards abundant and wild. There were men leading strings of ponies burdened with bundles of silk or sacks of other desirable goods, such as spices and finely-worked leather or woollen blankets. Street vendors had lit braziers upon which they prepared aromatic food, which they ladled into wooden bowls and pressed into the cold hands of hungry customers. All about us were shouts and cries in a dozen languages, with beasts of burden being cajoled and corralled, wares being advertised, deals being struck. Many fairgoers wore distinctive and outlandish clothes, proud to display their origins and their heritage, each marking himself out as to his birthplace, his station, and his business.

The fair is a vital fixture in for the commerce of the region, for without it the town would not survive. The rest of the year it is a deserted place where nothing occurs to alter the rhythm of life in a small, forgotten part of the country, with little trade or commerce beyond its own boundaries. Merchants travel to the fair from all corners of the Empire, bringing with them all manner of commodities unobtainable on any other day, so that I do not think there is anything to match it in any other place in Russia or beyond. Even Ada, tired and sickening as she was, could not fail to be cheered by such a spectacle and such a riotous clamour upon the senses.

Music added to the cacophony, provided by drums and horns. Ada and I turned to see the crowd part so that a procession might wind its way through the market square. At its head was a priest, elaborately dressed with towering hat and a proud bearing, swinging a smoking censer as he performed the official opening and blessing of the fair.

One of our guides found his way to us and spoke briefly with Ada in Russian.

She smiled at me. 'He says he has found the merchant you were told about; the one who might know of the herb.'

We eagerly followed him through the crush. If we had thought to find peace and quiet in a hostelry we were disappointed. The inn to which we were led was filled to the gunwales! There was barely room to squeeze two thickly-dressed women into the low-ceilinged space. At least a fire blazed in a broad hearth, though the price for this was choking smoke, thick enough to feel gritty on our tongues, but which seemed to bother no one but us. The revellers were all furnished with jars of liquor or bowls of mare's milk, some also clutching pipes. Even through the smoky miasma it seemed to me that no two faces were alike, no two costumes similar.

We were conducted to a low table, behind which sat a strikingly large man, broad shouldered with a moon face which was weathered and tanned no doubt by years traversing the tundra to many such remote places. When he smiled his face creased into a line for each mile he had travelled, his eyes twinkling. He gabbled at his men to make way for his visitors, and space was cleared for us. There were not chairs. Instead we were invited to sit cross-legged on stiffly stuffed cushions. No mean feat in our padded layers of winter clothing!

'Ada, ask him if he speaks Russian.'

She did so, and he responded with a mighty laugh.

'My travels have furnished me with many languages. English among them.'

I smiled. 'How very fortunate for us,' I replied.

He regarded me closely as he spoke. 'When I heard tell of two English ladies travelling alone in winter I was incredulous! How could this be? Who would permit such folly?'

I opened my mouth to defend our mission, but our guide placed a hand on my arm signalling for me to be patient.

The silk merchant was enjoying the sound of his own cleverness. 'I said to myself, Are these women who have lost their minds? Have they, perhaps, been thrown out by their husbands because they made poor wives?'

He paused so that the listening crowd might laugh long and loud at this and I had to force myself not to retort.

'But,' he held up a hand, 'I was told no! These women are unmarried. This led me to believe that they have come to Irbit in search of husbands!'

This, of course, elicited yet more laughter. I feared that by now my expression was as icy as the Siberian tundra itself, and yet I must not cross this man, for we needed his knowledge. But the merchant had not finished his joke yet and slapped his thigh.

70

'I think that now I see what fine women they are I am tempted to make room in my life for two more wives of my own. Where is that good for nothing priest? If he is not yet drunk and fallen on his backside in the snow, let him be fetched so that he might perform the ceremony without delay. My bed will be warm this night!'

Laughter in the inn reached rabid levels. I bided my time. At last the clamour subsided and the merchant raised his eyebrows, curious now to hear my response. I kept my tone polite yet firm.

'It is as well the Esteemed Merchant is not a native speaker of English. If I were to hear my own tongue more eloquently employed I might be moved to agree to the match. As it is, I find I am able to refuse his kind offer.'

There was a moment of charged silence. The merchant frowned deeply, narrowing his eyes at me, and then exploded into laughter, slapping his thigh again. The assembled company joined in.

I went on.

'Having escaped the onerous duties of becoming husband to two mad English women, perhaps the Esteemed Merchant might feel inclined to answer one or two questions?' When he nodded I continued. 'On your far-ranging travels have you come across any lepers?'

'Of course. The disease plays no heed to borders. The wretches may be found everywhere. Why would two English women, mad or not, wish to know such a thing?'

'It is my purpose, my mission, and my dearest hope, to find those outcast and suffering from this blight.'

'Are you shaman?' he wished to know.

'I am a nurse and a foot soldier for the Lord.' Seeing his blank face I elaborated. 'I follow where God leads me, sir. I do his work.'

The chatter quietened somewhat, the merchant's expression grew more serious.

71

'Then I shall say a prayer for you,' he promised. 'What do you wish to know of these lepers?'

'It would aid me greatly if you could show me, on a map, where I might find them. I wish to take them God's word.'

'They may not wish to hear it. Suffering can bring a man closer to God or drive him fast in the other direction.'

'I wish also to tell them of the hospital I intend building in Yakutsk. There will be a place for all of them. Clean, warm, safe, with medical care. A community. A life.'

The merchant stroked his chin. 'This they will wish to hear. Mad women must have many riches, to bring such a costly gift.'

'This particular mad woman has the support of the Tsarina herself.'

As others in the crowd translated this there was a murmur of astonishment around us. I took the photograph of dear Maria Feodorovna from my pocket and handed it to the silk merchant, who was noticeably impressed.

'With God and the Empress on your side surely your mission cannot fail.'

'I am fortunate, though I lack one thing more. A cure. Tell me, have you heard of the special herb that grows in this region? I am told it has the power to heal the leper.'

'I have heard of it, but I have never seen it,' he said with a shrug.

He dismissed it as such a trifle! He could not have known how heavily I took his words, and how my heart laboured beneath that disappointment. Mercifully, he had more to say on the matter.

'But I know of a shaman, a way off in the *taiga*. Maybe he can help you with this.'

I leapt to my feet.

'Oh, can you take me to him?'

The merchant resumed laughing.

'Be still! Be still. You will have your shaman. And your wretches. Bring me your maps in the morning. Now...'

He clambered heavily to his feet, the table scraping back as he pushed at it.

'...now is not the time for such business. The fair has just begun, and we must celebrate that we have all lived long enough to come to Irbit to see it and trade with our friends and brothers. Now, we dance!'

A cheer went up. Cushions and benches and tables were swept away and space appeared where before there was none. Fiddlers and drummers emerged from the crowd and struck up a tune of frantic tempo. Within moments everyone who could find an inch of room was dancing, wildly and without apparent method or design. Ada and I staggered backwards, seeking a corner from which to observe the merrymaking, but the silk merchant had other plans for us. He took my hand, without so much as a bow, and pulled me to the centre of the dance floor. I was aware of one of his companions steering Ada in just such a fashion. Before either of us could protest – though how we would have made ourselves heard I cannot imagine – we were whirled and spun and polka'd around the room, so that soon the laughing onlookers became no more than a blur of colours as we sped by.

There were occasions, during our time in Wellington, when money became such a concern that it rendered thoughts of all else insignificant. Mother fretted and railed and blamed my refusal to find a wealthy husband. As much as I sought to reassure her, I knew I would have to take drastic steps if we were not to become destitute. Had we been living in poverty, surrounded by others in similar circumstances, and had I been alone, I might have let us fall low and seen it as God's will. But we were in what passed for society, Mother wished to maintain the little status we had acquired, and she had already suffered so much loss. I cannot expect those who have known only the comfort of a secure income to understand that we who are less fortunate must sometimes choose between what is right and what is necessary, but such is the way of things. Such were the choices I faced.

I suppose it was a beautiful place. Or rather, there was beauty to be found in it. I am not, as some are, a lover of nature for nature's sake. A wilderness is an empty, hostile place. The *taiga* did not seem lovely to me at all. The mighty River Lena would tolerate boats upon her broad back, but would swallow up any unwary sailors who had the misfortune to fall from their vessels. The biting flies and insects without number that inhabit Siberia see all other life forms simply as food. The summer sun is too hot to enjoy, and the winter cold too severe to survive for more than a few hours at a time. Such untamed, uncivilised places make up the greater part of the world, and for the most part humans have no business being in them. And as it is God's greatest work, those he fashioned in his own image, who command my attention and interest, I am not given to lyrical thoughts about the vastness of the tundra, or the savage splendour of a bear. That does not mean, however, that I cannot appreciate the intricate beauty of a snowflake through which the low November sun glints. Or the perfection of a songbird's voice drifting down from the towering pines.

Perhaps it is something lacking in me that prevents me from finding loveliness in a place where man is not welcome. I would rather think it that I am a civilised being, and this civilisation – education, society, faith, the modern way of living, and so on – have elevated my tastes to a point beyond the naturalistic. I see prettiness in an icicle because it puts me in mind of the chandeliers at the Winter Palace. I find beauty in the blue of a harebell because it helps me recall the blue of Rose's eyes. I need a reference in the world in which I am best suited to thrive in order to appreciate the beauty of a world other than that. I believe God will forgive me this limitation in my ability to see the beauty in all His work. He has made me as I am, after all.

We were prevented from returning to the silk merchant with our maps the next day, however, as Ada fell ill. She took a chill, and then a fever set in. For three days I kept to her side in the desolate lodgings we were obliged to put up with, doing my best to keep her comfortable and to nurse her, all the while impatient to hear more of the shaman who had knowledge of the precious herb. As the days and then hours passed, even as Ada began to recover, it became clear to me that she would not be strong enough to continue with me on the trek. I chided myself for ever having agreed to take her as my translator and companion. She was so frail, so young, so untested. The privations, the cold, the poor meals, all had sapped her strength and left her vulnerable and susceptible to illness. As soon as she was sufficiently recovered, I would send her home. As I formed this thought she woke from her first fever-free sleep for many hours.

As she stirred she moaned lightly. I picked up the face cloth, dipping it into the chipped enamel bowl which I had begged from the owner of the guest house, and wrung out the warm water and alcohol I had prepared to keep her cool. Slowly, methodically, I mopped her face with it.

'Hush now, Ada.'

Her eyes fluttered open.

'Oh, Kate,' she said, her voice hoarse. She looked up at me and I saw that she knew that for her the mission was at an end. 'I am so very sorry,' she said.

'You must not reproach yourself for becoming unwell, my dear. If anyone is at fault it is I for bringing you so far...'

'I have become a burden.'

'Nonsense, you will soon be well again.'

'But I am holding you up, delaying everything, the shaman, the flower...'

'Have waited for me many long years. They can wait a little longer.'

This appeared to satisfy her. She closed her eyes again. I left her sleeping and went to make arrangements for her journey back to Moscow.

※

We lay on the picnic rug beneath the chestnut tree, the hems of our summer dresses still wet from paddling in the river, our feet and legs bare. Rose had her eyes closed, but I could tell she was not asleep. It was blissful to lie drowsy and quiet, with no need for words. We had feasted upon a lunch of cold chicken, tomatoes and fresh bread, all washed down with elderflower cordial. The decision to take a little nap had been an easy one, but now I could not sleep. Not with Rose so close. I sat up. Rose had taken her hat off some time earlier and her skin was tinged pink from the sun. A bee buzzed around the hamper for a moment and then flew on. From somewhere across the field came the sound of the kakapo, its booming call reminding me of the bitterns of my English childhood trips to Norfolk.

'You like to watch me, don't you?' she asked suddenly without opening her eyes.

'I'm sorry,' I began, not knowing what to say next.

'Don't be.' She opened her eyes then and sat up, grinning. 'I watch you too, sometimes when we are working together. Of course, you are always too busy to notice, busy being Sister Marsden. But I watch you. I like to.'

I did not know how to reply. I felt horribly flustered. She could have teased me about my consternation, but she did not. Instead she said, 'It is different, being watched when you *know* you are being watched. It's a special thing. Don't you think?'

'I have no idea, I'm sure I've never...'

'I'll show you. Lie back.'

'What?'

'Go on, lie back and shut your eyes.'

I did as she asked. It was the most unnerving experience, to lie there knowing that I was being looked at, being scrutinised, being seen, in a way that I had never before considered. Then, to my astonishment, I felt a light touch upon my ankle. Rose's fingers against my flesh!

'Oh!' I said, opening my eyes and making to sit up.

'Shh.' Rose put her hand on my shoulder and gently pushed me back. 'Lie still. Close your eyes. Keep them closed.'

Once again I complied with her wishes. My heart was racing. My breath sounded horribly loud. Rose placed her fingertips on my ankle again and softly traced my shin bone up to my knee and then back down to my ankle. There was nothing ticklish about her touch, and yet it set my nerves tingling. Wordlessly, she continued to stroke my leg, up and down, up and down, her fingers light and soft and cool. The sensation was exquisite. I knew I should stop her. I should say something, or open my eyes. But then the spell would be broken. She reached over and touched my other leg in the same way, sometimes using the pads of her fingers, sometimes using her neat little nails. My whole body began to awaken, began to respond to her touch in a way I would not have believed it capable of. With a gasp I sat up, backing away against the trunk of the tree. I was breathless.

'Rose...'

'Come on,' she said, springing to her feet. 'Time for another paddle. Bet I find a fish before you do.' And with that she ran back into the water. 'Come on!' she called over her shoulder, and I followed, all awkwardness forgotten.

The gentleman who stood before me was not young, but still retained the vigour of a man of determination and good sense. He was pleasant-looking enough, though we were all disguised by our outdoor clothing so much of the time that one became adept at recognising people by their eyes and their gait, rather than their faces.

He spoke good French, for which he had been singled out by the governor of Tomsk as a suitable translator for me, now that poor Ada had been forced to return home. My own command of the French language was not impressive, but it was sufficient for us to be able to converse, and so I was not to be left to manage only with my few words of Russian. I was immensely grateful for him.

'I am at your service, madame,' he assured me in French. 'With the governor's compliments.'

He made himself sound like some manner of gift, which indeed I suppose he was.

'I am delighted to meet you, Monsieur Vilenbakhov. It is good of the governor to spare you.' I offered him my gloved hand, which he shook in a manner that was more English than it was Russian.

He smiled at me then, and I realised this small action was designed to put me at my ease; to make me feel he understood a little of my Britishness. Such kindnesses were to be his habit, and I thanked God for putting this good and caring person in my path. Along the testing route ahead his was a comforting and reassuring presence. The other men treated him with a slightly cautious respect. He was, after all, an official person, one of the governor's attachés. This deference had the effect of quietening them a little, and though they had never treated me with anything but the utmost courtesy, I felt a general improvement in my circumstances beyond that of my translator's skills as a linguist.

One evening we stopped at a 'hotel' between two of the larger towns. This building resembled more a forest cabin, though we were in a village which boasted both church and school. Our accommodation consisted of one large room, into which we all, guides, drivers, soldiers, officials and curious English woman alike, filed wearily in search of supper and sleep. It had been a long and gruelling day. The snow lay so thick and deep in parts that we spent more of our time getting in and then out of drifts than ever we did travelling forwards. I had lost count of the occasions where I was required to scramble out of the sledge and stand helplessly at the roadside whilst all others pulled and pushed at the horses, harness, and conveyance. As I watched the cold would seep through my many layers until its icy fingers touched my skin. Monsieur Vilenbakhov worked with the other men, despite being a man not accustomed to such labours, and it was well that he did, for it took every bit of strength they had to free the sledge.

There was a fireplace set in the far wall of the cabin, and upon this a kettle was set to boil and a pot hung over the flames. We had black bread in our reduced store, and this was crumbled into the pot, whereupon blocks of frozen milk were added to the mix, stirred, melted, brought to boil, and coaxed into producing a grey porridge. On this particular occasion, I recall there being tinned fish to add to the feast. We were fiercely hungry, the food was hot, and washed down with piping, sweetened, black tea it tasted far finer than it looked, and much better than it might sound here.

I had taken off my reindeer coat so that I was better able to move. The smoky room was warm, and would quickly become unpleasantly hot, with so many people crammed into it. Monsieur Vilenbakhov sat beside me, his bowl of supper hugged close. He set his tea at his feet. We ate in companionable silence for some time before he spoke.

'This is a wonderful thing that you do, Madame Marsden. To travel so very far, to endure such hardships, such privations...' here he gestured expansively with his spoon.

'I disagree,' I told him, indicating my gruel, 'this is quite the finest food I have ever tasted.'

He smiled sheepishly. 'Of course you are right. All things are relative.'

'And we are far more fortunate than the people I have been sent here to help.'

'That is what you truly believe? That God has sent you here?'

'Are you not a man of faith, Monsieur Vilenbakhov?'

He looked a little uneasy at the question. 'But of course, and yet... Forgive me, madame, I cannot help thinking that God might have chosen differently had He known the nature of the landscape He was asking you to cross.'

'Surely you cannot think Him ignorant of a single footstep of His own creation?'

'In which case I must think Him cruel. To send a woman...'

'Ah, we come to it. It is my sex that offends you, not my frailty specifically.'

'Madame, I did not mean—!'

I held up a hand. 'You are not the first to question my suitability for such a journey, monsieur, I doubt you will be the last. However, I am fortunate in trusting God's judgement. If He deems me suitable, then suitable I must be.'

He regarded me keenly. 'Truly, it must be a great comfort, to travel through life with such...certainty.'

'I could not progress one mile without it.'

'Madame Marsden I envy you.'

'There is no necessity, Monsieur Vilenbakhov, for are you not travelling with me?'

He gave a light laugh, not mocking, rather fond. 'And do you have God's assurance that I too will escape being eaten by a bear?'

'Oh, I'm afraid I cannot promise you that.' Seeing his disappointment but keeping my face implacable I added, 'Finish up your supper. You may need all your strength to fight them off.'

You do want to remember, don't you?

It is not a matter of wanting to or *not* wanting to. My memory will do what it will do, and I am no longer in charge of it.

You remember places, people...

Of course, but sometimes...

Sometimes...?

I think I know something, I believe that I am certain and then, it changes. It comes to me differently and that certainty is lost.

Perhaps if you try to tell the story it will become clearer.

I fear the opposite may be true: the more I attempt to recall the shadowy past the less clear it is, the more versions present themselves, so that I am afraid soon I may not hold the truth of it in my mind at all.

The Hotel Normandie was a place in which I had stayed on several occasions when visiting New York. It was comfortable, yet the tariffs were reasonable, and being centrally placed I could attend meetings and give talks in a number of venues in a short space of time, with the minimum of inconvenience. During my fundraising tour of America, I had enjoyed my times there, and always found the staff and clientele to be helpful and friendly. My last experience of the Normandie, however, was memorable for quite the reverse reasons.

I had been in the city for three days, and had already given two talks, both of which had been well attended and well received, and had garnered many promises of donations towards the building of the hospital. I was returning to my room, which was situated on the third floor, when a boy of about fourteen years, apparently accompanied by his mother, spied me as I walked along the corridor.

'Aren't you that woman who roamed across Russia on a leper hunt?' he asked, bold and free, without so much as a word of greeting nor introduction. I looked to his mother for some application of manners, but none was forthcoming.

'I am Kate Marsden, yes,' I replied, wary of his tone but always ready to put forward the best representation of myself. I had learned even then how quick people are to cut down a tall poppy. One of the challenges that faced me during those times of pleading the cause of my lepers was to push myself forward so that their plight might be heard, and yet to remain humble and not to seem self-serving. It was ever a fine line to tread. This boy, however, had other, more specific questions on his mind.

'It is her, Mama,' he said to his parent without for one second taking his scrutinising gaze from my face. 'She's the one I heard tell of. Walked into leper colonies, stepped right up to those cripples with their rotting flesh and shook them by the hand, she did.' When his mother gasped at this he added, 'Embraced them too, true enough.'

Three more residents of the hotel were now walking down the passageway and could not help but overhear our conversation. They slowed their pace, the better to listen, and I could see at once there was a reluctance on their part to pass close to me.

I said clearly for all to hear, 'I did indeed visit many settlements where sufferers of the terrible disease are forced to live out their lives. Their misery is very great, and if you have heard of me, you will no doubt know that my mission now is to see a hospital built for them.'

The boy's eyes were bright with mischief. 'And you sat and ate with them, it's been said. Slept in their filthy hovels.'

'There was neither the space nor the necessity...'

'And some people say that you caught the lepers' curse yourself.'

This time there was a collective gasp from all who stood around me. The boy's mother instinctively put her hand on her son's shoulder and pulled him towards herself and away from me.

'That's the truth isn't it?' he demanded.

I fumbled for my key in my purse, but such was my sense of being surrounded, of being hounded, that my hands were trembling. 'I am not prepared to answer such accusations.'

'Why not?' came a shout from one of the other guests, a man dressed in an expensive overcoat and carrying a silver-topped cane. 'Let's hear it, madam. Are you a leper or no?'

'I refuse to be harangued in this manner! I must ask you to excuse me...' At last I retrieved my key from my bag, but another guest – I will not call him gentleman! – had put himself between me and the door of my room.

'We've a right to know,' he insisted.

'Sir, kindly allow me to pass.'

The boy, delighted at the excitement he had stirred up, would not be stopped.

'She is a leper herself!' he declared, pointing a finger, though taking care not to get close enough to inadvertently touch me.

A woman in the crowd gave a sharp cry of alarm. Two chambermaids had come upon the scene and I noticed them hurry away, no doubt bearing the news to others.

'I simply refuse to be accosted in this fashion!' I said, raising my voice to be heard above the growing clamour. With the route to my room still barred I found myself slowly beaten back along the corridor. As I reached the lift the doors opened and the manager, evidently alerted to the commotion, stepped forth.

'I am pleased to see you indeed,' I told him, but before I could ask his assistance, the man with the cane was berating him loudly.

'This is monstrous!' he cried. 'That you should allow a person known to consort with lepers... to allow her into your hotel...'

'What were you thinking?' demanded the other man. 'If there is a risk of infection, we have a right to be told!'

The manager lifted his hands and adopted a soothing tone, but they would not listen. I tried to get into the lift, but more guests and staff had appeared and I found the only path left me was along the passageway. I turned and walked briskly to the stairs, but by the time I was at the top of them I was being chased!

'Stand back!' 'Do not let her touch you!' 'Leper! Leper!' came the shouts behind me, so that I was forced to run.

I tore through the foyer of that establishment and out of its gleaming doors as people recoiled in front of me, hurrying from my path, lest they come into contact with this foul, leprous creature!

We came to the shaman's *yourt* late in the afternoon and the sun was hastening to meet the horizon. The snow was already tinged pink with the dusk. There was smoke pluming from a hole at the centre of the roof of the padded dwelling. Monsieur Vilenbakhov and I were helped from our sleigh by our guide. The shaman's home was set apart from the rest of the village, and most of the other dwellings were closed against the cold of the encroaching night, their inhabitants nowhere to be seen. Our guide hailed the shaman, we heard a gruff answering word or two, and we were shown through the reindeer-skin door.

Inside there was little by way of natural light, and small oil lamps threw irregular patches of illumination through the smoky gloom. Richly coloured rugs formed the inside walls of the space, and there were many low cushions and curious collections of stones and feathers about the place. In the centre stood the shaman, a man of Mongolian appearance, impossibly old, his bright red coat adorned with intricate embroidery, ribbons, bells and more feathers. His headgear was equally ostentatious. We exchanged polite bows. With a curt gesture he invited us to sit upon some reindeer skins which I feared were not free of vermin. Once seated, I asked Vilenbakhov to translate for me, though it was quickly apparent that the shaman spoke scant and corrupted Russian. My young translator did his best.

'Tell him,' I instructed, 'how honoured I am that he has agreed to see me. Tell him...'

But he interrupted me, holding up his hand. He uttered a few words.

Vilenbakhov translated. 'Madame Marsden, he cannot speak with you until you have accepted his hospitality,' he explained.

The shaman picked up a stone jug. He took the stopper from it and poured a greyish foamy liquid into a bowl. Next he picked up a feathered stick tied with bells and this he proceeded to wave above the bowl while he uttered some strange words. He held the bowl out towards me.

'Is strong drink,' my translator informed me. 'Traditional.'

Gingerly, I took the proffered bowl and set it to my lips. The fumes of the alcohol alone in the fermented mare's milk were sufficient to give this follower of temperance a dizzy spell! Still I forced myself to take a sip before offering it back to my host. He shook his head, frowning.

Monsieur Vilenbakhov said somewhat apologetically, 'The guest must drain the bowl, madame.'

There was nothing to be done but drink, or our journey would have been wasted, and the precious herb no nearer. Closing my eyes and holding my breath I tipped the entire serving of the sour, powerful liquor down my throat, fighting the urge to retch. At last it was gone. I kept my face as impassive as I was able and returned the bowl to the inscrutable shaman.

As he spoke, Vilenbakhov searched for meaning in his words.

'We are both people of medicine. Healers,' the shaman said.

'It is for this very reason that I have sought you out.' I waited while my reply was translated, and so our halting conversation continued.

'I know what it is you want,' the shaman told me. 'You want the flower.'

'You have used it yourself?' I hoped that the translation would not carry my own breathless excitement.

The shaman merely nodded.

'Where might I find it?' I asked.

'A nurse from Moscow must have much medicine in her bag,' was his reply.

'We have many medicines, it is true, but none yet that can cure a leper.'

'I have heard Moscow doctors speak of an elixir that can trick the mind so it no longer hears the roar of pain. And another that brings on sleep.'

'Yes, we have these things.'

The shaman shrugged. 'We have them also. I am told you have a device to take the blood from one person and give it to another?'

'Indeed, this is true also.'

The shaman waved his hand dismissively. 'We can do this without the use of a device. The magic of a shaman is powerful. And your doctors use a machine to listen to the workings of a man's heart?'

'A stethoscope. A useful diagnostic tool.'

'What need have I of such a machine when I can listen to the heart of a man with my ears and look into his soul with my shaman's eyes?' He paused to allow his words to sink in and then continued. 'Medicines can be used up. Devices and machines cease to work. Yakutsk people are better served by their shaman. Which is why you have come, for only here is the plant you seek to be found. And yet,' he added, shaking his head, 'there is nothing I want from you.'

His suggestion that I had nothing with which to bargain was clear.

'I hope,' I told him as levelly as I could, 'that a fellow healer will understand my wish to help rid the world of this terrible disease.'

'A Yakutsk shaman understands more than you will ever know,' he stated boldly. 'He understands that the world is a wide place, with many people. There is not enough of this flower for all of them. If I show you where it grows you would take every plant until there is nothing left.'

'No. We would take only seedlings and seeds to grow the plant ourselves.'

'It will not grow somewhere else. It will not work unless given by a shaman. Will you harvest all the shamans in Yakutsk also?'

'Might I not be taught by one such as yourself? Shown how to use it?'

'A shaman is born not made. You must find the medicine of your own for your own people.'

'But I wish to help your people too, do you not see that? Monsieur Vilenbakhov, make sure he understands. He must understand! Tell him about the hospital. It will help the families of Yakutsk who suffer so. Will you not share your knowledge so that, together, we can help them?'

The shaman leaned back, his face impassive, his heart unmoved.

'Our people do not need you. They have their shaman.'

He picked up his pipe and sucked deeply upon it. The conversation was at an end.

I strode from the *yourt*, infuriated, my frustration threatening to overwhelm me. Vilenbakhov followed and stood helpless behind me as I strode about in the gathering dark, icy snow crunching beneath my feet.

'Such short-sightedness! Such arrogance! Does he think God made him alone keeper of the cure? Why will he not see my motives are pure?'

My translator said gently, 'The shaman is unaccustomed to sharing his patients.'

I stopped pacing then and stared at him. 'He is protecting his income? Ha! He will not share the whereabouts of the flower because he fears he will lose business if his patients are cured by someone else. Such shameless self-interest!'

I was all for charging back inside and confronting the shaman again, but I heard shouts.

Vilenbakhov put his hand on my arm. 'Look,' he said, pointing towards the village.

Down the frigid path came a rag-taggle group of people, shuffling, stumbling, lame and blindly groping. They were clothed in rags, and the smell of them reached us before the poor wretches themselves were close enough for us to discern their ravaged features. My lepers had found me! Our local guide looked terrified and backed away, all the while shouting at them to stay back.

'No,' I told him. 'Let them come.'

The shaman emerged from his dwelling to see what was happening. One of the lepers stepped forward, chattering in a dialect so thick it defied translation so that Vilenbakhov had to ask him to repeat himself more slowly.

'They heard of the English nurse who was come to help them. They are begging you for a cure,' he said, stepping backwards to distance himself from the rotting limbs and sore-pocked faces which slowly advanced.

I saw them and I wept. Not out of pity, for I had surely seen many such afflicted patients by this time. I wept because the scales had fallen from my eyes and I could see the truth. The truth of the flower, that no doubt grew nearby, and that the shaman no doubt used and made a profit doing so. But it was no cure. How could it be? For if the Yakutsk people had within their reach a remedy that might free their loved ones from the dreadful curse of leprosy they would surely have used it, and the hellish scene that was before me would not have existed. Even the self-serving shaman would not have passed up the chance to heal had it been within his power. I saw now that it was not. That flower I had travelled so very far to find did not, after all, hold within its fragile leaves the promise of a cure.

'Do you ever wonder if we could have lived different lives?' Rose put her hand behind her head as she reclined further on the wicker chaise. Her hair, ordinarily so neatly tamed, had come free of its pins and she was too languid, too hot, too at ease to bother with it. Its soft, tawny curls framed her face prettily. She closed her eyes against the sunshine that filtered through the cane blinds of the verandah, so that I was able to sit and gaze at her. Her skin was translucent, and I found myself burning with a desire to touch it, to feel its delicate perfection beneath my fingers. Instead I clasped my hands in my lap.

'Different lives?'

'Yes. I mean, might we *not* have become nurses? Might we have found other paths to tread? Other versions of ourselves? Do you not, on occasion, wonder what else we might have been?'

'I have always known I would be a nurse.'

'I know you have,' she said with a sigh, 'but there are times when I think, what if I had thrown caution to the four winds and become a painter?'

'But, Rose, you do not care for painting.'

'That's just a for instance, silly. I could have said opera singer, or ballerina, or... oh, I don't know, a fortune teller with a travelling circus!' She laughed, opened her eyes, and threw a small cushion at me when she saw how serious I looked. 'Kate! Your face!'

'I didn't realise you were... discontent.'

'I am not. I am merely dreaming.' She sighed again, all the laughter quickly gone out of her voice.

'I believe we are what we were meant to be,' I said.

At this she rolled her eyes. '*Please* do not tell me it is God's will that I spend my life as a nurse. Not that.'

'I cannot help what I believe,' I told her.

'And do you think *we* are God's will? Us? Do you think He approves of us?'

I had no answer for her then. I have no answer still.

It was such a small church, and plain by the standards of the region. No gilt or purple paint here, simply whitewashed walls and wooden panels, simply carved. I know not how long I sat in that empty place, wearing that weighty silence. I had reached a point of epiphany the day before, on coming to the realisation that there was no magical cure. The flower might be a soothing balm perhaps, but it was not the miracle I had been led to believe. Not the wondrous deliverance I had hoped to find. There I sat, thousands of miles into a strange land, a land I had traversed on the promise of this hope. I listened for the voice of God in that church more keenly, more desperately than I had done in my life before. I had not needed to hear him so badly ever, I believe, not even as I nursed my siblings to their cruel end, nor watched helpless as a soldier died upon the battlefield. I waited for Him to give me a sign, to show me what I should do next, but all that came was more of the heavy silence that held me to that pew.

I started as I heard the stout wooden door open, scraping upon the flagstoned floor. Footsteps, and then Monsieur Vilenbakhov appeared at my side. He had taken off his hat and carried it in restless hands. He looked anxious. I confess I found it difficult to meet his gaze and returned to staring at the modest altar.

'Madame Marsden? The packs have been loaded. We are ready to depart.'

I nodded and did my utmost to appear composed but he saw at once how I battled with my innermost thoughts.

'Forgive me,' he said, shuffling his feet. 'I should not have intruded...'

'It cannot work. Do you see that?' I asked of him, unfairly, of course.

'You are referring to the plant...?

'The flower. The thing they guard so fiercely, it cannot be the cure I had been promised. If it were, why would the shaman not use it, if only to line his own pockets and improve his exalted position further? I have been chasing a myth, Monsieur Vilenbakhov. A powerless whisper of hope. Nothing more.'

The young man came to sit on the pew beside me then, clutching his hat in his hands.

'You will turn back?' he asked.

I stared at him then, astonished.

'I most certainly will not.'

'But without the cure, that is to say, I understood...'

'It is a blow, I admit it, but to give up? To abandon those I have been sent to save? Never!' I jumped to my feet. 'What manner of nurse would I be to do so? What poor shadow of a Christian woman? There is now more than ever a need for the hospital I will build, for what else can we offer the afflicted now but solace, comfort, companionship and care?' I saw in that moment that God had indeed sent me a sign. This well-meaning young man had questioned my resolve, and I had found it to be every bit as strong as ever it had been. I strode down the aisle, calling back as I did so. 'Quickly, if you please, monsieur! Many miles lie ahead of us.'

Lying here, my limbs so frail, at times I believe I have a sense of what it must be like to feel one's body dying by inches. There are days I can wriggle my toes, but I cannot feel them. I can move my fingers, but not stir strength in them. As now, today, my entire being seems almost weightless. But then, I am fortunate to be resting in a comfortable bed, with clean linen, the care of trained nurses, food that my poor dear Yakuts could only dream of, placed in my hand. Not a sack of turnips and potatoes left such a distance from my sick bed that I would have to crawl to fetch it.

I found many Yakuts lepers frozen in the snow having failed to reach their pitiful supplies. If we happened across them in summer the animals of the forest would have reached them first, so that their bones were scattered and gnawed. How many, I wonder, lost their lives to the bears? Those fearsome beasts were, for me, the spectres of the *taiga*. We were ever alert for signs of them. Scratchings on a tree. Scent markings. Spoor. A distant sound among the woodland. The horses sensed them, of course, hearing and smelling what we could not. So terrified were they that they would take off, galloping from the path, running blindly. I knew that to fall would be catastrophic, but staying aboard was also perilous. My legs were bashed against rough trunks as the animal twisted and turned at speed. I was compelled to throw myself forward, clinging to the pony's neck, in order to avoid being cracked upon the head by a low bough, or knocked to the ground.

And how was it that you fell from favour in New Zealand?

There were misunderstandings.

Surely it was more than that! The newspapers vilified you. You were accused of... well, would you like to defend yourself now?

There will always be those who seek to make themselves look better by making someone else look worse.

But don't you want to clear your name? You tried to do so before. You even brought a law suit.

Which I chose to drop.

Which lack of money forced you to drop. How that must have rankled! To have to let your accusers go unchallenged. Their accusations unanswered.

I did answer them, many times. Those who know me know the truth of it. As does God.

There were some who said you hid behind God. That you were not, perhaps, the pious, godly woman you would have everyone believe.

I was only ever engaged in God's work.

Lucky for you that work saw you elevated, then. Mixing with royalty. Money being given you in the name of your causes.

You seem determined to goad me into anger. I can't think why. What is it you want me to say? Do you expect me to defend myself all over again? Do you truly believe that now, at this point in my life, I have the strength to do it all again?

And yet you are writing another book, aren't you?

I do that to order my thoughts. I do that so that I might remember clearly.

I wonder what it is you wish to remember most? Tell me just this: what was the most hurtful accusation? Which blow caused the most pain?

What would that reveal? If you seek truth, that may not be the path to it.

I could give you a list, to make it easier. Where shall we start?

Please, do not.

Fraud. Embezzlement. Lying. Self-aggrandisement. Assault.

✦

The only sensible way to travel from Irkutsk to Yakutsk was, of course, to use the river. This wide, smooth waterway was the main connection between the two places before the completion of the Trans-Siberian railway line. I am a fair sailor, not given to sickness, and I could, if called upon to do so, swim passably well, so that I was not anxious when considering this section of the journey. I had not, however, understood the nature of the vessel on which I would be berthed. This was no recreational river boat. Indeed, it was not designed for passengers at all. It was a barge, no more no less, and its cargo potatoes. My billet was atop the sacking that covered these muddy, musty vegetables. We were fortunate that the journey was no more than 3,000 miles, for 3,000 miles was quite enough.

We had not long begun the task of reorganising the hospital linen cupboard, but already the store room was half-filled with stacks of neatly folded sheets and pillow cases. I had two nurses to help me, Nurse Wilson and a newcomer, Nurse Treharn, a shy little thing given to blushing. Ours was not a difficult task that day, but it was an extra bit of work on top of our normal duties, and as such we all viewed it as a nuisance. Still, it could not be put off indefinitely.

'Nurse Wilson, put the newest linen upon the far end of the table. I wish to sort the wheat from the chaff. We will inspect each piece and anything requiring further mending can go on a separate pile over there.' I indicated the top of the cupboard in the corner of the room.

'We are up to date with the needlework, Sister,' she told me. 'We should find nothing that is not suitable for use.'

'We should not, but I wager that we shall,' I replied, handing her another armful of whiteness. The smell of bleach and starch was disturbed the more we unloaded the cupboard. Nurse Treharn scurried back and fore with the pillow slips. She reminded me of a house mouse, darting for the skirting. 'Nurse Treharn, kindly fetch the stepladder. I shall need it if I am to reach the top shelf.'

She did as she was instructed, and together we positioned the wooden steps as near to the cupboard as was possible.

'They seem very rickety, Sister Marsden. Are you quite certain they are safe?' she asked, her voice little more than a whisper. She had the perplexing habit of not looking one in the eye when she spoke.

'They are perfectly serviceable, Nurse,' I told her. 'Now, you hold onto them like so,' I took her hands and placed them upon the wooden uprights. 'That's it. Just to keep them steady. Really, Nurse, you must learn to raise your face when someone is speaking to you.'

'Sorry, Sister.'

'It truly is disconcerting to be always addressing the top of your head.'

'Sorry, Sister,' she said again, only this time she lifted her chin and met my eye. At once her face flushed deepest pink.

'That's better. Now, don't let go,' I said as I mounted the ladder.

I recall reaching the penultimate step and finding that still I could not reach the back of the highest shelf of the tallboy. 'Hold tight, I shall have to stand on the top.' Even as I spoke I felt the steps give a slight wobble. I placed my feet squarely in the centre of the tread, my shins leaning my weight forwards against the hand rail above it. By stretching forwards I was able to take hold of the last bundle of linen and pull it towards myself. It was as I did so that I the ladder gave way. I heard both nurses cry out, there was the sound of snapping wood, and then I fell. I fell heavily, I landed awkwardly, my head connecting with the hard tiles of the floor so that I was instantly rendered unconscious.

The barge, or *pauzok*, was typical of its kind in that it was designed to float in shallow water, so that I was able to embark directly from the pier at Irkutsk. As I reached for the hand that was offered me I wondered if this was not to be a more testing mode of transport even that the dreaded tarantass. It was little more than a covered raft. The covered part providing not accommodation for passengers – for this was in no way a pleasure cruiser! – but protection for its cargo, in this instance potatoes. There was a small area to the rear which was open, and upon which deck the pilot of the vessel and his single crew member stood or sat so that they might navigate the river. At times one of them would stand at the front of the boat to use one of the long poles with which he would punt to help steer the boat, another being similarly employed at the rear. As I set foot aboard I was immediately aware of two things. The first was the uneasy movement of the boat, for something with no keel can only bob and bounce upon the water, even though it be a river free of larger waves. Whilst I am not given to suffering from *mal de mer* I did wonder if I might not fall victim to *mal de rivière*. Happily, this proved not to be the case. The second unforgettable characteristic of the barge was its smell. There was a musty, damp, dankness that emanated from the hold that seemed to cling to one's clothes, so that in the days and weeks to come I would feel myself as reeking as the vegetables with which I travelled. The odour placed a bitterness upon one's palette, so that it tainted every morsel eaten or drunk for the entirety of the voyage.

The Lena is a majestic river, the proportions of which it will be hard for me to adequately describe to anyone who has not travelled beyond the small countries of Europe. Imagine, if you can, a steel grey surface that stretches towards the horizon in both directions. You might conjure this spectacle if you think of looking first up and then downstream on the longest stretch of river you have ever encountered. Now adjust your thinking to comprehend that this is not the length of the river, but its *width*. Indeed, on some days, it was only possible to see one bank of the river. To see the other, we must travel past the midway point. This gave the curious impression that we were off the coast on some swirling sea, rather than following the course of an inland waterway of freshwater, rather than salt.

The owner of the vessel – the name of which I was never told – showed me with unconcealed pride the quarters that were to be mine during my stay aboard. These consisted of a pile of sacking placed atop the cargo in the hold on the left hand side, as near to the entrance as it was possible to get. This position at least allowed for some air and a little light. My billet was in the corner curtained off on the remaining two sides by further hessian, and included a tiny area next the wall, which was sacrificed to my needs, being free from potatoes, so that the boards of the deck were revealed. Here was space enough for me to use the bucket provided when nature compelled me to do so. In addition, there was space for my cases, upon which I would be able to sit, and a small tin cupboard for my food. The sight of the limit of my comforts for the coming weeks gave me a moment of near despair, causing me to think I would prefer to take my chances with wolves, bears and thawing ice, if only it meant fresh air and freedom of movement. But then I thought of how comparatively quickly I would cover the thousands of miles between Irkutsk and Yakutsk on the barge, and how every moment which delayed me prolonged the suffering of my poor lepers, and I silently rebuked myself for my selfishness.

After the first few days I believed I had settled into a way of managing the new challenges presented me. The captain of the boat and his crew spoke nothing but a dialect of Russian that was impenetrable to me. Indeed, having enjoyed the services of two translators I had acquired very little Russian at all. The few guides who travelled with me and who still included Yuri, the trusty Cossack and his dog, chose to 'camp' on top of the cover of the barge towards its prow, beneath a tent of their own construction. To reach them would require scrambling over the uneven rooftop, so that we would be able to do little more than wave acknowledgement of one another occasionally, unless we put into a port along the way. How I missed Ada. How I missed Monsieur Vilenbakhov. It is such a fundamental human desire to communicate. I would have to content myself with directing my thoughts and fears to the ready ear of God.

I decided routine was key to making the journey tolerable. I arose with the dawn, which was signified by a grey light creeping through the cracks between the boards forming the sides of the covered area. This early in the season – it was nearing the end of March – daylight did not visit this distant land until nearly nine o'clock. I would rise and fetch water from one of the tin cans stored on the other side of my curtain. With this gritty liquid I would do my best to make my ablutions, before pinning back the hessian so that there was sufficient light by which to read. I spent an hour or so then with the Gospels, happy to set my thoughts on higher things, to strengthen my resolve and remind me of my purpose. On the fourth day, however, when the temperature had risen considerably even, it seemed to me, before the sun was up, the air in the hold was oppressively thick with potato fumes. What was worse, this warmth brought other changes, for it stirred from slumber other passengers with which I shared my billet. Of course there were mice, and I was so accustomed to these I barely registered their presence. If I spied a rat I called out and one of the men would appear with a shovel and dash about beating at the sacks and floor until the thing had either escaped or been despatched. If he was successful the captain would treat me to a gummy smile. If he was unsuccessful he would merely shrug, a gesture which he sometimes chose to underline with a hearty spit.

But there was something else. As I sat upon my chair of luggage, my book in hand, my mind happily taken up with the familiar words and their message, I became dimly aware of a movement. Thinking it likely a mouse, I ignored it and read on. I then felt something nudging against my foot. Slowly, cautiously, expecting a particularly bold rat, I lowered my book so that I might see what company I had.

I am not given to shrieking, and I am of the opinion that when a woman screams from fear of something she finds repulsive it does our sex no good at all, for it underlines that spurious notion that we are but a muddle of hysterical female physiology, and should be kept silent and at home. However, the sight of the monstrous centipede that was now lifting its front legs to climb my boot brought forth from me such a screech as wolf and bear had so far failed to elicit. The thing was longer than any rat and almost as broad. As I leapt from my seat, dropping my precious copy of the Gospels, the vile creature wriggled and undulated, its orange body raising up as its countless black legs felt about it for my boot. There was no space to step away from the thing, and even as I hesitated in horror I watched it gain purchase on the leather toe and begin its ascent with terrifying speed, so that I knew in seconds it would scale my leg. I cannot say I was in control of my actions as I beat at my skirts and hopped and jumped and shook my foot. When the captain appeared in the doorway it was to see a woman in a frenzy of violence beating at the twitching corpse of the assailant with a (mercifully empty!) bucket. He uttered words that needed no translation, the astonishment on his face being entirely eloquent.

I took myself up on deck, such as it was, and exchanged incomprehensible good mornings with the captain and his crew. The sight and sound of the samovar was always able to lift my spirits, and the men appeared cheerful enough, and content to have me sit with them. They laughed as they chatted on this occasion, and I feel certain their amusement was at my own expense, but I was too shaken to care. It was only as I sipped my tea and watched the smooth water of the Lena slipping by that I began to feel calmer. The captain had led me to understand, through an elaborate mime, that many more of the loathsome centipedes inhabited the cargo. I feared I might never sleep properly in my 'cabin' now that I knew whom I shared it with, and the thought depressed me. I must find a way to endure the weeks ahead, and refreshing sleep was a crucial part of this. It occurred to me that such insects preferred to dwell in darkness, and so I reasoned that Yuri and his companions were not troubled by them in their 'encampment' out in the open on the top of the boat. I finished my tea, and then, to the amazement of the captain and his man, climbed onto the roof of the barge and made my precarious way to the front of the boat. Yuri and the others were sitting or reclining and on seeing me attempted to stand up. I signalled to them not to bother. Yuri's dog wagged his tail in welcome. Through halting Russian on my part, great patience on their part, and no small amount of mime, I was able to tell them my plan. I was shamed by my inability to speak their language and determined to use the remainder of the voyage to learn what Russian I could from them. The rest of the day was taken up moving my bed and extending their canvas shelter to accommodate it. Most of my things I kept below, so that I could still return to them during the day when I needed to, to give the men and myself a brief period of privacy.

Oh, how much better it was to be sleeping beneath the stars once again!

When people at home heard of my mission they tried to stop me with accusations of the crime of being unwomanly. When this failed, they turned the thing upon its head and accused me of the greater crime of being a woman in a man's arena. What business, they demanded, has a fragile female, a delicate daughter, being in so terrible and cruel a place? Her slender bones will surely snap. Her thin skin will blister and ruin. Her frail womanly heart will break. They chose to forget that the very thing I sought, the object of my quest beyond the lepers themselves, was a flower. A tiny plant, blossoming somewhere hidden in the vastness of the Siberian steppes. Could a thing be more fragile, more dainty? And yet it had the greatest power: the power to heal. It had strength beyond all those learned men of science, all those knighted sons of medicine. A secret flower. I had heard it spoken of in awe in India, in wonder on the battlefield thousands of miles away, but in Russia it was mentioned only in whispers. A secret guarded by its rarity and protected by its inaccessibility. I would not stop until I had found it. Until I had seen for myself what it might do.

After a week aboard the potato barge the weather began to change. Chill nights and still, frosty days gave way to warm, wet winds. These buffeted our makeshift camp on deck in the most tiresome manner, making our outdoor living altogether less tolerable than it had been to that point. While it was a relief to be free of the cold that had accompanied me on my journey since leaving Moscow, the rise in temperature brought with it these wearying breezes which soon grew in to gales and, eventually, spring rain. Ceaseless, heavy, beating rain. We reinforced our tents and shelters as best we could, but it was now impossible to sit outside them at all, and even within them we were constantly and consistently wet through. I was, at last, forced back down to my quarters below.

The rise in temperature had brought about another change; the smell of the cargo had increased tenfold, so that now I felt I was breathing in more vegetable than air at times. The stink was so overwhelming it made me nauseous, and to add to my misery, I acquired a chill and a cough that sapped from me both strength and resolve. I lay for days at a time upon my hessian bed, using the last of my feverish wits to banish thoughts of scuttling roommates from my mind. I had no alternative but to lie at the mercy of any creature who cared to investigate me. To dwell upon what might wriggle or crawl upon me in the night was to give way to nightmares. I sought solace in the Gospels, copies of which I had brought with me to distribute among those I met upon the way. What comfort there is to be had in those dear, familiar words, and I thanked God for them.

'You have a visitor,' my mother announced, standing in the doorway of my bedroom. She wore a disapproving expression which I had suffered under many times before. Her brows were lowered, her lips pursed, and she held her hands clasped across her bosom as if in an attempt to make herself larger and more important. She stepped to one side, reluctantly it seemed to me, and Rose appeared. I struggled to sit up in my bed.

'No!' Rose shook her head as she hurried towards me. 'Do not exert yourself, and especially do not put strain on your poor back. I have spoken to Dr Ferber, and he is adamant you need plenty of bed rest.' She was off duty, so not wearing her uniform, but instead had chosen a pale yellow cotton dress, so that it was as if a little drop of sunshine had entered the gloomy room. She came to stand beside the bed, tugging off her white lace gloves. 'See what I've brought for you? Freesias,' she said, holding the blooms forward for my inspection. 'Don't they smell divine.'

'You shouldn't have...'

'Nonsense. I know you,' she said, plucking some wilting carnations from the vase on my bedside locker, 'you'll be fretting about the hospital and worrying yourself into all manner of imaginary horrors about what we nurses are doing or not doing while you're stuck in here. A few fragrant flowers will be a soothing influence. There! Isn't that better?'

From the doorway came a harrumph from my mother, who then, mercifully, left us.

'It was good of you to come, but really, there is nothing to be done but let time heal. And I am certain you are needed at the hospital.'

'I've changed my shifts to nights so I can come and see you,' she said brightly, sitting herself on the edge of my bed. 'Can't have you brooding up here on your own all the time, can we?'

'I am not brooding.'

'Well, can't be much fun. I mean, I don't suppose many visitors get past your mother,' she giggled.

'Rose, hush!'

'I thought for a moment she was going to refuse to let me in.'

'She isn't used to people coming to the house.'

'She didn't like the look of me, that much was obvious.'

'It is only that we've lived a quiet life since we came to Wellington...'

'Well I am going to see to it that you have regular doses of cheering up. I'd tell you all the gossip but there isn't any. To be honest, it is deadly dull without you at the hospital. Everyone is quite lost without you to tell them what to do, and they fall to bickering, which is tiresome. You have to get better just as soon as ever you can. Let's plan another picnic! That will give you something to look forward to.'

'I fear it will be some time before I am well enough to travel anywhere.'

'Yes but it's good to be able to think of it. Motivate the mind and the body will rally, that's what you've always told us. So, a sunny day by the river, paddling in the water, an *enormous* picnic hamper full of goodies, all day with nothing to do but please ourselves.' She put her hand lightly on top of mine. 'How does that sound?'

I smiled. 'I believe I feel better already.'

By the third week in June, we were ready to leave for the final and most challenging part of my journey. How much the weather and the landscape had changed since the commencement of our mission in the winter months. Gone was the pristine snow and bone-aching cold. Instead we faced the dual enemies of heat and biting flies. Our party numbered fifteen in total, consisting of local men, guides, two Cossacks, a local official who had a little French, and myself. The tracks and paths upon which we were to travel were too narrow and rough to accommodate carriages of any sort, so we were all to make the journey on horseback. I have since received criticism for my decision to ride astride, but in truth there was no choice to be made on the matter. Ahead lay thousands of miles of rugged terrain which would cause our small, wild-headed horses to plunge and leap. Then there were the constant alarms set up from bears or wolves, which would also provoked our mounts into panic, which sometimes involved them bolting through the dense forest. Were I to have ridden side-saddle I would have been unseated before very many miles, and my mission would have come to an inglorious end. And of course, these stout, hardy ponies had not been schooled to carry the sort of saddle preferred by ladies. The beginning of such a trek over such dangerous territory was not the time to start persuading them to tolerate one.

As a consequence, I had to choose clothing that would allow me to sit astride my horse, allowing me sufficient freedom of movement to control it, whilst giving me protection from the rough bark of the trees I would be squeezed against, from the summer rain when it fell in great downpours, and from the armies of biting flies. To my riding trousers and jacket I added thick leather boots and a deerstalker hat which I had purchased in London, and over which I draped a net veil. In addition, I had ticketed upon my left sleeve the badge of the red cross. Glamour and elegance were left behind, and in their place I took up practicality and good sense. If my selections resulted in an outlandish and less than ladylike appearance I make no apology for it.

Our cavalcade was a curious one. Fifteen men commanded thirty horses, carrying stores and supplies, and armed against bears. I myself wore a whip and revolver at my hip, though with the ardent hope that I would not be called upon to use either. I had heard such terrible tales of attacks by bears upon travellers that I felt I would be reckless to go unarmed. However, it chilled me to the marrow to consider the circumstances in which I might be compelled to fire on a charging beast.

His Grace the Bishop of Yakutsk held a special service for us, where we prayed for God's blessing and protection. I was deeply touched to see this singular collection of men and one strangely-attired English woman receive this benediction of the eve of our perilous mission. I had not wanted to draw unnecessary attention to our party upon our departure, but we naturally aroused no small amount of curiosity as we gathered for the off. I felt a nervousness assail me, for though I had already covered vast distances to reach this remote point, it was now that I considered the true test, the most exacting and important part of my quest, to begin in earnest. At last, on the morning of June 22nd, 1891, all preparations completed, we started on our journey of 2,000 miles.

I had considered myself well-equipped for the ride through the forests, but I had not, it transpired, properly understood what faced me. The *taiga* was no ordinary forest. It laid no claim to dappled shade or pretty glades, but was a dense tangle of towering trees, knitted together with briars, brambles and creeping vines in such a way as to best repel the advances of any who would travel through it. The ground was far from even, consisting mostly of mud rutted and potholed by the severity of the winter weather, now dried in parts, while in others it was little more than a bog. This meant that our horses must plunge and stagger their way ahead.

And to those of you imagining horses similar to mounts one might hire back in England I say you have never met a Siberian pony. These horses were small, hardy, and nimble, which was all to the good, for I believe none other could have managed in such terrain. Their natures, however, were less helpful, being only half-tamed, and given to acting upon their wild instinct to flee from any perceived danger. This would compel them to plunge off whatever path there was into the near impenetrable undergrowth, forcing themselves – and their hapless passenger – between trees no matter how small the gap, so that my legs were mercilessly dashed against the rough trunks, and I was forced to crouch close to the terrified creature's neck for fear of being swept from my saddle by a low bough. Time and again my mount put us both through this ordeal for fear of a sound or smell that might or might not have heralded the arrival of a bear. The upshot of this activity was twofold. First, within a few hours, my gloves hung in useless shreds from holding the reins of plaited horse hair which wore through them to my soon blistered palms. The second was that I dare not, for a moment, take even one hand off my grip of these reins, for to do so would have certainly resulted in a fall, so that I was unable to swat away the dreadful flies and mosquitoes which set up a ceaseless assault. My veil proved useless against most of them, and by the end of the first day my face and neck were horribly bitten and swollen. We were none of us immune from these relentless swarms; people, horses, and dogs alike all suffered their attentions for the entirety of our journey.

It had been a singularly tiring day at the Wellington. In my capacity as Lady Superintendent of Nurses I was responsible for overseeing the training of all new staff coming into the hospital. As we had recently received a large donation, a new ward had been built, so that we had increased capacity for patients, and therefore had taken on four new nurses. Two were very junior, one had several useful years' experience of a surgical ward, and the other had held the position of Sister at her previous place of employment. I had spent the day apportioning duties for all, and finding other nurses to oversee the new arrivals. I was also required to attend a difficult meeting concerning the conduct of one of the surgeons towards a young nurse. It seemed the matter might be taken to court, which would do the reputation of the hospital no good at all, which led me to speak up for the surgeon involved, for the good of the Wellington. By seven o'clock that evening I was drained of all energy and sat at my desk attempting to summon the strength to go home. There was a knock at the door and Rose stepped into my room.

'Dear Kate, you look quite done in,' she said, coming to perch on the edge of my desk. She too must have worked a long and demanding day, yet she appeared to me as fresh and as pretty as her name suggested.

'I am all the better for seeing you,' I told her, reaching out to place my hand upon her knee. The heavy fabric of her uniform felt gritty with starch, but still I could detect the curve of her dainty knee beneath my palm.

'What you need,' she said, putting her hand on mine, 'is a little fun. You know what they say, "All work and no play makes Jack a dull boy".'

'I fear I am far too weary for anything that could be described as fun.'

'Nonsense.'

'Truly, Rose, I should get myself home, see that Mama is well, and at least take supper with her before I fall into bed.'

'Dear me, what a very dull evening that sounds!'

'It is what is required of me.'

'Not *every* evening. No, I won't hear of it. Not this time. A little cheerful diversion can have a beneficial and restorative effect – I'm certain I read that in a nursing manual somewhere.' She got to her feet, leading me by the hand. 'Come along, before someone else appears to ask something of you.'

'Where are we going? We can hardly go out to dine in our uniforms.'

'But of course we can! Two hard-working nurses eating a well-earned supper in a respectable establishment. What could be more proper?'

I went with her willingly, of course. I would have followed her anywhere. How our lives might have been different if only one of us had had a fortune of our own!

We put on our coats and walked ten minutes away from the hospital, turning into a narrow side street. I had imagined a quiet restaurant where we might take a corner table and go unnoticed, but Rose had something quite other in mind. It was dark, and quite cold, yet there were plenty of people turned out to enjoy the evening. It was a lively part of the city with which I was not familiar. Rose, on the other hand, appeared perfectly at home, and took me to a charming café, which had about it the look of a Parisian bistro. I don't believe I had ever been to a place like it before. There were lots of low gaslights and mirrors on the wall, and the furnishings were either of gleaming brass or burnished wood, so that the whole place glowed. There were warm fires in the hearths, and tables and banquette seating set close together, and already filling with happy diners. The ambience was lively and welcoming. We took a table against the far wall, with Rose upon the green leather seating, myself with my back to the room but able to view it in the mirrors opposite me. The effect was curious, as if the room and its inhabitants were repeated over and over, doubling and trebling the numbers of revellers, amplifying both sound and activity, as white-aproned waiters hurried from table to table.

'What an unusual place, Rose.'

'Isn't it fun? I discovered it last summer,' she told me, raising her hand to acknowledge the proprietor, who seemed to recognise her at once.

'You are a regular diner here, it seems.'

'On a nurse's salary? I think not. But I like to treat myself when I can. I would have brought you here sooner, I was certain you would like it, only...'

'Only what?'

'It is not very... discreet, Kate.'

I looked about me. Now I noticed that some of the clientele were already in their cups, despite the early hour. I saw also that people were happy to sit embracing one another, couples snuggled close as they drank, some sharing food, others lost in close conversation. All of them seemed so wonderfully at ease. And not all of the couples were comprised of a man and a woman. I felt my mouth dry. Rose was watching me closely.

'Have a glass of wine, Kate. Oh do, just this once. It is very good here, and really quite reasonably priced.'

She was not, I knew, inviting me merely to try the wine. She was waiting to see if I would flee the place, or if I would be bold enough to stay. Up until that moment, I could not have said myself how I would respond. But then, at that moment, with the seductive warmth and carefree atmosphere of the place, and with my darling Rose looking at me with such hope and such love, I knew there was not a place on God's earth that I would rather have been. I felt reckless, and it was a new experience for me.

'I think, on this occasion, a small glass of wine is a perfectly lovely idea,' I told her. I had never been a drinker of alcohol, and later became known for my support of the Temperance movement, but that night was truly a night when I was entirely in Rose's thrall, and I am not sorry for a second of it.

Soon the bistro was filled to capacity, abuzz with good-humoured noise. Rose was familiar with the menu, and we feasted upon battered fried squid and a French loaf, which we ate with our fingers, dipping the salty fish into flavoured oil, and mopping our plates with the crusty bread. She introduced me to the most delicious of all puddings – a bitter chocolate mousse liberally laced with Cointreau. Before we left the hospital I had sent a note home informing Mama that my duties would keep me late, that I would find something to eat, and that she was not to wait up. It was liberating to know that I was excused the duties of a daughter, if only for a few hours.

We rounded off our little meal with strong French coffee and then it was time to leave. We buttoned up our coats against the cold of the night outside and walked the short distance to a busy street where we might hail a cab. Rose looked at me then, her face solemn.

'Don't go,' she said. 'Don't go back to your house. Stay with me.'

'At the nurses's quarters? But Rose, what if we were to be discovered...?'

'We won't be. I promise you. It will be all right, Kate, only stay with me tonight.'

I knew that I should not. I knew if we were found out I should be ruined, and I heard my conscience cry out in protest at my sinful longing, but oh, how I loved her. How I loved her!

Siberia revealed itself to me as a place of extremes in so many ways, and none more so than in its climate. When I began my journey it was winter, so naturally I anticipated snow and low temperatures. Nothing, however, could have prepared me for the cold I was to experience. When the air is lower than -30degrees, and a knife-sharp wind circulates it about you, you stand before it as if naked and defenceless, and this despite the overwhelming weight of winter clothing.

Next came spring, which had up until that time signified to me rebirth, hope, blossom, and cheerfulness. Hereafter I can only ever think of it in Siberian terms, and those are simply thaw and rain. The first brings about a terrifying transformation of the ice that had, for the winter, been the surface upon which all must travel. That solid paving now began its melt. We could no longer head across a frozen lake or river without first sending some stalwart member of our company to test its condition. More than once his report caused us to clamber from our heavy conveyances and into lighter ones, to guard against cracking the surface of the lake and taking a deadly plunge into the water below.

And the rain. The rain!

And then came summer, and with it the mosquitoes and biting flies that were so many and so set upon their task of tormenting us that we were driven half-mad by the things, and never found any effective method of evading them.

Yet again the summer heat had driven us to travel by night. Aside from avoiding the testing temperatures, this also allowed us respite from the majority of the flies that so plagued us during the daylight hours.

The darkness was not so deep as to make our progress impossible, though we had still to rely upon the superior eyesight of our horses. They picked their way through the tangled forest, following the rough path that the villagers along our route had been employed to clear for us. Without their efforts, our progress would have been woefully slow. As it was the cavalcade moved at a cautious speed.

After twenty or so miles of our riding that day, by which time parts of my body had fallen to numbness, while others were in persistent pain from the wooden saddle, the uneven movement of the horse over the difficult terrain, the constant wearing of the same clothes, drenched by rain and dried upon my unwashed body, I was weary in the extreme. Even with my senses so addled, I became aware of an unfamiliar smell. The air tasted acrid, almost smoky. Indeed a few more minutes and I could see smoke, and then flames. At first I imagined we had happened upon an encampment, or even a village of some sort, but no, it was the forest itself that was alight. Not the trees, but the ground. At the same moment, my horse's hooves began to make a curious sound, as if the earth upon which it trod was hollow.

There were shouts up ahead and we came to a halt, all peering forward into the darkness. What manner of infernal forest had we found? Beyond the lead rider, in all directions as far as the eye could see, flames shot upwards from the soil in myriad colours. There were such blues and violets and even green bursts of fire as I had never in my life thought to see.

Further shouts came down the line, some in Russian, some in Yakuts, few that made any sense to me. Despite this, it was evident my guides were conferring as to what must be done. After a short exchange it was decided; there was no other way but forward. We were to ride through those very fires! There were more shouts and whips cracked as the poor, frightened horses were made to step between the flames. There were no paths to follow here, so that we each had to find our own way. The brilliance of the tongues of fire, and their vivid colours, jumping and leaping about our very heels, gave the impression we had entered the borders of hell itself. In some places the flames spluttered short and wavering, whilst in others they leapt high and straight one minute before disappearing the next, only to burst forth from the ground again, like subterranean prisoners escaping their confines. So unnerving and out of kilter with my own understanding of the world was the sight that I was almost relieved to see my companions similarly disturbed, lest I thought I was imagining the scene entirely.

With faltering words, one of the guides who had a little French explained to me that this part of the region has fires combusting beneath its surface in many places. The lower level of earth is burned away, so that we are indeed treading upon hollow ground. Eventually these fires find their way to the surface, emerging in the terrifying spectacle in which we now found ourselves.

My horse snorted and trembled at every burst of fire, and I had to hold tight to the reins or be thrown. I slipped my feet to the edges of the stirrups so that I might free myself quickly if the need arose. Gritty smoke assailed us, so that we all coughed and choked until we nearly retched. My heart pounded wildly, for it was clear that at any moment a wrong turn could result in calamity. As there was no way to predict where the next flames would erupt one had simply to trust to the horse's will to live, attempt to calm the animal as much as possible, and trust in God to see us safely delivered to the other side.

We had all but cleared the burning ground when a commotion from the back of the cavalcade set up cries of alarm and warning. In seconds the cause of the clattering and crashing became clear, as a bolting pack-horse charged towards us. The poor creature had stepped into the fire and the pain had caused it to bolt in terror, its packs banging against its sides or bashing against others as it passed. It was barrelling towards me and I could do nothing but wait for the inevitable. Only the actions of my quick-thinking guide, who urged his own horse in front of me and brought his whip down on the charging animal, turning it in its course, saved me. We all had to hold fast to our mounts, for every one of them wanted nothing more than to gallop off with their panicking stablemate.

When I awoke this morning the room was filled with a pure white light. My mind was quite clear, so that I knew I was here, in my hospital bed, and yet the light that surrounded me was not of this place. I wondered if the moment of my death had come. The thought brought with it a surge of joy, for at last I should be with Him! I felt my heart pound beneath my breast, but then I reasoned if my heart beat so, surely my body was not yet ready to relinquish my soul? I was at a loss to understand what was happening, and then, from the midst of this brightness, stepped a figure, small and slender. I squinted against the glare, shielding my eyes with my hand, trying to see more clearly. The figure came to stand at the foot of my bed and now I knew beyond doubt who it was!

'Tsarina? Tsarina!'

'Good morning, Katerina.' Her voice was as soft and sweet as ever it had been.

'You are here!'

She smiled. How had I ever forgotten the joy of seeing Tsarina Maria Feodorovna smile? I struggled to sit up.

'There now, Katerina, do not disturb yourself.'

'But I must, there is so much still to discuss, Your Majesty, so much still to be done.'

'Later. For now you must rest. Rest and get better, and then we will talk again and you can tell me of your plans. We will take tea together.'

'Just as we did before, all those years ago?'

'Just as we did before.'

She began to fade then, and I cried out, desperate at the thought of losing her.

'Stay!' I called to her, but she had gone.

The door opened and a nurse entered the room, coming to stand exactly on the spot where only a heartbeat before my dearest Maria Feodorovna had stood. She did her best to make sense of what I was saying, I know she did, but I was inconsolable, and she could do nothing to stem the flow of my tears.

❦

The black bread, which formed the bulk of our supplies, had soaked up the rainwater until it disintegrated, becoming a grey pap. It was salty from lying against the horses' sweaty flanks. Blocks of frozen milk were melted in a pan over the fire and the ruined bread thrown in. We ate the resultant gritty porridge with greedy delight, such was our hunger.

❦

We had not long recovered from the thunderstorm, all of us wet through, and horses and men alike exhausted from plunging in and out of the boggy ground, fighting fear and fatigue, when a new terror befell us. We were sitting beside the camp fires, our clothes steaming, our trembling hands wrapped around our cups of tea, when I noticed unusually excited chatter among the men. With my few words of Russian and halting French from one of the soldiers, I was able to understand that a large bear had been sighted nearby. It seemed it had been spied near the post-station up ahead and was believed to be at large in the neighbourhood. We mounted our horses as quickly as we were able, eager to get out of this dense part of the forest. The men were silent, hoping, I supposed, to creep past the bear without alerting it to our presence. However, they then decided that it was better to scare the bear away, or at least give it the opportunity to remove itself from our path. To this end we proceeded with as much noise and clamour as we could manage. Some of the men took to singing loudly, whilst others preferred to shout, as much to give themselves courage as to frighten the bear, I believe. Later we equipped ourselves with bells on the horses at the front of the cavalcade, and tin boxes half-filled with stone were passed out so that we could rattle and shake them to make as much of a clattering as we could. The resultant sound was so riotous and so discordant that after so many miles of it I began to wonder if I wouldn't rather face the bears. Even so, I knew this was false bravery, for I began to see every tree stump or fallen branch as a crouching bear, and when my horse shied at some unseen terror my heart would gallop. We saw tracks, and heard tales, but yet again it was our own fear that followed us through the forest far more effectively than the bears themselves.

Do you remember that particular rumour? The one that circulated about you only days after your return?

I have no wish to recall the malicious words that were put about by jealous people.

When they couldn't sully your reputation one way, they tried another, didn't they?

Many people said many things. That doesn't make any of them true.

His family feared there might be some truth in them, didn't they?

I do not know to what you are referring.

Don't be coy. In a way it was flattering, wasn't it? Were you not just the tiniest bit flattered to be thought of as sufficiently alluring to win the affection of a dashing young attaché to the governor general?

Monsieur Vilenbakhov? You are talking of Monsieur Vilenbakhov?

The two of you travelled so many miles together. You became close, do you deny that?

He was my interpreter. He never behaved towards me other than with the utmost propriety.

All those hundreds of miles, with him your only means of communication with everyone you met, with your guides, and so on. No one else could understand what passed between you, what you spoke of. It is said you would stay up long into the night, chatting together.

Said by whom?

And that you often shared a room, sometimes a bed.

I slept where there was a place to sleep. We all did. There was no choice but to share a space with my fellow travellers. But I was never alone in a room with Monsieur Vilenbakhov, not once.

Is there anyone who can vouch for that?

You might ask Monsieur Vilenbakhov himself.

Someone a little more objective?

Why is that the burden of proof of innocence seems to be with the accused, rather than the burden of proof of guilt resting with the accuser? Why should I be forced to prove, over and over, what did or did not happen? How is it that my detractors and traducers are able to hurl slanderous abuse with impunity? I have letters of support, from people in positions of authority, vindicating my position, my journey, my mission... will this never be enough?

At last we came to a clearing in the trees. This was not some sunlit glade, it was merely a less dense area of forest, where a few pines had been felled and undergrowth beaten back. It was summer. June, I think, and the heat of the day had wearied all of us, so that for a moment we did not speak, but simply sat on our horses and gazed upon the scene in front of us. There was a tiny, ramshackle hut, built of logs and daub of some sort. Its roof was low and moss-covered. No smoke rose from the hole that served as a chimney. The windows were glassless, their shutters hanging limp and loose. There was no door in the doorway. In front of this meagre dwelling the ground was worn to firm, bare mud. One could too easily imagine the mire this would become in the rain, and the height the snow would reach in winter.

Yuri dismounted but would go no closer to the dwelling.

'Anybody there?' he called out.

One of the Yakut guides echoed the question in his own language.

There was no response. Stiffly, I started to climb out of my saddle. Yuri hurried to help me. Though I came to stand on firm ground I felt as if at sea, my legs weakened by so many hours, so many miles riding. A fierce thirst assailed me but it would have to wait. I began to stride for the hut. My guides cried out in alarm, shouting at me to stop, warning me not to go near. Yuri stood before me.

'Have a care, Nurse Marsden. You should not enter such a place.'

'Yuri, I thank you for your concern, but I have travelled halfway across the world to be here. I have not come this far only to falter on the last few steps.'

A slight movement caught our attention. Around us, all else became still and silent as we watched, our eyes fixed upon that small, dark doorway. The silence thickened, so that we were breathing it in with the loam-laden forest air. Another movement in the opening to the hut. A shifting of the shadows, a disturbance of the gloom within. And then a part of that gloom – or so it seemed to me – separated itself, came forwards, took shape. The shape of a person, too ill-clothed, too disguised to be identified as man or woman. Their arms were unnaturally short, finishing in rag-covered stumps. They hobbled on gnarled, toeless feet upon which no shoes could comfortably fit. Their gait was pitifully uneven, their movements painfully slow and clumsy. The figure paused, peering up at us. I looked into that man's eyes – for man I now saw that it was – and he returned my look. I saw pain and fear, yes, clearly this man suffered deeply, but I saw something else in the instant that he realised I would not turn away. I held him in my gaze as I slowly walked towards him, and he saw that I had come for him. And then, in that moment of quiet and stillness, I saw something bright and clear and beautiful. I saw *hope*. The deliverance of that hope was the reason I had made my journey. It was precisely why God had sent me there.

⚉

Bears were the spectres of the forest. Their presence permeated the very air of the *taiga*. The threat of them – of their great violence – both lay in wait ahead and shadowed our footsteps. We rounded every corner with the expectation of meeting one, and listened to every snapping twig among the trees as proof of their imminent appearance. Had I known we were to make the entire journey without ever directly encountering one, how different my experience might have been. As it was, they haunted my dreams while I slept and my waking moments while we rode the boggy paths, so that I, like the horses, grew anxious and weary from the anticipation of an attack. How true it is that the fear of a thing can be as debilitating as the thing itself. A fact that was not helped by the tales I had been told of trappers and travellers set upon by these fearsome beasts.

My mother bore eight children and outlived five of them. I was the youngest, but I enjoyed no privilege from this position. I was not a pretty or endearing child, my features being too bold, my physique too unladylike. In my favour, I had the strength to endure the illnesses to which my siblings succumbed. My lack of femininity might have been a source of disappointment for my mother, who would have rather had me fair and frail I think, but both my height and my somewhat determined nature were what made it possible for me to journey through the hazards and dangers that I faced on my mission. Still, I am aware, and was always aware, that my mother would have sooner seen me married than roaming the world in answer to my calling. I was not surprised by this, rather frustrated. I could never expect her to share my passion for my work. Nor was I able to convince her of the good sense of what I was doing in respect of our livelihoods. And of course, I could not explain to her how marriage was anathema to me. That was not a subject I dared discuss with her beyond my own determined refusal to consider it. How could I?

The villagers had at first regarded me warily, and I understood their reasons. I might be the only English woman any of them had seen, and here I was in outlandish clothing, travelling the world alone, tall, pale, broad-shouldered compared to many of them. I came, so they heard, to seek out the very people their society shunned and banished. What manner of stranger was this? And then there was my contact with the lepers, for they quickly understood that I had

121

already found some sufferers, and that I had not only approached them, but touched them. Might I be infected? Might I bring calamity to their village, their homes, their families? They hung back, afraid and disturbed by my presence. By my mission. I could not blame them, for they dealt with the disease in the only way they knew. I did not for one moment believe that it was easy for a son to banish his elderly father, or a husband to take his wife out to the wilderness and abandon her there. These were good people, many of whom had God in their hearts and their lives, and so I knew it must cost them dearly to follow such a desperate course of action. What else could they do, if no one came to show them that there existed an alternative? During my stay in Yakutsk one of the governor's officials had sought to explain it to me.

'Leprosy is not seen as other sicknesses are, not here. Our people have lost children to measles, to influenza, to smallpox, to all manner of diseases, and their hearts break when this happens, but they see them as sent by God, either as punishment for sins, or to teach them some lesson, however hard. But leprosy,' here he paused and shook his head. 'Leprosy is sent by the devil.'

The meeting of the newly-formed branch of the St John's Ambulance Society in Nelson had about it the air of a little party. We had at last secured the venue – in the shape of the Temperance Hall – for our weekly gatherings, and we would be able to use it for our demonstrations of first aid. As my injuries had continued to heal well, I was delighted to be able to put myself forward to tour the schools and factories in the region. There was something immensely satisfying about taking life-saving skills out into the community. While the cause still dearest to me remained the plight of the lepers, I knew that I could not set out upon that mission until I was sufficiently well again. My mother's health had improved, and I was confident she could withstand the voyage back to England. All that remained was to secure further funds. I felt certain I could raise more money once in Europe, but at this point my immediate needs extended as far as the price of our passage home. In the meantime, it was to everyone's good that I throw myself into my St John's Ambulance work.

And had I not done so, I might never have met Nell. She came to that meeting, she later told me, out of curiosity, not only about the organisation, but about me. It seems she had heard of this nurse who had served in the Russo-Turkish war. She had heard of my good works in New Zealand. And, happily, she had heard of my desire to travel the world in support of God's outcast lepers; a cause which touched her tender heart.

As the business of the meeting came to a close the society members took tea together, inviting our new guests to join us. Amid the pleasant chatter, the note of which was a shared desire to do God's work in whatever way we were best suited, I spied Nell in the corner of the room. She was talking with – or rather, being talked at by – one of our more strident members, Mrs Langley, who was, to my embarrassment, telling her how fortunate they were to have me on their committee. Nell seemed to be barely listening, as her gaze was directed at me. When I smiled at her she cast her eyes down quickly, as if caught out in some way. I threaded my way through the small crowd to stand beside her, and offered her my hand while we were introduced.

'Oh, Sister Marsden,' Mrs Langley beamed, 'we are blessed today to have won the support of this good lady, Mrs Duff Hewitt. She is known for her philanthropy, and has given generously of both her time and her own income in many instances. I am certain the two of you will share a great deal of common ground.'

Nell, or Ellen as she was to me at first, was an attractive woman, with soft, soulful eyes, and a freshness about her skin that belied the fact that she was several years older than me. She had, I believe, resigned herself to the solitude of widowhood without bitterness. Perhaps she knew, in her heart, that there was something more, another love of which she was capable.

'I am delighted to meet anyone who puts themselves forward in the cause of the sick and the needy. There is much work to be done, Mrs Hewitt.'

'And you are the person to do it, I've heard,' she said.

'I am a woman unsuited to inactivity,' I told her. 'Alas my recent accident forced me to resign my post as Superintendent of Nurses at the Wellington.'

'Their loss was our good fortune,' Mrs Langley put in.

Nell said, 'I do not think we should plan on having Sister Marsden to ourselves. From what I have been told, a little town like Nelson will not hold you for long. Is that right?'

'I do indeed have bigger plans, if I am to further the cause of the lepers of this world, and they will require my travelling extensively.'

'How I wish I had a fraction of your bravery. To journey to far flung places and nurse people afflicted with such a terrifying disease... Are you never afraid?'

'I put my trust in God, Mrs Hewitt. He will send me where He may. I know that He will not ask of me something that is beyond my doing.'

I found myself staring at her, quite without meaning to. Mrs Langley was called away and the two of us were left, surrounded by people, and yet alone for all the interest we had in anyone save one another at that moment. I could see confusion on Nell's fine face. It was easier for me. The territory onto which we now ventured was familiar. I thought briefly of Rose, and quickly turned from that fragile memory. I saw that a battle was being fought within Nell, where propriety fought with desire. I wanted to spare her such turmoil, and yet to do so would have meant walking away from her. She blushed beneath the boldness of my gaze, but I would not let her go.

'If you have an interest in my work,' I said quietly, 'I should very much like the opportunity to speak with you further on the subject.'

She nodded quickly. 'That would be most agreeable, Sister Marsden,' she said.

'Excellent! I know of a dear little tea shop where we might talk undisturbed while enjoying particularly wonderful cakes. And do, please, call me Kate.'

It seems to me I have made a lifetime's companion of death. Perhaps that is why now, as the end of my own life is near, I do not fear it. That and my longing to be with my Lord, of course. As a nurse I have witnessed many deaths. I have delayed or prevented others, but to spend one's time surrounded by the sick is to have death hover ever at one's shoulder. Some of my patients were not seriously ill but even so the fear of death, of imminent departure from this life, it was in their eyes, in every anxious glance or imploring look. The fear of death stalked them just as the fear of the bears in the forest stalked me.

And what was leprosy if not a slow death? Wherever I treated lepers, on whatever continent, under whatever conditions, they received their diagnosis with a dread of dying from the disease, but as time went on it was *living* with it that frightened them. In the end, many longed for the release of death.

If I retreated to my personal life I would find death waiting for me there too. My father had died when most of us were still children, his death signifying the end of our innocence, the end of our protection. And then my sisters embarked upon their painful journeys through tuberculosis to meet our Maker.

Were there times when I wished death upon one who suffered? I would not be truthful if I pretended otherwise, but to admit it causes me distress, for I know it is for God to decide when our souls will go to Him. No one else has the authority to make that decision. There were occasions – few, but seared into my memory – when I was pleaded with to bring about an end to suffering. To see a person beg to have you end their life is a terrible thing. Terrible because you cannot accede to their wishes. Terrible because you have no desire to see them in pain. Terrible because you have no words that can lift them from their despair.

Come then, death, when God wills it. I know you are near. You always have been. But you have no power over me, for the hour will not be of your choosing. I felt you close when the ice cracked beneath the runners of our sledge upon the frozen lake. I knew you were watching when the forest burned and my horse threatened to throw me into the blaze. I heard your rasping breath in the midst of the fever that gripped me so far from home. But God had a purpose for me, and he kept me to it.

It was not my first visit to the city of New York. During my time travelling around the states of America to raise funds for and awareness of the plight of my poor lepers, I had been there on several occasions. Indeed after two years of such campaigning I had visited the majority of the major cities of that country, and had, for the most part, been welcomed. Good people know good when they see it, and who could not be moved when told of such suffering? I was able to give a first-hand account of the conditions in which the lepers of Siberia lived, and then able to explain our plans for the hospital.

But this time was different. I arrived by train, and took a cab from the station to a hotel which I shall not name here, for fear of further trouble and litigation. I had been travelling a number of hours, having recently come from Hawaii, where business had taken me. The porter took my luggage, the doorman tipped his cap, and I entered through the gleaming revolving doors. The reception area of the hotel was smart rather than grand, and I had always admired its understated elegance. There was something refined about its style. It was important that people with whom I would hold meetings should have somewhere to come to that set the correct tone for our discussions. This hotel offered just such an ambience. I was greeted at the desk by the concierge and the under manager, both of whom knew me by sight and by name.

'Good morning, George. Mister Whitely. It is a pleasure to be here again. Oh, don't the lilies in the foyer look delightful?'

The under manager, was about to respond and was indeed on the point of reaching for the register for me to sign when the manager himself, Mister O'Dwyer, came hurrying through from the rear office. He put his hand on the register and pulled it back towards him across the desk, an action that seemed full of significance to me even at that moment.

'I regret, Miss Marsden,' he said in a voice so low I had to lean forward to hear it, 'we do not have a room available for you.'

'Not? How so? I wired to inform you of my arrival. Did you not receive my telegram?' I asked, my gloves already half-removed in preparation for signing my name in the book.

'We did, madam.'

'Then am I to understand there has been a sudden influx of travellers and your hotel is full?'

127

'That is not... exactly the case,' he fidgeted as he spoke and had difficulty meeting my eye. His assistant looked as nonplussed as I.

'I am sorry, Mister O'Dwyer, but I am at a loss to comprehend what you are trying to tell me. Do you have a room or do you not?'

He hesitated and then said carefully, 'For you, Miss Marsden, I regret we do not.'

Behind me a small queue was forming. Other guests were waiting to check in or to collect their keys. Even with the manager practically whispering, it was clear some manner of altercation was taking place, and I had no doubt those close by would be able to hear his words if they cared to listen.

'I see,' I said, making no effort to quieten my own voice. 'And may I have the reason for this... exclusion?'

The man's fidgeting reached its height, so that he all but squirmed in front of me.

'I fear I am not able to speak of the details behind this decision...'

'Not able! Come, man, I have a right to know why I am no longer welcome at this establishment. I demand to know!'

Now all ears were strained to hear his answer. There was no escaping it; I would not allow him to slink away without explaining himself.

At last he said, 'It is a matter of protecting our guests. The hotel has a strong policy...'

'Protecting them from *me*?'

'Not yourself as such, Miss Marsden, but from, well, to put it plainly, the risk of infection.'

There it was. The gossip that had started as a malicious whisper had found its voice and progressed from city to city with breathtaking speed. There is a saying that a lie will travel around the world before truth has got his boots on, and indeed that seemed to be the case. I took a steadying breath. I let myself be strengthened by the knowledge that by being so shunned I was in the smallest of ways knowing the suffering of those I had given my life to help.

'Do you call me a leper, sir?' I asked, making my words loud and clear for all present to receive. There was a collective gasp. The couple nearest me took a step backwards. Aside from this all movement in the foyer ceased. The door did not revolve. Luggage was not wheeled in or out. Guests stopped mid-stride, uncertain whether to remain and listen further, or to flee. Such was the power of the word.

The manager flapped his hands as if he would silence me.

'Miss Marsden, please try to understand...'

'I understand perfectly well. You have allowed rumour and slanderous hearsay to influence your judgement. You are badly advised, Mister O'Dwyer. Your facts are nothing but fabrication.' I pulled my gloves on and straightened my shoulders. 'I shall take myself to an establishment where good sense and sound judgement are still the order of the day.'

So saying I strode from the hotel, the bellboy trotting after me with my cases. I swept from that place with my head held high, but I felt the disgust and fear of all I passed, and I shall never forget it.

That morning the sun was slow to rise above the horizon, the frozen tundra revealing itself in pale, faltering degrees. There was a light wind sighing about me as I stood waiting for the men to break camp. Their gruff voices seemed to recede, so poignant was the sound of the wind, and as I listened I was transported back to another time. To another dawn. To Rose. And the sighing was her own sweet voice. I closed my eyes then, allowing myself to be taken by the memory, experiencing a surge of love as I glimpsed her golden skin, her long limbs, her languid expression. It was but a moment, vividly brought to mind by the moaning of the Siberian wilderness, and yet it moved me so.

I opened my eyes and blinked away the bittersweet memory, pushing my hands into my pockets. I found a wrapped piece of Christmas pudding. Carefully I folded back the Fortnum and Mason paper and took some of the sugary contents. The taste alone was reviving, restoring my mood. I walked over to my waiting pony and fed him a little of the pudding, watching his delight as he enjoyed the treat and nuzzled my hand with his soft nose, hoping for another morsel.

I sat across the desk from the doctor, this time not as a nurse waiting to assist him, but as a patient, come for my diagnosis. It was a hard thing to find myself in such a position, and yet I should not have been surprised. After all, was not the fear of contagion what had driven those Siberian families to carry their dear mothers, fathers, sisters, brothers out into the cruel wilderness and leave them there? Was it not the nature of the disease to strike those who came close to it? Why should I escape then, when I had spent so many hours, days, weeks, years with lepers in all stages and conditions of the disease?

The room was cool, the blinds lowered against the glare of the Hawaiian sunshine. the doctor was a local man, born, raised and schooled on the island. He had grown up knowing of the ravages of the disease, and like me, he had dedicated his life to helping those who fell victim to it. Unlike me, he had not, thus far, been compelled to undergo the tests and examination that would confirm or reject a positive diagnosis. He cleared his throat as he shuffled the notes in his hand, reading quickly. From outside came the sounds of children playing in a nearby park. A dog barked somewhere. A carriage sped past, the ironclad hooves of the horses ringing louder, then softer as it raced away. All was normal and ordinary and as it should be. And yet there I sat awaiting the words that would decide my future.

The doctor looked up at me then and gave a gentle, kindly smile.

They said you were mad.

I was not.

Yet you did not defend yourself.

I could not.

Could not or would not? You should surely have been indignant, outraged, shouting your denial from the rooftops.

I imagine that might only have confirmed their suspicions.

You could have demanded a retraction. What was it William Stead said of you? That your experiences had brought about 'Painful maladies which disturbed her mental balance.'

He was quite wrong.

And yet you did not say so at the time. Not publicly. Why was that?

I had neither the time nor the inclination to answer every slur upon my character.

Wasn't the truth rather more personal? Wasn't it the case that being thought mad was preferable to being thought bad? After all, an insane woman can hardly be held to account for her behaviour, however abhorrent. Insanity might have proved a rather useful diagnosis to hide behind, is that not so?

The chief advantage of travelling in a tarantass rather than a sledge was speed. Despite the idea that one might move more swiftly on runners over snow, the conditions of the winter roads were such that

131

progress was both painfully uncomfortable and painfully slow. Once summer had arrived properly, it was possible to negotiate the roads in one of these heavy vehicles with three or more horses pulling it, often at a gallop. Indeed, the chief disadvantage appeared to be the recklessness with which the drivers of these fiendish conveyances controlled them. They were often inebriated, having taken frequent nips from a bottle of vodka to fight off the chill of the night, or to ward off fatigue. Their judgement thus impaired, they would urge the horses on, faster and faster, seemingly without regard for their own safety, nor apparently that of their horses, and certainly not that of any passenger.

On one occasion I was travelling alone in a particularly bone-rattling tarantass, and was already clinging on in a state of some terror as we tore through the evening with ever increasing speed. The driver cracked his whip and shouted at the horses, urging them on as if we were being pursued by the devil himself. Within a few miles I came to think that we were in point of fact being driven by him, as we began to descend a steep and rugged slope, and still the driver did not rein in the wild-eyed steeds that pulled us. I did not believe it possible that we could complete our descent safely at such breakneck speed, but worse was to come. Jolted from his seat, as one of the horses stumbled, the driver was pulled forwards, so that he fell, still clinging to the reins, between the bolting beasts. His cries were terrible as we galloped on, and I could do nothing to help. I could barely haul myself forwards to the empty seat, and, even then, there was no possibility of my retrieving the reins, which meant all I could do was hold fast, listening to the dwindling screams of the poor driver, waiting for whatever end was to come.

I confess my stomach lurched with terror just as the tarantass lurched and bounced down the hillside. But then I reminded myself that I was in God's hands. I trusted that He would see me safely delivered, for how else could I complete His work? Comforted by this thought, I resigned myself to the fate He had chosen for me. At last the animals tired, the slope levelled out, and we came to a slithering halt at the side of the road. Another vehicle happened upon us and its occupants hurried to our aid. Miraculously, the horses were unharmed, as was I. The driver, alas, had been severely trampled and did not survive his injuries.

The sitting room of our house in Wellington was not grand by any measure, but it had a pleasant window seat overlooking the garden. In summer the lawns became a little brown and the gardener struggled to stop the beds of flowers from wilting, but as autumn approached there was a softening in the weather and of the landscape in general, so that the aspect was cheerful enough.

After my accident I was compelled to spend far longer than I had patience for recovering at home. This inactivity was a testing state in which to find myself, as my natural inclination was for useful activity. My mother, of course, made the most of my company, so that after a few weeks she had become accustomed to sitting with me in whatever room I put myself. I tried to read, or to attend to my correspondence as best I could in her presence, but she was rarely content to sit quietly.

'Another letter, Kate? It is a mystery to me whom you find to write to. Your pen is ever scratching at a page.'

'I may not be able to work in the hospital at present, Mama, but there are still many matters related to my position that demand my attention,' I told her.

'Surely that must be for someone else to worry about now? I cannot see that the quality of your rest is as it should be if you are always concerning yourself with the hospital.'

'My body may be injured, but my mind is in perfect health and ready to be used. I cannot simply sit and wait to heal.'

My mother gave a grunt. 'It seems to me you make a good nurse but a poor patient.'

'Believe me, I am eager to be well and return to work.' I bent my head over my paper again. The little writing tray I had taken to using allowed room for inkwell, blotter and a sheet of paper, giving me a steady surface upon which to work. I was completing yet another letter to the insurance company who appeared intent on avoiding their obligation to me if I gave them the slightest opportunity to do so. Since my fall, I had submitted all the correct papers and documents in order that I might obtain the full and fair payment due me. After all, what is the point of an insurance policy if not to draw upon it in times of need? That is its very purpose. Why the insurance had been so obstinate I could not fathom. I did not, however, allow their behaviour to unsettle me. I had already filed another claim, I knew what I was about, I was confident I was in the right and ultimately they, and indeed the hospital, would pay out as they should. There was no question that the stepladder's poor condition had caused my fall. It being hospital property, the responsibility to maintain equipment lay with them, and therefore they were liable for any injury caused to any of their employees because of it. It had taken four lengthy letters before they had capitulated on this point. I did not anticipate my insurers proving any more difficult to persuade of the merits of my case.

Much as I disliked being unable to go about my work, the accident had in fact eased our financial situation considerably. Wages brought up to date. The roof, at last, got its repair. I was even able to organise a trip or two for myself and Rose, who had shown herself to be such a devoted and caring friend. I could not have wished for better.

'If you are feeling quite up to it,' my mother interrupted both my letter writing and my thoughts of Rose, 'I should like to invite the Morrisons to dine with us. And possibly the Devlins.'

'A dinner party?'

'Why not? Nothing elaborate, you understand, something simple. Refined. A way of thanking them for their sympathies when Annie died. And for their concern over your own health.'

'If any of them have shown any such concern I am unaware of it.'

'Oh, come now, Kate, Mrs Morrison sent flowers the day you came home from hospital. And the Devlins asked us to take tea with them...'

'Safe in the knowledge I was unable to accept!'

'You seem determined to see problems where there are none! Do you wish me to live out my years in solitude?'

'Of course not.'

'You have your work. Your hospital, your vocation, as you never tire of telling me. And your nurses, of course.' She paused here, but when I said nothing, pressed on. 'A simple dinner, that is all. It is common courtesy, and I should like it. Need there be better reason?'

'Have I raised any objection?'

'I have not heard you speak in support of my idea.'

'Mama, if it would make you happy to invite the Morrisons and the Devlins to dine with us, then by all means, let us fix a date and dispatch the invitations. I am sure you will have no objection to my inviting a friend to join us.'

'A friend?' There was no hope or excitement in my mother's eyes, only a wariness that pinched at something tender in me.

'The nurse who has had to shoulder a great deal of my work since my accident. Rose Farley. You have met her more than once.'

'Indeed I have.'

Ignoring the barb in her voice I turned back to my letter. 'That's settled then. It will be something for us all to look forward to.'

My mother's silence was as eloquent as any I had heard. I paid her no heed. To include Rose in the dinner party was important, for me and for her. The more the respectable people of Wellington saw that ours was an entirely respectable friendship the better. I was not immune to the cruel whispers that followed us about, and I was certain they had reached my mother. I wondered what thoughts she entertained on the matter in her private moments. I knew there was no possible circumstance in which she would begin a conversation on the subject, for to do so would give it credence, and her mind would not, simply could not, shed light on such a dark possibility.

In Jessy Brodie I found a fellow nurse whose determination to help the lepers of the world matched my own. She was a mature woman, considerably older than myself, who had established herself as a nurse of repute in New Zealand, and together we worked to set up the St John's Ambulance in the town of Nelson. We talked often of how we might travel to India to seek out those unfortunates outcast and abandoned, who needed us most. She understood, however, that after my accident my health was compromised, as was my income. Indeed, when it was decided I would not be fit to return to my post at the Wellington Hospital, it was Jessy who came to my aid.

'Truly, Kate, my house in Nelson sits barely used. I am so often about the country, and in any case there are more than enough rooms for us all. You and your mother would be most welcome to stay until you are completely well again.'

'But, Jessy, it is such an imposition.'

'Nonsense. Think how much better able to form our plans for the future we will be when we are under the same roof.'

'It is a fact that I am finding the upkeep of our house here in Wellington… difficult.'

'I cannot stand by and see you so taken up with worry over money when I have it to give, Kate.'

'I confess, since I was replaced at the Wellington I have relied entirely upon the payments I received for my injuries. They never seem sufficient to cover our needs, particularly now that Mama requires tempting with good food if she is to eat at all well.'

'Then let us decide it here and now. You will be my guests.'

And so we were. The house was small, and the garden lacking in any plants of note, but it was a comfortable and quiet place for us to stay. Mama resisted the idea at first, not wishing to give up what she considered to be her domain. When I made her understand how much easier life would be without the financial burden of our address in Wellington, however, she agreed to the move.

As time passed we came to see the little house as our home. Jessy was, as she had predicted, often away, so that more and more Mama and I inhabited the place without harbouring a desire to move on or take on a lease ourselves elsewhere.

※

I have always acted out of love. Our Lord told us to value faith, hope and love, but that the greatest of these is love. He instructed us, clearly, to love our neighbours as ourselves. That is all and ever what I have tried to do. How was it that people were unable or unwilling to see that? Why were they so determined to find some other, baser motivation for my actions?

And then, are there loves that are wrong? How can this be so? Why would God equip us with the ability to care for and cherish someone if it were wrong for us to do so? Surely real love can never be a malformed thing.

Our small party eventually halted at the leper settlement at Hatignach, an innermost area of Siberia. My guides were anxious at our proximity to the leper hovels and held back. By this point in my mission I had encountered many lepers, and seen for myself the terrible conditions in which they were forced to live out their pitiful existences, but still I was unprepared for the sight that greeted me at this place. It was too horrible to fully describe, and so I summarise here. A dozen or so men, women and children inhabited two tiny *yourta*. They were each and every one of them scantily dressed in ragged clothes, so that they must huddle together due to cold or lack of space. The dwellings themselves were riddled with vermin. One of the men was at the point of death. Two of the others who had lost their feet had tied boards to their knees so that they might drag themselves where they needed to go. Many there had only fingerless hands, and I leave it to you to imagine the hardships this brought about in a place that already offered only a harsh life. When one of the men attempted to make the sign of the cross without the aid of fingers it would have brought tears to the most callous of hearts.

They were all quite terrified of us, anticipating our loathing, borne of fear. They had learned to expect the roughest of treatments, and no words of sympathy. When they were at last helped to understand what it was we were about they fell to their knees, praising God for his mercy, blessing Him that had sent me to help them.

At one point I heard voices raised in anger and found that the Yakuts were driving away the lepers who were trying to approach me. They wished only to speak to me, but my guides and guards feared contagion, for myself and for them, and so angrily attempted to send the lepers away. I at once went towards them, an action which met with horrified objections from my travelling companions. I refused to be kept from those I had journeyed to help, and spent time reassuring them, as best our language shortfalls would permit, of my plans. My Russian was still woeful, but they heard the sincerity in my voice, and understood the true affection in my gestures. Once again I believe a shared love of God and His own language transcended the difficulties in our communications. They soon came to see that I was there because of Him, for them. They were tearful in their gratitude, and begged me to work swiftly so that a hospital might be built for them. In the meantime I promised to see that the bread that was taken out to them be of good quality, as many of them were falling ill through eating putrid food.

I arrived in Chicago for the World Trade Fair in the unshakeable belief that when the story of my journey to Siberia was heard, when my dream of the hospital for the lepers living there was explained, and when the suffering of those same people was laid before the gathering, my request for funds would be swiftly answered. God had chosen me for his instrument in this task, but I knew that He also dwells in the heart of every good and right-thinking person. And those people would be moved to act.

The city was abuzz with excitement for the Fair, the hotels and guesthouses filled, and the streets crowded. It was as a result of fighting my way through these excited crowds that I was a little late for my meeting with Mrs Elizabeth B Grannis, President of the national Christian League for the Promotion of Social Purity.

'Please forgive my tardiness,' I said as she bid me sit down in the charming room she used as an office. 'I am sorry if it has put you to any inconvenience.' I would have expected a lady of good manners to have quashed my fears and reassured me that the opposite was true. I was surprised, therefore, when no such assurance came forth from Mrs Grannis. Indeed her demeanour was cool and distant. She asked me to wait, and then left the room. On her return she had with her four more women, whom she identified as members of the board of the League. Once we were all introduced and seated she started up in a manner that quite amazed me.

'Miss Marsden, I requested you attend this meeting because certain facts have come to our attention. And these facts, given that you wish to speak at the conference, cannot be left unchecked. I'm sure you will understand that I have a duty to the League to be certain of the... nature of the speakers whom we engage.'

I think it was that use of the term *nature* that so alarmed me. That and the stiff and wholly unfriendly manner in which Mrs Grannis and her colleagues held themselves in my presence. At first I did not say a word. This was not a matter of judgement on my part, simply an inability to trust myself to respond calmly on the matter on which I believed we were about to speak.

Mrs Grannis continued. 'I have here a letter,' she said, picking up a sheet of paper from the blotter on her desk. I could see that it contained handwritten lines, but I could not make out the signature. 'The writer says he has reason to believe you are not entirely trustworthy. Indeed that you are not the pious and Christian soul you profess yourself to be. He states that he knows of your actions in New Zealand, and that there are people in that country who are willing and able to corroborate the facts that he has brought to my notice.

New Zealand! Had it been anywhere else, had she said Turkey, or referred to my time in Bulgaria, or in Siberia, or even Paris... I might have reacted differently. But, New Zealand.

'Oh!' I cried, my still-gloved hands flying to my mouth. Before I knew it I was weeping, and my words were an outpouring of emotion. Of guilt. Of confusion. Of shame. Of self-hate. For my truth was discovered, laid bare, and I could no longer deny it to myself or any of my inquisitors.

'Miss Marsden...!' My accuser attempted to quieten me, but my confession now flowed from me loudly and wildly and would not be stopped.

'You cannot know how much I despise myself, good ladies!' I told them. 'That you should be forced – by dint of your good standing in society and your being a part of such a noble cause – that you should be forced to listen to tales of my misdeeds, to find that I am such a flawed and wretched creature...' Through my tears I saw their shocked faces. They paled before me as I spoke. Some stared at me as if I had run mad. The others looked away, no longer able to meet my eye. And why would they wish to? 'I do not seek to excuse myself,' I insisted. 'I only ask you to find it in your hearts to put aside your revulsion, for the sake of my poor lepers. It would be wrong, surely, for them to suffer further as a result of my own failings, when all I wish for in the world is to do God's work in helping them.'

Now it was the good ladies' turn to be silent. As I spoke they regarded me, mouths agape, some pallor being replaced by blushes, shocked as if hearing the details of my past for the first time. I knew they would judge me, for was that not their reason for summoning me? And yet I continued with my plea, for the Fair was too great an opportunity to be missed. 'Ladies, I can only tell you this: the rigours and trials of my journey in the Siberian wilderness will have been for nought if I do not likewise withstand the tribulations facing me now. For if I am unsuccessful in raising funds for the hospital, those poor children of God will be abandoned forever to their suffering.'

I fancied I saw then a softening in their resolve to expose me and punish me. I made haste to capitalise on their compassion. I sprang from my chair and prostrated myself on the floor in front of them. 'Please, do not force my lepers to pay the price for my sins.'

'Miss Marsden!' Mrs Grannis was on her feet. 'Will you please stop this... display, and return to your seat.'

'Alas I cannot, I will not! Not until I have your assurance that my transgressions will be overlooked so that I might give my speech at the Fair. It is for my mission that I beg you, not for myself, for I know I shall never have your respect again. I do not ask for it. I ask only your help for God's sake.'

'I must ask you to control yourself and be seated. Only then can we resume this discussion in a civilised manner.'

Reluctantly I pushed myself up from the floor and sat heavily in my chair. Mrs Grannis consulted *sotto voce* with her companions while I awaited their verdict. Although in truth I knew I could only ever be found guilty. No, it was more their sentencing I waited for. Would they denounce me publicly? Humiliate me? Tear my reputation to shreds and scatter them on the winds of scandal? I prayed silently that God would guide them, for I had to believe that He at least had already forgiven me.

After a lengthy deliberation Mrs Grannis cleared her throat and spoke with a calmness which did not entirely match her expression.

'We are of the opinion that such matters as you have... explained, here, today, are not for open debate, certainly if the very mention of them might bring the League into any sort of disrepute. We would prefer it if you would leave Chicago this day...'

'No!'

'Miss Marsden, think of how such revelations would reflect upon our organisation. We cannot be seen to be associating with someone whose conduct is so perfectly at odds with all that we stand for!'

'But why must it be known?' I challenged her then. Challenged them all. 'What I mean to say is, you have there a letter, Mrs

Grannis. True, it is a damning epistle, one that could condemn me to oblivion should its contents be known.'

'But they are known,' a lady in an elaborately feathered hat spoke up. '*We* know of them.'

'And is it not your reputations you wish to protect?' I asked. 'I do not ask you to care for mine if you cannot, and why should you? But surely, if I were to withdraw from my scheduled talk on the programme of the Fair, then questions would be asked. Then the contents of that letter would fall beneath the harsh light of public scrutiny. Surely your League, and your good selves, are already associated with me, for am I not here to give my talk at your invitation?'

This interpretation of the situation in which we found ourselves gave them pause. Again they consulted one another, heads bent low, voices soft so that I might not hear their debate. When Mrs Grannis spoke again I detected a note of anger in her words, but it was the faintest trace, for she kept herself tightly reined.

'Given the lateness of the hour, we are prepared to permit you to speak, so long as you confine yourself precisely to details of your mission, to your proposals for the hospital, and to your request for donations for the cause.'

'Of course, you need have no fear, Mrs Grannis. That is all I ever wanted.'

She offered no response to this. Indeed, the good ladies sat silent as sphinxes, not for one moment taking their eyes off me, as I then proceeded to outline for them the shape of the talk I intended giving. I was greatly relieved to once again be allowed to focus my energies and my attention on the needs of the lepers, and found solace in talking of them, the shame of my earlier confession fading slightly as I did so.

The Silver Spoon Tea Shop in Nelson was a little taste of home, offering cakes and biscuits such as one might find in the best bakeries of any English town. It was Jessy Brodie who first introduced me to it, and it became our habit to meet there when her work schedule allowed so that we might make our plans.

We sat at our favourite table in the window, overlooking the busy high street. I lifted the pretty china tea pot and poured carefully through the strainer. 'Now, Jessy, I know you are bursting to tell me what you found on your trip to the north of the country, but first, I myself have news.'

'Oh?' She took off her gloves and placed them on the table on top of the small, pink and white, beaded bag she always carried. She was a rather plain woman, and wore her years of widowhood somewhat heavily, but she made the best of herself. Her late husband's money enabled her to dress well, and to indulge in her weakness for the occasional frippery. Such as the beaded bag. 'What news is that, Kate?'

'Well, on Tuesday last I attended a meeting of the St John's Ambulance committee, and I must say by the by that we shall have to keep a close eye on the manner in which they are running things, Jessy. I am not sure they are yet meeting your exacting standards.' She blushed a little at this compliment. I went on. 'But, committee matters aside, I was introduced to an interesting person, a widow like yourself. She has given of her free time, and of her own funds I am told, to help the organisation, and when I spoke to her she became most interested in my plans to seek out lepers in need of help and support.'

'*Your* plans?'

'I mean *our* plans, naturally. A little sugar? There. The lady in question is named Mrs Duff Hewitt. You might have heard of her? No? She is very well connected. I was impressed, I confess, by the calibre of person she calls friend. Two bishops and a state governor, no less. Not to mention the chair of the board of trustees for a highly reputable charity, I forget which just now.'

'And how is Mrs Hewitt to be of help to our cause?' Jessy asked, helping herself to a Viennese pastry.

'She is keen to be involved, to help in any way she can. Oh, a slice of Battenberg! How delightful.'

'Is she then a nurse? Is she willing to accompany us on our planned visit to India?'

'Dear me, no, Nell has no medical training. And she does not pretend to be any sort of traveller.' The idea made me laugh a little. I felt Jessy watching me closely, as if my very thoughts were being observed. It was not a pleasant feeling at all, to be so scrutinised by one who called herself my friend. Not for the first time I reflected upon the somewhat jealous nature of that friendship. It was as if Jessy disliked the notion of my having any friends at all besides herself. I had already given up Rose to satisfy this apparent need for an exclusive friendship, even though the manner of our relationship was not, and could never be, of the kind Rose and I had shared. Now, once more, I felt the burden of her disapproval and wondered how high a price I was prepared to pay for her continued support.

'Then I do not see,' Jessy said after sipping her tea, 'quite how Mrs Hewitt is to assist us.'

'She is a lady of some means,' I explained. 'She is grateful for her good fortune, and wishes to share what she has to help others.'

'My word, she sounds to be the perfect philanthropist,' Jessy said, though her tone suggested she might think otherwise.

I thought it best to ignore the subtle resistance she was putting up to even the notion of including someone new in our plans. There were greater matters at stake than her pride. 'Indeed,' I agreed cautiously, 'her motives are entirely Christian. I see in her a kindred spirit.'

145

This simple statement of fact caused Jessy to sigh and turn to gaze out of the window. There were times I questioned her commitment to our cause. Was she truly sincere in her wish to travel to wherever might be necessary, to give up her life to help the most wretched and needy of God's children? Or did she simply delight in make believe, enjoying the fancy of planning such grand endeavours without ever, ultimately, putting them into action? Certainly, in recent months, I had detected a reluctance on her part to spend money where it was needed. Only the previous week she had flatly refused to purchase the new trunks we would need in order to travel. Quite how she imagine we could journey halfway across the world without them I could not fathom.

'Jessy, come along, your tea is getting cold. And these scones are delicious, you must try one.' I reached across the table and patted her hand in what I hoped was a reassuring manner.

The gesture seemed to cheer her, for she smiled quite sweetly, placing her other hand on top of mine.

'Oh, I almost forgot,' I said, withdrawing my hand from her grasp so that I might search in my portmanteau. 'Here, I received the drawings from the seamstress we were recommended. She has produce sketches of the travelling nurses' uniforms we shall need for our trip, see?' I handed her the papers. 'I think they are very fine, don't you agree?'

As I watched, Jessy gave the images only a cursory glance before turning the page in search of the price the work would command. In truth, I was beginning to find her constant concern with the cost of everything more than a little tiresome.

While I believed the loveliness and kindliness of the Tsarina had no equal, our own dear sovereign was undoubtedly the most queenly woman, and the most womanly queen. Her support for my work was steadfast. She was above such malicious tales and scandalous gossip as had turned others from me. Such talk did not reach her ears, or if it did, she chose to treat it with the scorn it deserved. She had been determined to give her blessing, and indeed her great name, to my mission through Siberia, and her endorsement had paved the way for my being accepted into high society in Russia also.

Later, in the dark years after publication of my book, when many jealous foes had allied themselves against me for their own base purposes, still our glorious queen deemed me respectable and worthy. I remember, in 1906 I believe it was, being presented at court for a second time, breaking with all tradition, as I was neither coming out into society as a young woman would, nor was I married. Even so, she invited me, showing surely that no others had the right to turn me away. I had a gown made specially for the occasion, for it would have been unforgivable of me not to show that I was worthy of her continued patronage by appearing in any way less than I should. I selected a rich, navy blue brocade, with details of dark lace upon the sleeves and neckline, of modest cut, flattering, yet conservative, but with no expense spared as to quality of both cloth and workmanship. I was pleased with the results, and had my photograph taken to mark the occasion. I of course wore the beautiful brooch with which Her Majesty presented me when first I returned from Russia.

I did consider taking Nell to the picnic spot by the river that meant so much to me. But Nell was not Rose. And in any case, by this time I was residing in Nelson, and the journey would have been unfeasibly long for an afternoon. Instead I had to content myself with enjoying her company, for the most part, with others. It was, I believe, as much a trial for her as it was for me. My mother took to her more than she had done Rose, perhaps because Nell was nearer her own age. Or it might have been that she simply refused to believe that the good Mrs Duff Hewitt could be other than she appeared. Either way, the absence of tension around the dinner table, or when we three sat playing cards, was brought about by this welcome change in Mama's behaviour.

I recall one evening that will be forever special in my memory. It had been a day of strong sunshine, and even though it was not far off midnight, the air remained heavy and warm. We had shared a fine supper, and Mama had retired. Nell and I took ourselves out into the little garden to the rear of the house. During my time there I had taken the trouble to have a pergola constructed at the far end of the lawn, with a cushioned swing seat fitted beneath it. The bougainvillea had established itself without any difficulty, and now its papery scarlet and purple blooms hung decoratively from the trellis above us.

We sat side by side and I set the seat to swinging, taking Nell's hand in my own.

'What a pretty dress this is, Nell. The colour suits you so very well,' I told her.

'Are you certain? I thought perhaps powder blue was a little young for me.'

'Nonsense. It is your colour now, and it shall be when you are a hundred.'

She laughed at this. 'I doubt I shall live to such a great age.'

'I insist upon it! We shall grow ancient together.'

'That would be most agreeable, Kate. I shall hold you to it.'

'You and I will wear our years as women who have travelled, have done great things, have lived!'

'And there was I, doing my utmost to live a quiet life. Until you stepped into it.'

I squeezed her hand and then, impulsively, lifted it to my lips and kissed it. Nell gave a little gasp, but she did not snatch it back. She was content to sit just so, with her long fingers pressed gently to my mouth. We looked into one another's eyes, and I felt a strong affection pass between us, wordlessly but clearly. She was a handsome woman, with soft grey eyes and beautiful skin. She had about her a radiance, and at the same time a sadness. I thought that she must have loved her husband very much, and that the years she had spent alone since his death had etched such a loneliness onto her heart as could only be removed by someone who understood that. Someone who saw that here was a woman capable of great and generous love, if only she would permit herself the freedom to take it when it was offered.

'I am so fortunate that God saw fit to bring you into my life, Nell.'

'God and the small society that Nelson has to offer,' she smiled.

'We shall be the firmest of friends, my dear. I am sure of it,' I told her.

She looked down then, a little nervously. 'But of course you have other friends. Younger than I. More...alluring.' She hesitated and then went on. 'I should be saddened to think I am keeping you from those whose company is special to you.'

'I shall always be happy to make time for you, Nell.'

'But you are so occupied, caring for your mother, planning for your mission, raising money... Rose, for example, a dear girl, I'm sure, but she is not so well placed to assist you as I happily am. I can help you achieve your goals, Kate. You know I am eager to do so. My concern is that you will wear yourself out in attempting to be so much to so many. Would it not be better to confine your attentions to what is truly important? Better to leave alone alliances that can, that must, come to nought?'

I examined her face for traces of guile but found none, yet the meaning of her words was clear. Rose was a compromise she was unable or unwilling to make. Rose who I believed I could not exist happily without. And yet here was Nell with the means to enable my mission, my future.

There are times now when I awake from a fitful sleep and have no understanding of where I am. The room is clearly a hospital room, but beyond that point I am at a loss. My mind casts about for reason, for sense, for something to stand out from the white walls and white bedclothes, from the blankness of it all, something to speak of why it is I am here. And then my deadened limb, my weakened legs, my groggy thoughts remind me that there is nowhere else I could be. Even so, when a nurse enters the room I cannot say with any certainty that I have seen her before. I make a point of running through a list in my head: the young cheerful one, the old impatient one, the short one, the one with the bright blue eyes. And then, as I try to properly recognise whoever it is who tends me, I see instead something that sends me back to the past. Tawny hair like Rose's. The sad eyes of my mother. Nell's elegant hands. And then I am transported to sharper images, to clearer thoughts, and the present is lost to me.

I think, upon reflection, that it was a mistake to agree to another picnic with Rose. Our special place by the river had been a site of joy, of happiness, of escape from the crueller, harsher aspects of our lives. By taking her there for our farewell I had tainted it, tainted its memory too, with sadness.

It was such a pretty day, late in the summer, with the leaves still on the trees and nothing more than a warm breeze to disturb them.

As we lay on the tartan rug beneath our favourite oak I saw a kingfisher flash above the river's surface. I pointed it out to Rose, but her mood would not be lifted.

'I shall never come here again,' she told me.

'Oh, Rose, you must! You love it so.'

'Not without you,' she said, picking at a loose thread in the weave of the rug.

'But surely, if you visited you could enjoy the memory...'

'I am not an old woman, Kate, to spend my life looking back, living on times gone by and things lost.'

'Of course not, but...'

'It's all very well for you. You are to go out into the world again on a great adventure, while I must stay here. You have a new friend,' she added pointedly.

'I am sorry you do not care for Nell's company. I believe you would have a great deal in common.'

'It is *she* who does not care for *my* company, you must know that. And aside from our profession, the only thing common to us is you. Which is precisely her objection.' Here she left off unravelling the rug and started packing up our picnic, stacking plates and food and jamming them roughly into the basket. 'She does not properly care for you, you know,' she went on speaking without once looking at me. 'If she did she would not forbid you to see me.'

'She has not forbidden me. What makes you think she has? And why do you think I would agree to such a thing?'

'She is taking you away from me.'

'Rose, I have explained. I must be practical, I have my mission to consider, and Mama...'

'Oh, and there's another who will be happily rid of me.'

'She does not understand.'

'And does she *understand* about you and Nell Duff Hewitt?'

151

'That is quite different and you know it. Nell has offered generous support of my plans. I do not have the luxury of financial security that would allow me to refuse that generosity.'

She paused in her packing to frown at me. 'I would never have thought you a person to be so easily bought.'

'Rose!'

'It must be a very wonderful thing that she offers you, enabling you to take off on your noble quest to help the lepers. How sure you must be it will set you up and make your fortune to be known as the saviour of the afflicted! I should not like to think of myself given up for anything less.'

She got to her feet and stood facing me, her fists clenched as much against her own hurt feelings as in anger towards me, I believed. I stood up and tried to take her hand in mine but she snatched it away.

'Dear Rose, do please try to understand. I am also trying to protect you.'

'From what?'

'There is no place in this world for us, you know that. We are judged and found unacceptable.' I struggled to find the words, wanting desperately to help her understand that I was doing what I was compelled to do. 'You cannot think that I wish to give you up. You must know how much I care for you. In what deep affection I hold you.'

'Affection? You are too kind!'

She picked up her straw bonnet and pulled it onto her head but her hands were trembling so much she was not able to tie the ribbon beneath her chin. I leaned forwards and did it for her.

'One day you will see that I am only doing what I must. That what life's circumstances compel me to do does not reflect the measure of my feelings for you.' I curled the scarlet ribbon around my fingers and eased it gently into a bow. 'If there were another way, do you not think I would take it? And who is to say that, in the future, things will not alter again, but this time in our favour?'

'You know they will not. Why say they will?'

I tried to ignore the tears filling her eyes. The blue of them was more than a match for the iridescent wing of the kingfisher. How I wished she was no bigger than that jewel-bright bird so that I might tuck her in my pocket and keep her with me always! What part of God's plan for me did her suffering serve? Was it His way of showing me that I had transgressed? Was the pain I had to witness in her darling face my own punishment?

'No miles would separate me from you if I believed you wanted me,' Rose told me. 'But you have already placed yourself forever beyond my reach.'

I paused, unable to think of a reply that would not cause her deeper distress. 'Needs must...'

'...when the devil drives? Not God this time, Kate?' she asked. And then she turned and walked away from me.

'But Kate,' Jessy's voice had a childlike whine to it, 'you cannot mean to stay here beyond the summer, surely?'

'I cannot leave before I have sufficient funds for my mission, Jessy, you are aware of that.'

'And you must be aware that I have no more money to give. All that I have left is what I may get for my few pieces of furniture, and I cannot dispose of those while you and your mother are still living in the house.'

'Well, I am relieved to hear you do not expect Mama to sleep on the bare boards of the floor!'

'Why must you say things like that? All I ever wanted was for us to go about our work together.'

'Which is my dearest wish also, Jessy, but you must face facts. It is no good wishing things were other than they are. You had promised to see that we should both, you and I, be able to set out upon our plans for assisting the lepers together, but clearly, as you have not funds enough for this to happen, we must amend those plans.'

'I have not money enough because it has all been spent!'

'I really do wish you wouldn't allow yourself to get in such a state about this. I fail to see why you should be anxious about your future when you have already secured a post in an Indian hospital. It must be a comfort to know you will have an income, and that you will be setting foot in the very place I had hoped we would be travelling to together.'

Jessy closed her eyes briefly and then replied. 'I had no choice but to seek a position. You know my family have connections in the north of the country, and that is how I was able to find a promise of employment. I would far rather we went together. It was *you* decided against, I might remind you.'

'How could I, in all conscience, go anywhere before seeing Mama settled back in London? It is all very well for a person such as yourself, without responsibilities, to go where she pleases. I do not have that freedom.'

'I do not believe you have ever done other than as you please!'

She had become quite shrill, and set to weeping in the most dramatic manner. I gave her my pocket-handkerchief.

'Dearest Jessy, do not take on so. It is my earnest intention to follow on to India as soon as I am able. All will be well, you'll see. I shall remain here only until I can book passage for myself and my mother, and obtained the necessary funds to allow me to continue on after that.'

'Well I should like to know where you imagine finding those

funds without me there to provide them,' she sniffed in the most unattractive fashion.

'I am fortunate in having secured the patronage of Mrs Hewitt.'

'Oh! Mrs Hewitt...'

'She shares our vision, Jessy. Your own heart's desire is hers too.'

'That,' she said, taking a steadying breath and squaring her shoulders, 'I do not for one second doubt.'

I saw that she was calmer at last and patted her hand. 'You will be the pioneer in our mission, Jessy, think of that,' I told her. 'I shall sell up your pieces for you and I will bring the proceeds with me all the way to India so that I might put them in your dear, sweet hand. And then we shall work together as we have always hoped to do. And you will be happy again then, won't you?'

You never forgot her, did you? It was to her that your thoughts turned when you were in St Petersburg.

Of course I did not forget her. She was dear to me. As you were.

You did not write to me.

I could not.

You left her, just as you left me, and yet you continued to write to her.

I did.

To try to win her back.

She would not forgive me.

She tried to ruin you!

She was angry with me, for leaving her. I tried to make her understand. After all, she had always known my mission was to travel to wherever I was needed. She had always known my life's work would take me away. But not forever.

She didn't see it that way, did she?

155

Perhaps if I had been able to see her again, to talk to her in person, to hold her hand.

Instead you wrote letters, and she used them against you, didn't she?

She felt that I had chosen my lepers over her. Which was in some ways true. But she should not have asked me to give them up. How could I? How could I turn from God's purpose for me? She should not have asked me that.

You didn't give her up as easily as you walked away from me.

Oh, Rose, you know that was not easy at all.

I know what you said to her in those letters. Everybody knows because she let them put them in the paper. Your love letters to her, and she made them public, for all to see, for all to leer over.

She acted out of anger, out of hurt.

I read those newspapers. The whole world did. Everybody knew your secret then, but still you denied it.

I had to protect my reputation, you must see that. If I was ruined no one would donate money to the cause. The hospital would never have been built. I had to bring a suit against the paper. I had to silence their libellous reports.

But they weren't libellous, were they? They were true. I remember what you wrote. I read it and read it and read it and wished that it was my name at the top! Wished it was me you still longed for! My own dear Nell *you wrote. You talked about your appointments with the great and the good of Russian society who were to fund your trip. You said* The Ambassador cannot arrange for my official presentation until Monday next. I am, however, sure of getting at least £100 for my lepers from the Emperor and Empress, and I will give you £50 out of it to spend as you please. *How quick you were to spread the financial good fortune of the lepers among your friends! You might have sent me a little while you were about it.*

You must understand, Nell had spent so much of her own money supporting my mission. Without her I would never have been in St Petersburg.

You gave funds raised in the name of God and for the lepers of Siberia to your fancy woman!

I sought only to repay some of what she had spent. She had given enough.

Or did you seek to buy back her affection? I have the entire letter committed to memory, for it played so much on my mind I had to consider your words over and over. The money was not the worst of it, was it? Not for those pious ladies and gents you hoped to win over to your cause. Not for me. Remember how you wrote Be sure, my darling one, to wait at Berlin till I come. I will take you up the Rhine and to Paris, where we will have a nice time; then on to England in the lovely spring. Live without you I simply cannot. There is no work or pleasure of any kind in life without you. I love you with my whole soul. *How she must have enjoyed hearing you speak so.*

I felt badly that she was so unhappy.

You did not end there. You went so far as to plan your pretty future together. Don't you remember? You were to return to New Zealand to be with her. I will accept your offer, dear Nell, *you wrote,* to live with you there, because exist without you I cannot. Oh! my love, they do not know what love is. My love may be fiercer than yours, but time will mend that.

But time did not mend that. She would not be moved, my silly, stubborn Nell. She would not.

⬚

I closed the door as the last of the furniture was taken away. We had obtained a fair price for it, and I felt confident Jessy would be pleased. It had suited her to leave the disposal of her tables and chairs and so on to me, and I had been glad to do it. After all, Mama and I had lived rent free in her little house for quite some time, and had been happy to act as caretakers for it after Jessy had departed for India. It can be a worry placing such a thing in the hands of agents, and she had been so set on leaving when she did.

I was never entirely clear in my mind as to why she was so determined to go then. I had told her as often as I had patience for that if she were to wait we could all travel to Europe together. She had insisted that she had not the money to stay longer in New Zealand, and that she needed to take up the post she had secured as a nurse in India as soon as possible. This surprised me at the time, as I had thought we were making plans together. For weeks we had talked of little else but when we should go to India and how we should get there. Increasingly, she had concerned herself with the finer details of how our trip was to be funded, to the extent where I had eventually had to reassure her that if her own resources were running low, at least Nell would be able to step in and pay where she could not. This idea had not, it must be said, found favour with Jessy. Indeed, she had become so resentful of the time I spent with Nell that she avoided any activities or arrangements that involved the three of us being together at one time. As a consequence she and I saw less and less of each other. In truth, by the time she left, I felt we had grown quite distant. She had a pinched look about her that was not flattering, and I am certain it was a direct result of so much fretting about money, which never, in my experience, did anyone any good at all.

The items of jewellery which she had left in my care were harder to sell than the furniture had been. There was a rather charming gold pin in the form of a jewelled snake, as well as a ring and a string of pearls, and one or two other baubles. They were a little dated, but attractive in their own way, and in good condition, particularly the snake. I had sought the advice of a valuer at the jewellers in

Nelson, but he had offered me such a low price I had opted to hold on to the pieces for a little longer. I reasoned that they might command a higher value in London. From there I could more easily see to it that the proceeds caught up with Jessy, assuming that by then she would be settled at her new post on the sub-continent.

The Polytechnic Institute in London was one of the first places in which I was able to give my talk regarding the lepers in Siberia and my plans for the hospital there. It was a grand building, though with a utilitarian air about it. It was raining when I stepped out of the cab that had been sent to collect me from my hotel, but even so there was a sizeable crowd awaiting my arrival. Once inside I was taken up onto the stage and introduced, though I heard barely a word of what was said, such was my astonishment at seeing the auditorium completely filled. I steadied my nerves by thinking of those who now relied upon my success, and by asking God to give me a sound and commanding voice so that my message might be heard.

I recall that as I stepped forward to speak I experienced a piercing pang of regret that Nell was not there to share the moment. We had talked for so long about our plans, had travelled across continents and oceans together, and her support had been invaluable to me. And yet, she had gone from my life completely. My letters to her, heartfelt and sincere as they were, went unanswered. I did not, at that point, know the full extent of her fury toward me, nor what form it would take. I could never have imagined the harm she wished upon me put into such effective action. I believe still that she was cajoled into it by someone who desired nothing short of my ruin and would press all and everyone into service in order to bring it about.

An expectant hush descended upon the London audience. I took a deep breath, thanked them for sallying forth on such a rain-filled

159

evening, and set before them the facts of my journey, of the plight of the lepers, and of my dream of building a hospital. I talked for nearly an hour of a land most people present that night would never see; of a disease of which they had no experience save horror stories; and of a people who must have seemed as remote and alien to them as if they had been located on the moon. And yet, those good and ordinary people, they listened to my words, they heard my plea, and they revealed themselves to be true Christians! As I completed my speech they began enthusiastic applause, many rising to their feet to show their support. The sound of their approval rang throughout the hall, confirmation, had I needed it, that my work was worthwhile, and that it would be recognised as such. My host, Mrs Dunstead-Blythe, was forced to ask for quiet in the end, so that she could explain the procedure in place for those wishing to give donations. Such a great number wished to give money that a queue formed that wound its way twice around the auditorium, and it was an hour more before all funds had been taken in and I had shaken the hand of the last donor.

The SS *Ruapehu* was a fine ship, though not grand. Mama and I had taken the best grade of cabin funds would allow, but even so she protested at the meanness of its proportions.

'Really, Kate, we are to be cooped up like hens for weeks. Could not better have been found?'

'Mama we must make our resources last. You know my payments from the hospital ceased some time ago. We have only the small income from my insurance policies.'

'After all your hard work at the Wellington...' she puffed out her chest as she sat on the edge of one of the twin beds. 'Such little gratitude. And your arduous endeavours on behalf of the St John's Ambulance. Why did not they see fit to repay your service?'

'I gave of my time voluntarily, Mama, and the work was far from arduous. And really, this cabin is perfectly adequate for our needs. After all, it is a large enough ship. You and I will be enjoying its dining room and the decks. Why, we shall hardly be in here at all.'

'It will be my place of quiet solitude when you are busy with your friend, no doubt.' My mother's earlier acceptance of Nell had, to my dismay, evaporated as our friendship strengthened. Once again there was the familiar barb in her voice when she spoke of Nell. It had been the same with Rose. Only Jessy had escaped her disapproval.

'You know Nell has been generous in support of my cause. She is my greatest advocate. Without her my plans for taking aid to the lepers would come to nothing.'

'A fact she is not above holding over you when it suits her to do so.'

'You judge her harshly, Mama, and without cause. She is a true friend.'

'Friend,' my mother repeated, though she made the word sound unpleasant.

'I am surely not to be denied a friendship, Mama?'

'Oh, it is not for me to deny you anything, Kate, and I am certain you will not deny yourself! Now, I should imagine you will want to find the good Mrs Hewitt and see that she is content with her own quarters. I will set myself to unpacking, though heaven knows where I shall find to put everything.'

I left her then, happy to take the opportunity to go. We would be at sea for six weeks, and already that was beginning to seem an eternity. But Nell was with us. And Mama needed her naps. I would not be called upon to be her companion without respite. And in those times Nell and I could please ourselves.

I met Nell in the passageway.

'We are berthed on the same deck,' she told me, 'and close by. I am but two doors removed.' She pointed back the way she had come. 'Your mother is settled?'

'As well as she ever will be.' I linked my arm through hers. 'Come, let us see the last of New Zealand before it is too distant to make out.'

On deck there was a refreshing breeze. Other passengers milled about excitedly, some also taking their farewells of the land we left behind. Nell and I stood watching the stretch of water between us and home grow broader.

'Shall we ever return?' she asked suddenly, and I saw that she was sad.

'Don't be glum, Nell. Of course we shall, if it is what you wish us to do.'

'But there are so many other demands upon you, Kate. We are only at the start of your mission.'

'For which I have you to thank.' I squeezed her arm a little tighter. 'I cannot tell you how much it pleases me that we are setting out on this adventure together. We must see Mama to London, and then we go to Paris. Imagine what a time we shall have!'

'You will be taken up with your fundraising.'

'And you will be ever at my side.' I smiled at her. 'Nell, you must never see my affection for you as in opposition to my calling. The two are the mainstays of my life. I could not do without either. You must know that.'

She smiled then, nodding. 'Well for now I have you here, on this ship, and your causes must wait. I intend making the most of our time!'

After the maid had set down the tea tray, Reverend Francis closed the door to his study and came to sit opposite me. It was, I remember thinking at the time, a typically masculine room, devoid of the touch of a woman's hand, with somewhat heavy, workaday furniture, more books than the shelves could comfortably hold, and simple, somewhat frayed curtains at the long window. The main feature in the room was the handsome desk, upon which sat an inkstand and blotter, a magnifying glass, orderly piles of papers and yet more books. The reverend had offered me the only comfortable chair, covered in green velvet, which was next to a low occasional table. As he took his seat on the other side of it I noticed he did not meet my eye. Reverend Francis and I had known each other for some time, and our meetings had always been cordial, our shared enthusiasm for the building of the leper hospital giving us common ground and an identical cherished goal. On this occasion, however, I felt him to be unusually reserved and distant. I was at a loss to understand this change in his demeanour in my presence, but I was soon to discover the reason behind it.

He spoke as he poured the tea. 'It was good of you to find time in your busy schedule to come and see me, Sister Marsden.'

'I am always happy to be available, Father. You have done so much for the Leper's Association since its coming into being. I will be forever grateful for your hard work and support.' I took the proffered tea cup from him.

'As you know, I have always been an admirer of your work, Sister Marsden. The hardships you endured, and the sacrifices you have made, in order to carry out your mission... Well, I am humbled by your commitment.'

'Like you, I am God's instrument, Father. I do his bidding, and I am glad to do it.'

'Quite so.' He sipped his tea for a moment and then cleared his throat. 'In my capacity as treasurer of the fundraising committee, it is my duty to maintain clear and accurate accounts of all monies that are donated or otherwise raised.'

'Such as the royalties from my book sales.'

'Indeed. You will understand, I'm sure, the need for the Association to be always transparent in its financial dealings, and to remain beyond reproach as regards to payments and expenses necessarily given out to those who do work on its behalf.'

'Of course. Which is why you are such a boon to our organisation, Father, for who better to uphold the virtues of truthfulness? No one, surely, could ever question your integrity or honesty in handling the Association's funds.'

'Perhaps not, or at least, one would hope not. In this instance, however, it is not my own character that is being called into question.'

In an effort to discern what he meant by this statement I examined the expression on the reverend's face, but he kept his head low and his focus remained fixed upon the tea in his cup.

'Are you suggesting that it is I who am under some manner of scrutiny?' I asked.

'I have been sent letters, from a journalist in New Zealand, and another in London, and still another from America.'

'Journalists!'

'They raise several disturbing points.'

'It is surely what they are given to doing.'

'There are questions being asked regarding the... thoroughness with which you declare monies raised... there are grey areas...'

'What do they accuse me of, Father? I must know.'

'To put it plainly, Sister Marsden, they claim that you have been keeping the greater proportion of monies raised for yourself.'

'What nonsense!'

'They maintain that you have been, let me see, how did they put it... yes, "living the high life" on the donations, rather than seeing that they reach the coffers of the Leper's Association.'

'Reverend Francis, you know this not to be the case.'

'These are not my accusations, please understand that.'

'I take only what I need for travel and accommodation, with a small allowance for my personal needs.'

'It may be that this is where the criticisms are arising.'

'What these *journalists* simply will not see, is that to raise money one must move among people who *have* money. There would be no earthly use my pestering the poor to donate their meagre savings, would there?'

'This is true, but...'

'The only manner in which sufficient funds may be raised to build the hospital is for me to approach those who have sufficient funds to give. It is for this reason that I must be suitably attired and appointed. I cannot present myself to members of the royal family in rags, nor can I expect them to attend functions in a church hall.'

The reverend nodded his agreement. 'It is not me who is in need of convincing. I have been involved with charitable fundraising for as many years as I have been a member of the clergy, and I assure you, I understand how these things work. There is much in what you say. However...'

'However? Either you are satisfied of my innocent motives in spending a portion of the funds raised, or you are not, Father. I fail to see where there is room for a "however".'

'Firstly, as I say, it is others who appear to require some explanation of the way in which the donations are used. I believe a letter from me to *The Times*, perhaps backed up by another from yourself, well, that could be sufficient to pour oil on troubled waters. The second matter is of a more complicated, not to say more delicate nature.'

Now I feared I knew too well the reason the good reverend could not meet my eye. I set down my tea cup, for already my hand had started to tremble, and I feared I would lose my composure completely at the sound of it rattling in its saucer.

We enjoyed fair weather for the first two weeks of our voyage aboard the SS *Ruapehu*. However, at the beginning of the third week high winds got up. The captain was an able man, and I was confident we were never in any danger, but he could do nothing to calm the leaping and bucking of the ship, as it was at the mercy of the wild seas upon which we must travel. Many of the passengers on board suffered sea sickness, and others were fearful, so that the dining room and decks were all but deserted. Mama took to her bed, where I administered a dose of the soothing medicine given us by the ship's physician, Dr Ballard. I watched him mix the concoction myself, and was pleased to see it contain a liberal quantity of laudanum, for I knew Mama would not sleep through the storms without it, and without sound sleep her health would surely suffer and decline again.

Once I was satisfied that she was comfortably settled, I left her and went to Nell's cabin. When I knocked upon her door she answered quickly, and I saw that her own face was pale.

'Dear Nell,' I said, 'are you unwell?'

'I am not, which is a mercy indeed, but oh, Kate! The ship does fling itself about so. I fear every moment that it might turn over.'

As if to underline her point the vessel gave a mighty lurch, so that we were both forced to cling to the door jamb if we were not to be thrown to the floor. I pulled myself into the cabin and closed the door. Nell's room was smaller than our own, with only one narrow bed, but it was cosy, and warm, and I could detect the aroma of her favourite perfume, which had violets at its heart. I placed my hands upon her shoulders.

'Nell, you must not be afraid. This is as sturdy a ship as ever was, and it and its captain both have made this journey many times. What seems to us to be a tempest of unnatural strength is to sailors simply the way of the sea, and with God's hand upon the wheel they will steer us through it. Have no fear.'

'You are such a stalwart, fearless creature, Kate. You put me to shame,' she said, her admiration obvious in her expression. 'I wish I had half your courage.'

'Let me give you mine, Nell, for I hate to see you distressed. You look so very tired and pale.'

'I have not slept well these past days. I know it is silly of me, but I cannot help myself from laying there, eyes wide open for fear I will end my days in that bed, alone and terrified.'

'You will not,' I told her. 'Firstly, because Captain Watson will see to it that his ship reaches her destination with her full complement of passengers, and secondly because you will not be alone any more.'

'You promise?' she asked tearfully. 'You will stay?'

'I will stay. Now, come along. Sister Marsden prescribes good, sound sleep.'

So saying I turned her around and began unlacing the stays at the back of her dress. The fabric was of fine quality, a closely woven wool, soft and light, which flattered her slender figure. In the flickering lamplight the colour reminded me of damsons harvested from the hedgerows in my childhood. The pitching and rolling of the ship made us both stumble now and again, so that it was a full ten minutes before we had both undressed to our shifts and climbed into the little bed together. I turned Nell towards me, letting her rest her head upon my shoulder, my arm around her, so that she was held safe and close. I stroked her silky hair much as a mother might do to soothe a fretful child, and by and by I felt her breathing grow slow and steady and knew that she had fallen into a deep and peaceful slumber.

The greater part of my mission was, of course, to raise funds for the outcast lepers, to bring their sorry plight to the attention of the world, to rescue them from their pitiable existences in the wilderness, and to ultimately provide them with a hospital and a home that could give them their living and their dignity once more. But whilst I was about God's work I could not help but spread His word, and to that end I had taken among my supplies as many copies of the Gospels as I could crave space for. These precious pages I determined to give to the inmates of the prisons I had been given leave to visit en route. It was no small achievement to have gained, during my time in St Petersburg and in Moscow, the necessary papers and permissions that would allow me to do this worthwhile and Christian work. For does not God care for His sinners?

And so it was that I equipped myself with twists of tea and sugar, also, so that I might offer some solace to the unfortunates whose lives had turned from the straight and narrow and brought them to such sad circumstances. It was my fervent wish that this small gesture of kindness, given along with God's Testament, would engender in the prisoners a kernel of hope and a desire to seek His forgiveness. At the very least I would be able to report back to the authorities after my inspection upon the conditions in which the men were kept.

We reached the town of Kainsk, and were led to understand that there were in the vicinity some prisoners being taken on their way to a larger penal institution a fair distance away. I wished at once to visit these men, and enquired after their whereabouts, but my questions met with prevarication and avoidance. I asked at every post-station along the way, but it was some days before we caught up with them. When we did, and I asked if I might be permitted to see them, I was informed that the hour was too late, and that the prisoners were all locked up for the night. I thought of how they must be feeling after trudging through the bitter winds, no doubt poorly clad, and I could not but think how welcome hot tea would be to them after hours of such hardship. I pressed my case, and at last the person charged with their care saw that I was not to be refused.

I was taken to the place where they were housed, which was no more than two, large, dark cells. Soldiers stood on guard with guns and bayonets. The darkness inside was so deep that at first I could see very little at all, though I could hear all too well the rattle of chains and shackles. The guards shouted at the prisoners to have a care, for a visitor was moving among them. I felt the presence of human beings all around me, though I could scarce make them out. There were ninety, at least, crammed into the space, with no window to allow clean air in nor foul out. A prisoner with a candle stump was sent to lead me, sideways, due to lack of room, between the men packed upon the floor, their beds merely a few raised boards.

I was stared at, of course, many showing their astonishment at discovering a lone woman walking amongst them in the dead of night. They thrust their hands out to me and I thought they might try to kill me, but no! It was the Gospels they yearned for, and I gave them happily, along with the meagre packets of tea. I made my stumbling progress through the rooms, and rather than do me harm they blessed me for the little gifts of comfort that I brought them. At one point I tripped, falling clumsily over a wretch whose spine was curved and twisted. How gently I was helped to my feet! The rough hands of the men were as tender as a woman's. After an hour or so I was fatigued to the point of collapse, and the foulness of the air was starting to rob me of my senses.

I bid them good night, and as I went the clanking of their leg irons sounded in the darkness. Yet even so, they shouted their thanks after me. The doors were bolted, the padlocks fixed, and those ninety men were lost to all life's joys. I prayed to God to show them mercy, and that the Gospels would help those sin-laden men turn to Him.

I wanted to rest, but sleep was hard to find, and when at last I caught it up, my dreams were peopled with lost souls, and the chains they wore rang through my mind for the entire night.

I smiled at Nell. 'What a spinsterish pair we are, wrapped up in our knee rugs.'

This made her laugh. 'Whatever you may be described as, I defy anyone to call you "spinster"!'

The ship was sailing directly west that day, and the late afternoon sun was cheerful enough to entice us onto the deck to sit, though the air was rather fresh. Other passengers strolled arm in arm, some chose deckchairs in which to sit and read or chat. A game of deck quoits was being got up, and all about us there was generally an air of cheerful relaxation, the kind which often follows a storm at sea. We were alive. The SS *Ruapehu* had steamed steadily through. God and our good captain had seen us safely delivered to another day, and this was to be quietly celebrated.

'Is your mother better this morning?' Nell asked.

'Considerably, though I doubt she will leave her cabin for a while yet. The voyage is a trial for her.' I did not add, though I knew Nell thought it too, that at least this gave us time to be together without her disapproving eye upon us. Our friendship had deepened in the short time we had been at sea, and I was glad of it. Nell was not Rose. She would never be Rose. But her affection for me was genuine and it moved me. That she had come to feel for me as she did no doubt still astonished her, but I believe it no longer shocked her. She had emerged from the lonely solitude of widowhood into something thrilling and new, and the power of it had made her almost reckless with her reputation. I knew I could not afford to be careless, for much depended upon my being able to win over people of fortune and influence to my cause. Nell knew this too, and I knew that she understood my calling.

She leaned back and closed her eyes, the sunshine bathing her fine features. 'I am sorry your mother is not enjoying her time aboard our dear little ship,' she said, 'but for my part I wish we could sail around and around the world without stopping, and be together as we are now. Always.'

I reached over and took her hand in mine. 'How lovely that would be,' I agreed. 'Perhaps one day, when I have achieved my goal, we will be free to take a cruise at our leisure.'

She opened her eyes and grinned. 'Without troubling your mama to accompany us?'

'We could invite her safe in the knowledge that nothing would induce her to set foot on a ship again, not once she has reached the sanctuary of England.'

Nell sat up, serious now. 'And once there I will lose you to your work, will I not?'

'Not lose me, no.'

'No? But you must be forever knocking on the doors of those who might help. Petitioning and pleading, raising funds where you can. It will take up all your time. And I...'

'And you will accompany me, as my aide, as my indispensable

companion. Besides, it need not be a dreary time. Would not a visit to Paris cheer you?' There. It was said.

'Paris?'

'I have heard that the great French scientist, Monsieur Louis Pasteur, has announced that he is close to finding a treatment, if not a cure for leprosy. Imagine, Nell! If I were to ally myself, my cause, my mission to him, well, how much easier would it then be to persuade people to support me?'

'So we will go to Paris, just you and I?'

I hesitated. 'It would be so very helpful to me, Nell, but, alas... I fear I have offered you something that is not within my gift. By the time we are arrive in London my money will be all but used up. And I must see Mama comfortably settled. No, it is a fond dream, but you are right, I shall have to concentrate my efforts in London.'

'But I can pay! Oh, Kate, do let me. You know how I want nothing more than to support you, to see you succeed.'

'But my vocation is not yours, dear Nell. It would not be fair of me to expect...'

'Please, allow me to do this. Allow me to help in the way that I can, for I am no nurse, no adventurous traveller. Let me be a part of what is so dear to your heart. And we shall be in Paris together!'

'Well, naturally, I should love nothing better than to walk beside the Seine with you, to visit Notre-Dame, for us to see all the wonders of that romantic city... But much of my time would still be taken up with appointments.'

'Of course, and rightly so. But we will have our time too. Oh it is a splendid idea, if only you will let me. Say you will.'

She had both of my hands in hers now and her face was aglow with excitement.

'Very well, darling Nell, how can I refuse you?' I said, and we sat in happy silence, watching the sun begin to drop towards the silvery horizon. It was as we were about to return to our cabins, a little while later, that I spotted a young woman on the aft deck. She was slender, with tawny hair, wisps of which escaped their pins at the tugging of the sea breeze. Just for an instant I thought it was Rose. I knew, of course, that it could not be, but in that moment when my eyes saw what they wished so very much to see and before reason made sense of my wayward vision, I fancied it was my dear girl, come to find me, and my heart danced. And then the young woman turned, and I saw that she was a stranger, and a heavy sadness settled upon me that I struggled to disguise for the remainder of the day.

And Jessy never got her money, did she? Nor her jewellery.

I had always intended giving it to her. She trusted me to sell her furniture, to get the best price I could for her things, but it was not an easy task.

The selling, or the giving her the money? Because you did *find buyers, didn't you?*

Eventually, yes, though not for as much as I'd hoped. Our passage was booked, you see, upon the *Ruapehu*. There was no time left.

So you sold the furniture, Jessy's furniture, for next to nothing, and what money you got you took with you.

There were expenses, aboard the ship. And then, when we reached home, it was difficult. I had to set mother up somewhere, making sure she was cared for.

So that you and Nell could be on your merry way.

You make it sound so simple.

Was it not?

You know better than that, I think.

So you used Jessy's money for your mother?

I was going to pay her back. She had always been so helpful, so understanding, I knew she would not begrudge Mama her security. My intention was that Jessy should have her money back as soon as I was able to give it to her.

But first you had to go to Paris with Nell. How inconvenient.

It is not always easy to put the right person first. Nell had been so very supportive, it would have been wrong of me to leave her. I needed to go to Paris to raise funds for the mission, and if I could see Monsieur Pasteur... well, think how much gravitas his name would have lent – did lend – to my cause? I had to go. I had to try. Jessy would understand.

You would explain everything to her when you got to India.

Yes, that's right.

Except that you never got there, did you?

I... I can't remember.

You never went to India.

Jessy and I were going to go there together.

But you didn't because you stayed behind to be with Nell. Jessy went to India alone.

Yes, Jessy went to India.

You promised you would follow. You promised you would join her out there, didn't you? But you never went.

Never? I thought...

What happened to Jessy? Do you remember that? What happened to her?

But, I did go to India. I remember, I'm sure of it, I remember because of the flower, do you see? I remember because of the flower...

The air was sultry as only the time of the monsoon in India can make it. My uniform stuck to my body as I went about my duties, and I worked accompanied by a thirst that would not be quenched. I did not allow myself to dwell on my discomfort, for how could I when my patients suffered so very much worse? The hospital was well appointed, compared to many in which I had worked, but still those afflicted with leprosy were relegated to its outer reaches, to the meanest of buildings, shut away from sight. When first I had encountered the disease, while nursing during the war in Bulgaria, it had moved within me such pity for the suffering it caused that it would not be banished from my mind. Not when I returned to England. Not after that, as I continued my nursing. So it was that I made my way to India where the disease was known to be prevalent. Here I was able to learn about it; its causes, its progression, its pitifully ineffective treatments. I saw strong, able men reduced to penury and begging. I found whole families decimated. I encountered children beyond counting, orphaned or abandoned, disfigured and despairing. I did what I could, nursing, taking them the solace of God's word, petitioning the authorities for money, pleading with them to give more, to do more. And ever and always it was not enough.

One evening, as I was nearing the end of my shift, I assisted a doctor from the south of the sub-continent who had recently come to work at the hospital. He, like me, was passionate in his determination to help sufferers of this cruel disease and worked tirelessly to improve the treatment of his patients. Dr Bindari was an unremarkable man to look at, slightly overweight, his hair thinning and receding, he was given to frequently taking off his wire-framed spectacles in order to clean them with an ever available handkerchief that remained miraculously spotless. He had asked me to remove the patient's bandages and dressings so that he might inspect the condition of the old man's limbs. The heat of the long day had won out over the inadequate ventilation, despite the best efforts of the boy working the fan. That same heat was the enemy of healing. As I lifted the last of the lint from the fingerless hands the unmistakeable stench of decay was released. A nurse becomes accustomed to such odours and quickly learns to appear impassive, but it is a truly terrible smell, for it heralds despair. It heralds death.

Dr Bindari leaned closer, lifting one of the shortened arms with great tenderness, peering at the glistening stumps. Wordlessly, he repeated his examination for all the man's limbs. When he had finished he nodded to me. I would clean and redress the wounds. He smiled down at the patient and spoke to him in Urdu with such cheeriness you'd think they were taking tea together, not discussing the likelihood that one of them would not live to see the end of the monsoon.

A little later, when I had made the patient as comfortable as I could, I found the doctor apparently waiting for me in the courtyard. This spartan area separated the lepers' ward from the rest of the hospital. Ordinarily a dusty no-man's-land, recent rains had caused it to change to a dark pool. The water seeped into my shoes as I stepped forwards, and I confess the cool of it was a relief. Dr Bindari had taken off his sandals and was standing ankle deep in the water, smoking a cigarette. He smiled at me sheepishly.

'I apologise for my unseemly behaviour, Nurse Marsden. I gave in to an impulse that began with a need to lower my body temperature and culminated in a wish to celebrate the fact that I am fortunate enough to have both my feet.' He wriggled his toes as he spoke.

I waited, for it seemed to me he wanted to speak further.

'There are times,' he continued, 'when I believe that is all we are here for, to give at least temporary relief from suffering, and as good a death as it is possible to have when parts of your body are festering.' There was not bitterness in his tone as much as there was sorrow.

'We do what we can,' I said.

'But it is not enough.'

How could I argue when I so wholeheartedly shared his view? And yet I saw a fellow healer struggling to come to terms with his own limitations.

'You are a fine physician, Dr Bindari,' I told him. The words sounded trite even as I spoke them, but what more was there to be said? 'We all do our best...'

'And it is not enough!' He shouted this time, the sound so uncharacteristic from this mild, cheerful man as to be shocking. He flung his cigarette into the water. 'How many people have we watched die here? How often have you and I observed the march of this damnable disease, knowing that we could do nothing to halt its progress, beyond mumbling soothing words that avoid saying the truth? The simple truth. Which is *I cannot save you*!' He waved his arms in exasperation. 'People are brought here, left here like so much discarded rubbish, or they drag themselves here, all of them terrified, alone, their hearts broken... they know what they have. They know what will happen to them. Just as they know there is no cure, and yet each and every one of them looks at us – at me and at you – and whatever nonsense comes out of their frightened mouths their eyes scream *help me!* And the plain fact of the matter is that we cannot.' He let out a long, long sigh. 'Nobody can help them.' He took his glasses from his face, squeezed his eyes tight shut for a moment, and then took out his handkerchief and began polishing the spectacles.

'Forgive me, Nurse...'

'There is no need to ask for my forgiveness, Doctor. Absolutely no need.'

'It is simply that there are times...'

'I understand,' I said.

He gave me another of his smiles. He nodded. 'Yes, I know that you do.' After a pause he gave a shrug. 'What we need is a miracle, Nurse Marsden. Do you think one of our gods will send one any day soon?' Then, seeing my discomfort, he went on. 'I am sorry, that was... impolite.'

'Oh, I do not believe your gods or mine concern themselves with what is polite!' I found myself almost laughing, and I knew it was because I too was close to despairing over how little difference either of us seemed able to make to our patients.

The doctor lifted a foot from the water. 'The other day,' he told me as he hopped about, pushing on first one sandal, then the other, 'I met an interesting fellow who had travelled a great deal. All over the globe. He told me that in the wilderness of Siberia there grows a very special plant. Its name and its whereabouts are known only to the local shaman, for it is very precious. These people use it to cure leprosy.' His footwear fixed in place, he stood still and regarded me with a steady gaze then, a look of wonder on his face. 'Imagine that, Nurse Marsden. A cure, just growing there in the ground, waiting to be picked. Shall we tell our patients, do you think? Shall we tell them to go to Siberia and find that flower and they will be back at work by the end of the week?' He gave a light laugh, bid me goodnight, and made his way across the flooded courtyard, the wash of his steps rippling back to me as he went.

The view of Paris from our hotel room was spectacular. I threw wide the windows and leaned out onto the railing of the Juliet balcony.

'Nell, do come and see. Such a splendid city, laid out before us!'

She came to stand beside me, but already I could sense her reluctance to enjoy our good fortune. 'It is very fine,' she agreed flatly.

'Nell, please don't sulk, it is most unbecoming.'

'I am far too old to be sulking. Though if I were to do so, who could blame me?'

'We are arrived in this most romantic of places and you seek to spoil our time together here. I confess there are times I am at a loss to understand you.'

'Is it really so difficult? Am I really so complicated?'

'You wanted so very much to be here, for us to be here together.'

'Yes, that is precisely it!'

'But here we are!'

'For this moment, yes, and then you will be off at a run, pestering the great and the good, not least Monsieur Pasteur, I don't doubt.'

'He is one of the reasons we came here, Nell. He is working on a cure. How could I *not* wish to talk to him?'

'It appears he does not wish to talk to you,' she said tartly, turning to pull off her gloves and drop them onto the bed. She untied her bonnet and removed that also.

'He is a busy man. I should not expect otherwise than that he is constantly engaged in his work, with an endless line of people demanding his attention. I believe that once he knows I am here, knows why I have come and how much we might be able to assist one another in our common goals, well, of course he will see me.'

'Well, Kate, God knows you will see him whether he wants it or not. Unless he has a guard at his door.'

I moved over to where she stood but she pointedly turned away from me to tidy her hair in the dressing table mirror.

'Please come with me, Nell.'

'You mean to go now? We have just this minute arrived.'

'Then let us complete our business without delay, so that afterwards we will be free to enjoy Paris at our leisure.'

'Truly?' She stopped adjusting her pins and listened. 'Once you have finished with Monsieur Pasteur you will have time for me?'

'Time for both of us! Tell me where you would like to visit? The Louvre. Sacré-Coeur? We could take a boat trip down the Seine. You choose, my darling Nell.'

'Oh, I should very much like to cruise the river!' she said, her face aglow at the thought. 'We could take supper on board one of the charming little boats. They have musicians too, I believe. And then we could walk to Notre-Dame, could we not?'

'An excellent plan. Now, replace your bonnet, come with me whilst I attend to this important business as briefly as possible, and then I am yours to command, as is the whole of Paris, I promise you!'

The ballroom of the Winter Palace looked even more splendid than usual on that occasion. I recall the Tsarina telling me that she had put in more chandeliers and more mirrors and had even had some of the gilt repainted onto the plasterwork, just to make absolutely certain that everything was at is very best. When I protested that she need not have gone to so much trouble on my account, she was adamant that my cause and my success demanded nothing less.

'Katerina, all of St Petersburg will turn out to see the brave English nurse who travelled so very far, who endured such hardships, all for the sake of those suffering from this terrible curse. We must give them such a ball as they will remember until the end of their days. And of course, such a marvellous occasion that it will encourage them to donate generously to towards the construction of the new hospital.'

'You are too kind, Your Highness, I cannot thank you enough for what you have done for me. Without your patronage, without the letter that I carried with me all those miles, I would never have succeeded where I did.'

'Nonsense, it is we who must thank you, Katerina. Your diligence, your self-sacrifice, it has put all of us to shame. Where was the Russian man or woman prepared to face the hazardous journey that you have made? No, this will be an evening of celebration, and one that you deserve completely. Now, to the question of your gown. You cannot have had time to find a dressmaker since your return, so I insist that you use mine.'

'Oh, I could not presume...'

'I will hear no argument from you on this matter,' she declared, raising her hand with mock severity, even though her sweet smile gave her away. 'You must choose the most elaborate, most wonderful gown, which she will produce to suit your requirements exactly. This is not a moment for you to hide, Katerina. Everyone will want to meet you, to speak with you, to dance with you. And I know when they do they will be won over to your cause. This will be your night, my dear, and you must shine!'

I would never, without the Tsarina's encouragement, have selected a gown of such richness, such elaborate detail. It was dark gold, with exquisite embroidery covering the close-fitting bodice, and yards and yards of silk in the full, cascading skirts. The dressmaker was indeed an expert at her craft, and tailored the dress to flatter without being in any way frivolous or girlish. The lines were simple, the neck modest, and the overall effect one of sophistication and elegance. I had never felt so noble, so grand, and never did again.

Maria Feodorovna had been correct in her expectation, and it seemed as if every person of note, wealth or influence in the city had turned out that night. The Tsarina herself wore white, and I recall thinking, as she entered the ballroom, that she resembled perfectly my notion of a snow queen, as if she were clothed in the very icicles and snowflakes of the vast Siberian wilderness itself. She was at my side almost the entire evening, like a proud parent showing off her clever offspring. She took care to introduce me personally to so many people that they became a blur of faces and a jumble of names in my memory. I cannot conjure the individuals, but I can summon the mood of that evening. The thrill of it. The sense of being accepted by these people of high society. Of being lauded by them for my work. And that admiration they readily expressed in the liberal donations they made to the collection for the leper hospital to be built in Viliusk, so that by the end of the evening we had raised over four thousand pounds!

It was late in the afternoon by the time Nell and I arrived at the residence of Monsieur Pasteur. We presented ourselves at the gates of the large, square building, only to be told that the great scientist was too unwell to receive any callers. When I explained who I was and the purpose of my visit the porter yet insisted that we could not be admitted. Three times he refused to let me pass. I turned to Nell with an urgent whisper.

'Have you any coins in your purse?'

'What?'

'I recall you brought a sovereign with you, Nell. Do let me have it; this man is most obstinate, and you know I simply must see Monsieur Pasteur.' I hated asking her for it, but my darling girl understood the importance of my seeing the great man. She gave me the money, and sure enough it proved to be the price of my admittance. Alas if I had harboured any hopes of a lengthy interview where Monsieur Pasteur and I might discuss the treatment of the lepers it was not to be. Oh, how I wished to hear of his rumoured cure! And yet, it transpired that the porter was accurate in his description of the scientist's health. Although I did gain admission to his quarters, it was only for the briefest of introductions. I am not sure, to this day, that he was sufficiently well to know to whom it was he was speaking, and he could not, sadly, elucidate on the matter of the disease or its possible prevention. Instead I had to content myself with a few polite words, a handshake, and his assurance that any assistance I could take to sufferers would no doubt be greatly welcomed.

I hurried back down the stairs and out of the building, all the while turning over in my mind the most advantageous manner in which to present Monsieur's support for my work to the world. While it might be slight, any connection with such a fêted man of medicine as he could only serve to further my cause. As ever, it was the lepers who compelled me to take action, and to make that action the most effective action I could find.

Nell had waited for me outside those high gates and was surprised to see me return so soon. I glanced at my pocket watch and saw that it was nearing five o'clock.

'We must hurry,' I told her, taking her arm and steering her to the kerb so that we might hail a cab.

'Well, did you see him? You were so quick. Were you able to talk to him at all?'

'Of course, but he is indeed not in the best of health. Come now, here is a cab.'

'Are we going to find a river boat? Why must we hurry so?'

'It is vital that our meeting is reported in the press swiftly and as broadly as possible,' I explained, helping Nell into the cab and instructing the driver to take us directly to the offices of the correspondent of *The Times*. 'Once we have been there,' I continued to Nell, 'if we move with all speed, we might catch the office of the *New York Herald* before it closes its doors. If a telegram is sent the article should make the morning papers on both continents.'

'But, Kate, we were to dine together on the Seine. You promised.'

'All in good time,' I assured her, peering out of the cab window to make certain the driver did not take us past the building, for such cabbies are well known for their sharp practices. 'The news will be well received, I am certain of it. This is a small but significant step in our campaign, Nell. I am satisfied it will serve us well.'

'And how long will it take?' she asked. 'Must we go to both offices at once? Surely this is not urgent news and could as easily wait until tomorrow.'

'It cannot, Nell. We must make the most of it. We must fly our flag from the tallest mast, do you not see that? Ah, I believe we are close. Driver! I say, driver, set us down, if you please!' I was forced to shout and to rap upon the ceiling of the cab to obtain his attention.

I am pleased to say we were in time at both offices, and the meeting was reported in London and New York the next morning. My only regret is that Nell did not share my happiness. She complained at the length of time delivering the report to the papers took, and when it was clear we would not, after all, be able to take our wished for cruise that night she flatly refused to be consoled, and her mood darkened markedly.

You aren't going to write in your book, are you?

No. Not tonight. I am too weary. Sometimes I like to hold it, to think about what I am going to put in it next.

Why don't you open it? Why don't you look inside?

My eyes are too tired to read today.

That book won't tire them any more. Look inside, Kate. Look inside.

The book feels heavy suddenly. Its worn leather cover is cracked and has lost some of its colour at the edges. I do as she says, and I open the book. Its spine creaks a little as I flatten it open, pressing as best I can with my one good hand. And now I see that the pages are completely empty.

All of them empty.

It was not an arduous train journey, the one between Cologne and Paris, but our itinerary had been hectic, and our stay in Berlin previously also busy. As the evening wore on into night, Nell was lulled into sleep on her seat opposite me. Apart from we two the carriage was empty save for one gentleman on his way back to London. To pass the time we struck up a quiet conversation, and at one point I recall reading to him from a paper I had written, an excerpt from a report regarding an aspect of life in Russia which seemed to arouse his curiosity. When I explained that it was my intention to travel to St Petersburg and thence to Siberia in search of the needy lepers he became quite animated.

'Upon my word, madam,' he laughed, 'it strikes me there's money to be made from these lepers of yours. There's a sympathy for 'em, and that's a fact. Folks will give for such suffering.'

'Indeed, it would be a hard-hearted fellow who would not soften when details of the lives of these wretches are set before him.'

'And if you were the one to do it, Ma'am, I'd wager none could turn from you. Bless you, your voice when you were reading just now was like music. You've a commanding presence and a way with you.'

'It is my aim to give people the fullest account of the disease and its attendant horrors, else how can they know? And once they do know, I do not believe that their Christian souls will allow them to turn away.'

'There's an interest in this leper business, people's minds are on it, and the right woman could fetch 'em. I believe you are that very woman.'

'I must hope so. For my journey to find the sufferers will be long and dangerous, and all will be for nothing if I am not afterwards persuasive.'

'I've connections in America, and there's a country you could take your story to and money to be made. You come to me in London and I'll set you up. And do not trouble yourself to freeze, nor risk your neck unnecessarily, madam. Just go far enough to say you've been. Spot one or two of the misfortunates, then come home and write your stories and we'll see them published and sold before you know it!' He laughed loudly again.

Nell slept on, but my mind was too busy to find rest. This curious man with his business mind lacked the proper sympathy my cause should elicit, and I could not see him as a person to contract myself to. And yet I was cheered, in the most pragmatic of ways, for if such a man could see financial gain to be had from allying himself with a supporter of lepers, then others would too. Perhaps there was a truth, too, in what he said regarding the fashion, if such it could be called, for taking an interest in those struck down by the disease. Whatever the motives for this interest, it was my job to use them to the good. It did not, in the end, matter what compelled people to affiliate themselves to my cause, so long as they gave money in the doing of it.

On returning to our hotel room Nell became quite impossible. Much as I tried to attribute her bad temper to the lateness of the hour, and to our not having eaten, I was finding it more and more difficult to cope with her petulance.

'Really, Nell, need you make quite such a fuss?' I asked as I sat upon the end of the bed, glad of the chance to rest my feet which were aching from so much dashing about. In the distance I could hear the bells of the cathedral ringing and imagined people on their way to a late mass, incense filling the air, the priest's voice intoning God's words through the echoey space.

'Am I always to put myself in second place?' she asked, not looking at me, but choosing instead to stride up and down.

'Second to me? Surely you cannot think that.'

'Second to your blessed cause!'

'Forgive me, Nell, I believed we were both committed to this work. I thought you held it as dear and as precious as I do.'

'Well, it just might be that I do not, after all.' She fair spat the words at me now, standing over me, the anger welling up from somewhere she had kept it deep and hidden. 'I am sorry if that disappoints you, Kate,' she went on, 'to discover that I am not, in the end, as perfect as you!'

'Nell...'

'How could I possibly ever match the wonderful, courageous, pious Kate Marsden, with her Russian Red Cross Award, and all her vast experience of nursing, and her worthy cause? Well I tell you, I cannot, and nor do I wish to. I am a woman, flawed and sinful, and full of pride and wishes of my own that do not in any way relate to the poor or the needy. So there it is! Now you know the truth of your less-than-perfect-friend.'

I stood up, wanting to reach out to her, to hold her, to reassure her that I loved her exactly as she was. 'We are none of us perfect, my dear Nell. I do not claim to be, and I do not expect perfection of you.'

'Then you must be happy! For yet again you are correct. I am just a silly woman who wanted to dine on board a river boat and have a cheerful time.'

'And so we shall, for you must know how much your happiness matters to me. Now, why not take off your boots, you are weary. I promise you will have my full and loving attention the second I have written up my own account of my meeting with Monsieur Pasteur. It will take no more than an hour and then...'

But I did not finish my sentence, for Nell put an end to my speaking. She raised her hand, drew it full back, and struck my face with such force that I was put off my feet and fell back into the chair. I sat there, shock silencing my voice, my cheek afire from the stinging blow, my heart wounded yet more deeply.

Nell had fallen into petulant silence by the time we arrived back at our hotel room. I promised her we would take our river cruise the following day instead, but even so I felt sorry to have so ruined her earlier happy mood.

I watched her remove her bonnet for the second time that evening. Had she been angry with me I should have better stood it. Her disappointment was harder to bear.

'I am sorry, Nell,' I said for the umpteenth time. 'I simply had to ensure that the reports of my meeting with Monsieur Pasteur were dispatched this night. For them to make the morning papers in both London and New York, well, I think you'll agree such publicity for my proposed mission will be invaluable.'

'I'm sure it will,' she said, sitting heavily on the little brocade chair by the window. Behind her the shutters were still open, so that there was merely the blackness of the night sky beyond the glass, with here and there a light burning in a tall building.

All at once an idea came to me, and the more I considered it, the more certain I became that it was the thing to do. I hurried to my valise, for I had not even completed my unpacking before we had set off on our quest for an interview with the great scientist. Beneath my gowns, wrapped in a piece of beige chamois leather and tied with a blue ribbon, I found what I was looking for. I went to kneel before Nell.

'I have something for you,' I told her gently. 'Nothing extravagant, rest assured. Just a little token of my affection.'

'Oh? Why would you choose this moment to give me a gift?'

'I confess I was saving it for... another time,' I said vaguely, not wanting to talk of the moment when I would depart for Russia without her. 'But you have been so supportive, you endure all manner of disappointments while you are with me, and I do so hate to see you sad. Here.'

I handed her the small parcel. She took it onto her lap and undid the bow. When she folded back the leather to reveal its contents she gave a little gasp.

'Oh, Kate! How charming. How pretty the stones are!' She turned the brooch over, stroking the gold with her fingers, holding it up to the lamplight so that the precious stones gleamed and sparkled.

'You like it?'

'I think it is delightful!' she said, smiling at last.

'Ancient civilisations considered the snake a symbol of faithfulness, of continuity, of the continuous circle of life. Think of it as standing for our friendship, that has no end. Let me,' I said, taking it from her and pinning it onto her gown just above her heart. 'There. It suits you very well, does it not?'

'Dear Kate,' she said, smiling properly now and taking my hand in hers. 'I shall think of you every time I wear it, and it will make me feel that you are close. I am foolish to be so glum when I have you to care for me. Who could want for more?'

After a long day's ride we came to another collection of lepers, nine in all. Their condition was among the worst I had seen. One of the men, two women and two children were naked, possessing no clothes at all. It was shocking to imagine what their existence would be like in the winter months. They told me that when the frost and the biting winds came they would cover themselves in what rags they could find and add leaves for a vestige of warmth. In the summer months their sores were unprotected from flies, which so tormented their festering wounds that some of the sufferers could do nothing but writhe in agony. This *yourt* was so far from any settlement and so deep in the suffocating woods that I did not wonder the lepers there remained uncounted and untended, for who could ever find them? There were signs that bears inhabited the forest around them, and such was the misery of those cast out to live their blighted lives among them that I wondered many did not throw themselves in the path of the fearsome creatures to find an end to their suffering.

This thought troubled my mind for hours after we had left. As we rode onwards I could not think of anything else, not even the hope of a better place for those afflicted with the merciless disease. All that occupied my thoughts were the horrifying extent of their suffering, and the notion that to be mauled to death by a bear could come to be seen as welcome beside such an existence. We journeyed on slowly though the ever dense *taiga*, and as we did so my mood became so heavy, my heart so troubled, and my mind so tortured with these imaginings that my body succumbed to fatigue, and I swooned from my horse.

I recall voices, urgent, calling my name. Strange languages being both shouted and whispered as I was lifted from the ground and carried to a small clearing in the trees. My vision was muddled and unclear, so that I had the sensation for a time that I was underwater, though I knew this not to be the case. I felt almost nothing as I was lifted again and laid upon reindeer skins, as if my bruised and battered limbs were no longer in my own control, my mind being too distressed to manage them.

We made camp. I began to revive and was given sweet black tea. One of the horsemen, with neither English nor French at his disposal, came to me, proffering a small pot of ointment. He indicated that I was to use it to ward off the terrible biting flies. Gratefully, I took it from him and slowly applied it to my skin and my clothing, noticing at once how the numbers of tormenting insects around me dwindled. A few paces off, my little horse was under a similar assault, ineffectually stamping his feet and swishing his tail, his flanks twitching under the ceaseless biting. With difficulty, I rose to my feet. My guides tried to assist me but I signalled to them so that they understood I was sufficiently recovered to walk unaided. I made my way to the miserable pony and dabbed a tiny amount of the precious unguent around his weeping eyes.

'There, my trusty friend,' I said to him softly. 'That is so much better, is it not?'

'Will the Tsarina be arriving later?' I asked the attaché, a minor Russian nobleman, who had been sent to escort me to the ball. I had only just finished preparing for the occasion, and the seamstress had been busy stitching me into my gown. It had been such a kindness on the part of the Empress, to make her own dressmaker available to me. When I had explained to her that I had nothing suitable to wear for such a grand event, and that I would appreciate a recommendation from her, she had hesitated only a moment before offering me her own woman. I had spent a great deal of time and care choosing the right shade of golden silk, and discussing with the seamstress how much of the bodice should be covered with embroidery. I was pleased with the results, though felt the lack of jewels to wear, having only two strings of pearls to put at my throat, and some earrings which had once belonged to Jessy.

I was informed that the Empress Maria Feodorovna had been unavoidably detained on matters of state business, but that she would, of course, make all haste to join me at the ball as soon as she was free of her duties.

We were not, in fact, to use the grand ballroom in which I had spent happy hours all those months ago before setting off on my eastward trek. Instead it had been decided that the silver ballroom in the east wing of the Winter Palace would better suit our purposes. This was to be a fine evening, with almost a full complement of orchestral musicians, and a large gathering of wealthy and influential people of the city. Nevertheless, our numbers would not be so great as to fill the grand ballroom, and the Tsarina had explained that the atmosphere would be more convivial in the smaller room. It looked very pretty, with its gleaming white walls and silver-framed mirrors and liveried servants aplenty to wait upon the guests.

I made my way to the ballroom an hour after the official start of the evening, to give others the opportunity to arrive before me. I was announced at the door and descended the short sweep of stairs on the arm of Count Morsky, who was my senior by a good twenty years, but tall, straight of back, and with a proud bearing that made him a perfectly suitable escort. I was a little concerned that he might make a less satisfactory dance partner. After a pause in the music to allow for polite applause to acknowledge the arrival of the guest of honour, I signalled my thanks, and the orchestra struck up a lively waltz, and the Count proved himself to be lighter on his feet than I had anticipated.

Between dances I circulated among the guests. Count Morsky made the necessary introductions, enabling me to recount tales of my mission and to elicit promises of financial support for the building of the lepers' hospital where I could. After an hour or more, however, I began to notice that people were remarking upon the absence of the Tsarina.

'What can be so important that it keeps her from a matter that I know to be dear to her kind heart?' I asked her attaché, but he had no answer for me beyond that she would come just as soon as she could.

'*Pardonnez-moi*, Madame Marsden,' a gentlemen hailed me and continued to address me in French. I followed his thread with some difficulty, so was relieved when he agreed to speak English so that I might better understand him. 'I was saying,' he explained, 'that it is a curious thing, how you, a woman, succeeded not only in traversing the wild regions of our nation but also in finding the lepers who are so few and so elusive.'

'I assure you, sir, they may be far from civilisation, but sadly they are far from being few.'

'Oh? And how many of these wretched folk did you come upon?'

'They totalled upwards of sixty, and you must comprehend that this is only a small proportion of the true number.'

'How can you be certain? After all, your leper hunt was widely known, would not all of these misfortunates have rushed to see you? Surely they would have been determined to tell you of their sorry situation the better to obtain new homes and a good living from your charitable supporters.'

'You must appreciate that a leper cannot, by the very nature of his afflictions, rush anywhere, for his deformed and painful limbs or his failing eyesight would prevent him from doing so however earnestly he wished it.'

The man, who appearance was that of one given to overindulgence, with a complexion that suggested gout lay in wait for him, raised his eyebrows. 'Perhaps, Madam Nurse, you have fallen victim to the tall tales people of those regions like to tell. A woman may take into her head romantic imaginings of suffering, and see herself in the role of heroine in the story she conjures.'

There was a little laughter from his companions at this suggestion, and I became aware that several guests were now listening to our conversation.

'I assure you, sir, that I am not such a woman as is given to the fanciful dreams you describe. I base my opinions on what I found in Siberia. On what I saw there. On the very real suffering I witnessed. On the terrible conditions in which the lepers now exist.'

A woman stepped forward. 'Did you encounter these people at close quarters, Madame Marsden?' she asked.

'I did.'

'And yet here you stand, not scarred by the terrible freezing weather, nor infected with the dread disease, nor indeed bearing any single mark upon you that might suggest you have endured all you describe in the course of your travels.'

To my astonishment, this observation was met with a murmur of assent and some nodding from the little group around us.

'It was my good fortune to escape injury,' I said. 'As for infection, I am a nurse of many years' experience and am perfectly capable of taking all measures necessary in order to protect myself.'

'There are some,' came a voice from the serried ranks, 'who say you scarce stepped from your fur-lined sleigh, but instead sent others to inspect these festering wretches, keeping yourself at a safe remove.'

'Who says that?' I demanded. 'Let them show themselves, and I will tell them as I tell you, I sought out those to whom I had travelled thousands of miles to offer God's help and that of the good people of Russia. I went among the lepers fearlessly, for I was about God's work. They received me with tears and with joy, for they knew at last that they were not forgotten. Shame on anyone who would snatch from those poor innocents the chance that their suffering might be lessened.'

The first speaker, who now puffed out his stout chest, full of importance at having started this slanderous debate, had more to say. 'It would seem, however, that the lepers still languish in the snow, while you enjoy the splendour of the Winter Palace, and the hospitality of the Her Majesty the Empress. One might conclude that whatever good Nurse Marsden has done the lepers, they have certainly done her no harm at all!'

At this there was an outburst of laughter. It was too much to stand with good grace!

'The Tsarina is my most stalwart supporter. She will vouch for me! She will speak of my integrity.'

'Perhaps she might,' my tormentor continued. 'And yet, strangely, the Empress is not at your side. Why is that, d'you suppose?'

At this more laughter! As I looked about me faces loomed out of the crowd, jeering and vulgar, poking fun, amusing themselves at my expense, enjoying the slander that was being presented them. I tried to insist on what was truth and what was not, but there was such a clamour by now, and the orchestra had struck up again, and I could not make my voice heard. And still the Tsarina was not to be found. Still she stayed away.

'I simply do not see why there was such urgency,' Nell stomped ahead of me into the hotel room. 'Surely you could have waited until tomorrow to go to the newspapers?'

I should have been more understanding of her disappointment, perhaps, but the hour was very late, and I was exhausted from the effort of dashing around Paris and cajoling recalcitrant newspaper people into cooperation. 'There would be little point in my going to the trouble of obtaining an interview with Monsieur Pasteur were nobody to hear of it. News grows old with startling rapidity, Nell. It could not wait.'

'It seems nothing ever can,' she said petulantly, striding up and down the room in the most provoking manner. 'Nothing and nobody except me, who is always to wait while more important things demand your time and attention. Which is to say *everything*.'

'You are being ridiculous,' I told her, removing my hat and dropping it upon the bed. The lamps in the room were particularly bright and a fierce headache had taken hold of me. I rubbed my eyes for a moment. 'There will be plenty of time for sightseeing tomorrow,' I said.

'Until, no doubt, some other pressing business arises.'

'Why must you take this tone? When we planned our tour of France and Germany to raise funds you knew that my mission would be the main focus of our time here. This was never to be a pleasure trip.'

'I know that when you persuaded me to pay for all the railway tickets and hotels and such like I thought it not unreasonable to expect that we might also enjoy travelling together.'

'And you are not enjoying it, evidently.'

'Do you really care so little about me?'

'Nell, I am too tired to argue with you. I have a headache...'

'There are times I am at a loss to know how to win back your affection!' She was becoming extremely distressed, weeping as she spoke now, gesticulating and pacing faster and faster.

'You have never for one minute lost my affection!'

Suddenly she strode over to me and thrust her face close to mine, her eyes wild with a startling, pent up fury that had at last burst forth. 'Must I compete with the whole of Europe now as well as your precious lepers?' she shouted. 'It would appear I am nothing more to you than a source of funds for your grand plans. How are we to pay for all this gadding about? Nell shall pay! How will we dine, where will we sleep? Do not concern yourself, for Nell shall pay for it all! What am I buying with all this money? A few scraps of your time? Perhaps you do not care for me at all, but only my money, which will not last for many more weeks, given the rate at which it must be spent in the name of your cause!'

'You must not say such things!'

'I say what is evident to everyone else, what my friends have been telling me for months, but I would not listen. That I am nothing more than an income for the pious Kate Marsden, who will not stop even at prostituting herself to a silly, lonely widow in her desire to find fame in her great leper hunt!

Something inside me gave way. I acted not with thought, but from deep hurt at her words. I cannot excuse my action, I can only explain that it arose from an instant of heartbreak, so that I do not recall raising my hand. I remember all too well, however, the feel of her cheek as I struck her, the curiously slow manner of her falling, and the terrible sound of her face hitting the dressing table as she fell.

I remember the snow was red. As I turned my face to the west – for what? A glimpse of home? – the setting sun leached its colour into the thirsty snow. Ada commented upon it, remarking on the richness of the hue. She found it rather charming. I did not. It made me think of pain. Of the suffering of those I travelled to help. Of

Christ's blood spilled for us. It was as if that scarlet ice, that crimson stretch of frigid earth, held within it all the agonies of mankind.

'Who is that? Who's there?' My voice sounds horribly feeble. I hardly recognise it as my own. I should not be alive still, lingering in this hospital bed, waiting for God to take me to Him. I have lived too long. I have no future, only a long and distant past. My present is peopled with ghosts. So many of my brothers and sisters died young, and yet I had the strength to cross the wilderness and live on to old age. I have been of no use to anyone for many years now, existing on the charity of others. Why am I still here? And who is it who has come to me now? 'Show yourself,' I say as firmly as I am able, which is to say not at all. 'Come nearer so that I might see you.'

A figure moves in the corner of the room. The light is low, it is evening, I think, and there are no lights lit in here. All the illumination there is comes from the twilight through the window, and the tawny rectangle of light falling from the corridor through the open door. Into this patch of warmth steps a woman. I struggle to sit up a little and frown in an effort to make my eyes work better. I cannot alter my position greatly, as my stroke-afflicted body no longer responds to orders from my clumsy brain in the way that it ought to. My left side will not move at all now. I peer at the person who now stands at the foot of my bed.

'Who's there?' I ask again, my old woman's voice rasping across the space between us.

I am answered with a question. 'Don't you know me Kate? Have you forgotten me entirely?'

The voice is familiar. Yes. I know it! 'Jessy? Is that you, Jessy?'

She remains too distant for me to see clearly, her face still turned to the shadows.

'I waited for you to come to me for such a long time. But you never came.'

'You were in India. I couldn't go there. I had to go to Russia.'

'You *said* you would come. You promised we would be together in India. That was why I went ahead.' She still has the childlike whine to her voice, even after all this time. I recall hearing it when she objected to my spending time with Nell. I recall hearing it when I could not go with her as we had planned.

'I couldn't follow, Jessy. I wanted to, but there wasn't enough money...'

'There was never enough money.'

'And then I heard of the lepers in Siberia, and of the herb that grew there. Their need was so very great, Jessy, and if there was the slightest chance of a cure... How could I not go?'

'You were chasing a fairy tale. There was no cure. There is no cure still.'

'I had to find out for myself. I had to try.'

She moves a little closer, and now I can see she is wearing her nurse's uniform. The one she took with her to India. But it is filthy, covered in blood and stains and terrible things. And now I can see that her hair hangs loose and wild about her shoulders. I become aware of a foul smell, rank and bitter. I know it well. It is the smell of disease. It is the stink of death.

'I waited there for you,' she says, stepping forwards and turning so that at last I can see her face.

'Oh! Poor Jessy!'

'You never came. You left me there sick and frightened. I died alone, Kate. All those miles from home because of you, and I died alone.'

When the scandal took hold, like a beast that grips its prey and will not release it until it is limp and dead, I was in America. That scandal, those lies, those half-truths and calumnies, they chased me around the globe, snapping at my heel no matter how far or how fast I travelled. I was assailed from all quarters – the newspapers in New Zealand, *The Times* in London, any number of American papers. It was quite astonishing how much harm can be done, how far the reach, of a handful of determined people. I tried my best to answer the accusations when I could. I published my own letters in what papers would take them. I defended my name where I could, even bringing my own law suit to fight for my reputation. All came to nothing, however, for once such slanders are spoken and heard, once such libels are written and read, they are known, and they can never be unknown. People turned against me, people whom I had loved and revered. The hardest of these losses to bear was not, after all, my darling Nell. No, the deepest hurt I felt, I believe, was when the Tsarina spurned me. I was no longer welcome at the Russian royal court. I was told she said of me, 'Let not that woman ever set foot in Russia again!' What poison must have been whispered in her ear for such a woman as Maria Feodorovna to turn her back on someone she had supported once so wholeheartedly. If only I had been allowed to see her, to speak with her, one more time, I could have made her understand. I am certain of it.

This particular stage was well lit and helpfully low, which was all the better for displaying the model of the Lepers' Hospital. I was singularly pleased with the way it had turned out. I had found an architect who had employed a skilled craftsman to construct the model for me, perfectly to scale, painted and even planted with artificial trees and flower beds. It was a perfect representation of how the finished hospital and surrounding buildings would look, and it was an invaluable aid to my talks during my fundraising tour. My talks in England upon my return home had been well received and well attended, and had garnered positive words from reporters in the newspapers. Likewise, there had been a deal of interest upon my arrival in America, and my events there had attracted attention in every city I visited. I had permitted myself the hope that the hospital would indeed come into being, and that my fundraising efforts would continue apace across the country.

That was before I encountered Isabel Hapgood.

The venue in New York was filled to capacity, and I had spent the opening moments of my speech outlining my plans for the hospital, and explaining how the money would be used. I had then gone on to try, in my inadequate way, to tell of the dire circumstances in which the lepers lived. I encouraged questions from the floor throughout my talks, and at this point a young woman in the centre of the auditorium raised her hand and then got to her feet. Her own question was harmless enough, and was one I expected to have put to me each time I spoke.

'Miss Marsden, I wonder could you tell us something of the details of the disease? What exactly are the symptoms?'

I recall being surprised, in the early months of my tours, that this query was always made. Were people attending merely for the sensational aspects of the suffering that the lepers endured? Was I providing nothing more than some manner of travelling sideshow that would have been more profitable had I dragged with me the most hideously deformed patient I could find? I chose not to believe this was the case, rather I felt that people came to hear of the lepers because they were at heart good Christians who wished to do what they could to relieve the suffering of the poorest of God's children. It was only fitting that they be given all the facts before being asked to part with their money. However, I had developed a pragmatism that I am certain served both me and my cause well. When writing my account of my journey across the wilderness I had kept in mind this desire to vicariously experience danger and horror. Including what some might see as almost overwhelming details was necessary in order to pique people's curiosity and to move them, I hoped, so that they might feel inclined to contribute financially to the building of the hospital.

'The disease involves a dying off of the nerves at the body's extremities – fingers, toes, nose – so that the afflicted person loses sensation in these areas,' I explained. 'Pain is the body's defence against injury; without it we are unable to register the effects of, say, a contusion, or a burn. Keep in mind that without sensation a person becomes clumsy, so that he may cut his hand whilst preparing food without noticing he has done so. The resultant wound is not treated properly, does not heal well, and becomes infected. These constant infections break down the general health of the patient. Added to this is the gradual atrophying – the dying off – of the affected areas. This is why typically a person who has been suffering from the disease will lose fingers and toes, sometimes whole hands and feet.' There were murmurs throughout the audience. 'I have seen lepers with no feet at all, forced to hobble on decaying ankle stumps, handless, with faces disfigured terribly.' There were further gasps. I pressed on, as I knew I must. 'The disease often affects the eyes, causing painful sores and inflammation which in many instances leads to blindness, which in turn worsens the sufferer's clumsiness, confounding the initial problem with the limbs. Another common factor are the lesions, which can appear on any part of the body. Indeed, these are often the first indication that a person has the disease. Although progress of many of the symptoms is mostly slow, these ugly, rough lumps and scaly patches can multiply with alarming rapidity, so that faces are entirely covered. They can, indeed, give the appearance of scales, which is where the disease found its name, from the Greek *lepra,* which means "scaly".

There was silence in the room now as those present fell under the spell of their imaginations, picturing the poor sufferers in their hellish state. I allowed them a moment to dwell upon this, though I knew that nothing their minds could conjure could come close to the awful truth.

I continued. 'The disease is contagious, but can be avoided with careful management of the patient. Sadly, such is the terror of infection that society's answer in these faraway places is to banish the lepers to a place sufficiently far away from others that they are not seen as a threat. This, of course, condemns the sufferer not only to endure the disease itself, but to struggle, unwell and bereft, torn from family and loved ones, to manage in the harsh wilderness, banished and alone.'

By this time the young woman who had asked the question had sat down again, her face quite pale. Still she managed to ask, 'Is there no cure?'

I shook my head. 'None,' I said simply.

Now I heard another voice, from the rear of the auditorium.

'But you believed that a cure did exist, is that not the case, Miss Marsden?'

I squinted into the gloom, the brightness of the stage lights up close limiting my view. People turned to see who had spoken.

'Would you stand, please?' I asked. 'If you would stand up, so that we might know who is putting the question...'

I could see someone moving. She did not content herself with staying in the shadows, but moved along the row of seats until she reached the aisle. She then stepped forwards several paces so that she stood in a well-lit part of the stalls, a tall, expensively dressed woman in her middle years. She had a proud, confident bearing, and a strong, forthright voice to match.

'I understand that you went to Siberia in search of a fabled flower that you wrongly believed to offer a cure for leprosy. Is that not a fact?'

'It is true I had been told of a rare plant that was thought to contain properties that might provide a cure.'

'And you found this plant?'

'I did.' There were more murmurs from the audience at this.

'But it wasn't a cure at all, was it?' There was an unmistakeable hostility in this woman's tone. Indeed she made no attempt to hide her contempt for me in either her questions or her manner.

'Alas it was not. It does alleviate some of the symptoms in a minor way, but—'

'But it is not the magic remedy you believed would make your fame and fortune.'

At this there was even some laughter. 'A pity for you,' she went on, addressing the audience as much as she addressed me, 'having trekked so very far in such testing conditions, withstanding, no doubt, all kinds of discomforts, and all for nothing. No wonder cure. No triumphal return for Nurse Marsden, saviour of the lepers.' This statement was greeted with equal amounts of gasps and sniggers.

I kept my own voice level as I replied. 'My mission was to help the lepers in whatever ways I could,' I said.

'But if you could help yourself at the same time, so much the better, eh?'

'I assure you there are easier paths to take should one look for fame and fortune, as you put it. Easier than risking one's life in the bear-infested forests, crossing frozen lakes during the thaw, or enduring the extreme temperatures of the wilderness for weeks on end...'

'Yes, yes, the trials of Nurse Marsden the Adventuress are well known, for you are an able self-publicist, no one would challenge your claim to that title.'

'Madam, if I am to be insulted I demand to have your name,' I said, struggling to keep my temper on a short rein.

'Isabel Hapgood. You may have heard of me. Many here will have,' there were a few nods and yesses from the stalls, no doubt from her companions. 'I have had the honour and the pleasure of visiting Russia myself on many occasions, and my work as a translator of Russian literature is well known.'

'Then if you know that great country you will know, Mrs Hapgood, that Siberia is as far from the sophistication and comforts of Moscow as Moscow is from London. And that between the two places lie thousands of miles of brutal wilderness, and that it is there the lepers are sent to live their wretched lives.'

'So you say.'

'I do say!'

'And I say bunkum!'

Now the audience reacted with more gasps and some shouts and further bursts of laughter. They had come for a sober and informative talk, in the cause of philanthropy. Now they were enjoying an altogether different entertainment. Mrs Hapgood stood, feet firmly planted, arms folded across her chest, braced fearlessly for my response.

'Do you question the very existence of these lepers, madam?'

'I question the numbers you count them in. Is it not the case that there are no more than sixty people affected with the disease in the whole of Russia? Sixty, and yet you would have us build your glorious hospital, with rooms to house three or four times that number.'

'You fail to comprehend how far spread and remote are the current dwellings of the lepers. I saw for myself twice the number you have given, and have reliable accounts of many, many more in existence...'

'Saw for yourself? From the comfort of your luxurious sleigh, perhaps? Or the vantage point of your hotel?'

'I assure you there was no luxury to be had within a thousand miles of my lepers.'

'*Your* lepers! There's the point, is it not? This *mission* as you style it was nothing more than the travelling of a well-to-do woman who wished to make a name for herself and haul herself up into high society in the process.'

'These accusations are outrageous and without foundation!'

'Are they? You were told by numerous physicians and experts on Russia that this miraculous herb was nothing more than a balm for sores. You were further told by Russian officials in St Petersburg before ever you set off on your voyage that the lepers numbered so few as to make a nonsense of all your expensive preparations and calls for people to fund your whimsical travel plans. What is more, I have proof that you were afraid to venture into the lepers' dwellings, and sent others in your place so that they could report back to you, and you could present their findings as your own.'

'Madam, these are slanderous allegations, which I refute absolutely!'

Here she brandished a piece of paper. 'I have a letter telling the truth of the Godly Miss Marsden. Proof of the self-serving nature of your expedition; a letter written by none other than a respected Russian official who was required to travel with you and saw first-hand the way in which the mission was first and foremost for the benefit not of the few lepers who could be dragged before you, but for one pious English woman set upon self-aggrandisement!'

Now there was something approaching uproar. To my left, on the stage, I was aware of the organiser of the event getting to her feet and appealing for quiet. But the room was filled with shouts of 'Shame!' and 'Liar!' Some directed at Mrs Hapgood, but most, astonishingly, thrown with fury in my direction.

'Here we are, Miss Marsden. A lovely bowl of soup for your supper. Chicken, I believe, and this bread smells very appetising, I must say.'

The young nurse is setting the tray upon my bed. I have already been lifted so that I am sitting up and better able to eat. I don't feed myself any longer. I think I could, were I given time to try. But the nurses find it quicker to do it for me. Less fuss and less mess. Would I have done the same in their position? I do not recall ever having so little time for a patient. Perhaps I am mistaken about that. Perhaps, to my patients, I was every bit as absent, as elusive, as those who are now charged with my care.

The nurse repositions the tray onto my lap and begins spooning the soup into my mouth. She is kind and goes about her work with an earnest diligence that reminds me of Jessy.

'I wanted to go to India,' I tell her. 'I meant to go.'

'Of course you did,' she replies, pausing to dab at my chin with the napkin.

'But Nell needed me, you see? And I had to go to Russia.'

'Goodness. India, Russia... what a lot of travelling.'

'Jessy was in India.'

'Another spoonful? There, that's right. Got to keep your strength up.'

'For what, I wonder?'

'Sorry?'

'Why must my strength be kept up? I never leave this bed, nor will I ever, so why should I need to be strong?'

The nurse frowned a little. 'Now, now. It does no one any good at all to think like that. Everybody needs to eat well, you know that. You were a nurse, weren't you?'

'Yes. And so was Jessy. That's why she went to India ahead of me. But I couldn't follow.'

'Not sure I should like to work in India. Too hot for me, I'm afraid.'

'There was a terrible cholera outbreak.'

'Oh dear.'

'Jessy fell ill. She was nursing the victims of the epidemic and she fell ill. And I wasn't there to help her.'

'Try not to distress yourself, Miss Marsden. It was all a very long time ago, wasn't it?'

'Jessy caught cholera and she died. It was because of me that she went there. Because of me that she died.'

'Now I highly doubt that,' says the nurse, quickly scraping up the last of the soup and feeding it to me. 'There. All eaten up. Very well done.' She dabs my mouth again and, picks up the tray, and walks towards the door. 'You see if you can't have a little nap,' she calls over her shoulder without looking back. 'Dr Philips will be doing his rounds at three. So we must have you spruced up and looking your best, mustn't we?' she asks without expecting an answer, and then she leaves.

'Just like Jessy. Everything done as it should be done. No place for cut corners. Only that time she would not wait for me. She was determined that she should go. She died and I wasn't there.'

How long the night seems. The daylight hours move by in a more business-like fashion, with the brisk comings and goings of nurses and doctors and orderlies but, at night, it is as if the weight of the darkness slows all movement. The heaviness of the night deadens sounds and pulls at the heels of the passing minutes. How long have I lain here? I know it is more than weeks, but is it months or years now? I can see the icy expanse of the wilderness so clearly that I can taste the falling snow as if it were landing upon my tongue, but I cannot bring to mind the moment of my coming to this hospital.

This night I am aware of a curious odour, one altogether different from the usual scent of human frailty and the harsh smell of treatments. It is something as dark as the night itself. Something earthy. I have smelled it before, yet I cannot place its origins. The air is so tainted with the odour that it catches at the back of my throat and triggers in me a primal fear. I can hear the fluttering of my own disturbed pulse beating on the drum of my ear. It is one of the many ironies of ageing that as my ability to discern noises outside my own body dwindles, I hear more clearly the stuttering sounds within. The quality of the silence around me, however, is not pure, for I can just detect the rasping of breaths taken that do not match my own flimsy rhythm. These are deep, gruff gulps of air, swiftly snatched and then grunted out, fetid and used up.

I sense rather than see movement, at first. There is a slow shifting of a large, heavy form in the darkest corner of the room. As my visitor moves nearer I am at last able to put a name to the familiar odour. If I could scream I would. I would scream on and on with my dying breath, but I find I cannot make a sound. The stroke left me with only a stammering whisper of a voice that has not the capacity for screaming. If I could run I would, but I cannot so much as raise myself up, nor turn away from the approaching horror. All I can do is shrink back on my pillows, drawing in what little of me is left, pulling myself in close to that tiny light that still insists on burning deep inside me. Beyond that there is nothing left but prayer. Oh God! Let it be a swift deliverance now!

And so it comes out of the gloom and into the half-light of the lamp, and I find I cannot look away but must stare right into the face of the great, hungry bear as it towers over me, its golden eyes fixed upon me, its savage gaze burning into me. At last the moment is come, and the terror of the *taiga* has found me, alone and unprotected, save for what mercy God might choose to show me.

Was it worth all the sacrifices? In the end, was it worth it?

Why do you ask me that? You of all people.

Perhaps I am the only one who knows, who truly knows, what it cost you. Your mission. Your cause. Your beloved lepers.

I had to go. I had to.

Everyone thinks you wanted to be famous, to go about in high society and live a celebrated life.

Mixing with people of wealth and influence was a necessary part of attempting to raise funds.

Even so, a rather pleasant necessity, wouldn't you say? Balls at the Winter Palace. Being received at Windsor Castle. Taking tea with the Empress and accepting gifts from the Queen of England. I should have liked some of that necessity *myself.*

I would have exchanged it all for one more picnic with you. I believe you know that, in your heart.

And what of your heart, Kate? Did it ever mend?

My pain was part of my penance.

And my pain?

I am so sorry, Rose. I would not have hurt you for the world, but...

...not for the world, but for God...? For your conscience?

210

It must be summer, I think. Or at least, an unusually sunny day, for the light falling through the window has bleached my room white. The linen of the bed, the paint of the walls, even the tiles of the floor, all are rendered bright, sharp, white without blemish. Or am I again on the tundra? Yes, this purity is too absolute for anything formed by man's hand. Such spotlessness, such flawlessness can surely only be found in the vast, wild places that are God's splendid work. I wish my eyes were not so feeble. I can only squint into the dazzle, searching for form or shape, for shade or shadow. But I am certain I am treading on the uncorrupted snow of the wilderness. How wonderful it is to stand again. I can see me feet are bare, bony and gnarled, but I do not feel them freeze. The snow has a crust of ice where it has melted slightly beneath the fleeting sun, and then frozen again, and again, and again. I stand upon this glass-like rime, yet my skin does not burn, nor stick, nor send jabbing pain upwards through my body.

I see now that my hands are gloveless, and yet they retain a healthy pink hue. It is as if I have a warmth from within that cannot be doused and quenched even by this arctic cold. I am accepted here at last. The elements no longer seem set upon my destruction. This vast emptiness allows me to be a part of it, and I find I am at last at peace with myself. How far I have travelled to come to this point. And look, there! Low buildings, arranged in a rectangle, with a church atop the hill. All white, and pristine, and newly built. And I can hear the church bell ring, summoning the faithful to worship, and there they go, arm in arm, nurses and patients, the old and the young, safe and sound.

The SS *Ruapehu* for the duration of the voyage from New Zealand to England was home to a curious mix of people. People who might otherwise never have found themselves in close proximity. It was not a grand ship, so that we were not treated to the company of people from the highest ranks of society. Nevertheless, there were those who interested me, and those I judged might listen to my plans with a sympathetic ear.

Upon a calm sea, we sailed into evening, having dined early, and retired to the saloon. Those with a yen for card games got up a four for bridge. A young businessman and a gentleman returning home to Scotland challenged one another to a game of chess. Mama was engaged in conversation by an elderly lady from Hampstead who wished to debate the curative properties of taking the waters at Bath, and whether better treatments could be found on the Continent. Nell and I took peppermint tea with Mr and Mrs Rawlings, a refined couple enjoying the freedom of travel now that their family were grown, and a rather brash man by the name of Harris who was, he told us, 'in entertainments' in the north of England. I quickly learned that both the Rawlings and the entrepreneur were of a philanthropic nature and had funds with which to indulge this inclination.

'Tell me, Miss Marsden,' Mrs Rawlings sat forwards on the red velvet chair, 'how is it that you have committed yourself to seeking out these lepers? What compels you?'

'As a nurse I am called to help those who suffer, wherever they may be.'

Mr Harris puffed on a stout cigar, not troubling himself to remove it from his mouth as he spoke. 'I heard you were out in Bulgaria. It's brave woman who puts herself in the way of the Turks. You went to help the Russians, though, not lepers.'

'That was early in my nursing career,' I explained, 'and I was asked, along with four fellow nurses, to assist at a field hospital during the war. It was there I first encountered patients afflicted with leprosy. I have never forgotten them, and I never will.' I looked directly at

Mrs Rawlings as I spoke. 'Imagine if you will a disease that robs a person of every shred of dignity, inflicts upon them cruel suffering and hideous disfigurement, on top of which that person must be cast out, to survive or not as he is able, away from loved ones, away from all Christian charity... no right-thinking person could turn their backs on such torment.'

Mrs Rawlings shook her head slowly, not in disagreement, but in disbelief at the cruelty of chance, no doubt, and the callousness of man. 'They are surely to be pitied,' she said quietly.

Her husband put his hand on her arm, sensing her distress, for she was a tender creature. 'But all hope for them is not yet lost,' he said. 'Not while there are people such as Nurse Marsden in the world.' He smiled at his wife and then asked me, 'Have you an idea of where you will go next to help these sufferers? I understood you have talked of going to India.'

'It is true, the larger portion of the world's lepers reside there, and I had indeed intended to seek them out. In fact, a colleague of mine, a dedicated nurse who shares my passion to take God's care to these poor people, she is already in India, working at a hospital known for giving what treatment there is for this disease. But...' here I hesitated and glanced at Nell, who gave me a small smile of encouragement. 'I believe I have found another group of lepers who are even more in need of our help. These outcasts inhabit the remote and desolate wilderness of Siberia, and are beyond the reach of either Christian solace or medical treatment. It is to them that I intend travelling.'

Mr Harris gave a gruff bark. 'Siberia! I've heard tell of it. 'Tis the other side of the world, and a place men fear to tread. There are wild animals and people near as wild themselves. Hundreds of acres of nothing, save snow and air so cold it could kill you in an hour. Forgive me, Miss Marsden, but it is no place for a woman.'

'And yet women live there.'

'Aye, women born to it. An English woman such as yourself? No, it would be folly to go there, I have to say it.'

'I am confident God will provide me with both the courage and the people necessary to succeed in my mission,' I told him. He refrained from commenting upon this theory, so I was able to say more. 'I am not afraid of hardship, and I know that others will want to assist me in doing God's work. Nell and I are to go to Paris and Berlin to raise funds for the expedition.'

Mr Rawlings looked surprised. 'You cannot find supporters closer to home?'

'I hope to do so, but I must spread word of the mission as far as I can before I leave for Russia.'

Mrs Rawlings took on an eager countenance. 'We would like to offer our support, Miss Marsden.'

Her husband nodded his agreement. 'Indeed we would. You must come to our house. We shall hold a dinner and invite others who might be willing to contribute. There are many like-minded people in England. I think you'll find it an unnecessary use of your time and resources to travel around Europe.'

Mr Harris put in his halfpennyworth. 'I'm with Rawlings on this, Nurse Marsden. There's much effort can be spent in such tours, and often there is little to show for it. I know plenty as would be happy to put their name to a venture such as yours. I count myself among them. It does a business no harm at all to have itself allied to a worthy cause. Makes folk feel better about paying for their own leisure if they think a portion of that money is doing good works. And it is no more than good business sense after all: the more money you can save in the raising of it, the quicker your mission can get under way.'

Beside me I felt Nell stiffen slightly. This was, after all, what she had feared on several fronts. That my time would be taken up with other people, that my leaving for Russia might come sooner rather than later, and now that our cherished idea of travelling to Paris together might be lost. I could not afford to disappoint her, nor did I wish to. However, I had, it appeared, struck upon people who could provide vital investment in my endeavours, and I could not let such a chance slip away.

'I should be delighted to visit you, Mr Rawlings. And Mr Harris, a man of such sound business acumen as yourself would indeed be an asset to my fundraising efforts, for where others see such good sense and philanthropy happily wed they will wish to follow.'

'Ha!' Mr Harris at last removed his cigar so that he might wave it in the air for emphasis. 'I see you are a woman with an eye for opportunity, Nurse Marsden. You might be just the woman to tame that wilderness after all!'

⚉

As I wake up I become aware that I am not alone. I have another visitor. This one does not hide in the shadows, nor linger shyly on the periphery of my vision. She sits, straight backed and elegant as ever, in the chair beside my bed. She is wearing the brown woollen dress with the russet velvet collar that suited her so well. It flatters her skin and her warm eyes. She was never a beauty, but had poise and a handsome face. I imagine, many years ago, she made a sophisticated bride. Mr Duff Hewitt would have been rightly proud.

'You are here to see me at last, Nell. I wondered when you would come.'

'You knew that I would.'

'I thought if you were not careful you might leave it too late.'

'I thought I might see you when you returned from your mission. I thought after you left St Petersburg you would come back to me.'

'Truly, Nell? Had you not cast me out from your heart long before then?'

'I wanted you to miss me. I hoped that you would.'

I give a long sigh. My body is full of aches and pains this morning, and I find I have little inclination to persuade Nell of things that I can do nothing to change. I do my best to sit up a little so that I can at least look at her more easily, but in truth I am no longer able to command the movements of my own, frail limbs. Nell does not move to help me. She was not a nurse, after all. And this aged version of her lost love has not the power to charm her now.

'You never loved me,' she says suddenly, looking only at her hands in her lap.

'I cared deeply for you.'

'But it was not love,' she insists. 'Whatever it was.'

'I never treated you with anything other than sincere affection and respect.'

'What cared I for your *respect*?' she snaps. 'It was not your respect I wanted.'

'I gave all that I could,' I say. 'I hoped it was enough.'

'It was not.' Still she will not look at me, and I know it is not from timidity, but because she does not want me to see the tears that threaten to spill from her eyes. She does not want me to witness her lose her composure again.

'I am sorry,' I say, 'that I caused to you much sadness. It was not always the case. Do you remember? When we first met we shared such hopes for the future. You were so supportive of my work.'

'I was supportive of you. I did not care about your precious lepers, but that they mattered to you.'

'Without your help I would never have reached St Petersburg, let alone Yakutsk. None of it would have been possible without you.'

'But it was not me you loved.'

I can find no response to this that would not hurt her. She waits, but I stay silent, and at last she stands up and walks towards the door. Before leaving she turns and looks at me one last time.

'It was always Rose,' she says plainly. 'Rose you loved. Never me.' And then she goes, letting that thought linger after she has left. And I know it to be the truth. And I know it to be the thing for which she was never able to forgive me.

⁂

The Reverend Alexander Francis had agreed to meet me at the hotel in which I was residing. I had been in Philadelphia for some time following my tour of America, and was considering settling there. Until I could find a suitable house I had taken rooms at a modest hotel in a quiet area of the city. It was wet that morning, with grey skies and slanting rain, casting a gloom over the day that seeped into the sitting room of my suite. I had the lamps lit and a fire burning in the hearth, but still there was a sombre mood to the place that would not be lifted. When the Reverend arrived I called for tea, and we sat on the small sofa by the fire, side by side. I should have suspected, when he did not choose the chair opposite me, that there was a reason why he did not wish to sit facing me. I should have known then that he had come to talk to me on a matter that caused him such discomfort that he would rather not confront me with it at all. But it seemed he saw no alternative. And such was the upsetting nature of our dialogue that I was unable to realise how catastrophic it would prove to be, for me, and for everything that mattered to me.

After a brief exchange of niceties, he came to the point.

'I am afraid I have received some... unsettling news,' he said, choosing his words with care. 'Some reports, of disturbing talk, about your conduct.'

'My conduct?'

'I confess, Miss Marsden, this is not an easy subject for me to raise with you, but raise it I must. As treasurer of the Leper's Hospital Association, and as, I hope, your friend...'

'You may speak plainly, Reverend. You know me well enough to know that.'

'Indeed, and yet I hesitate to do so.' He picked up his teaspoon and stirred the tea in his cup with great concentration.

'Since my mission I have met with great support and appreciation, both in England and here in America. However, I have also had to suffer having my integrity brought into doubt, both where funds for the association are involved, and even as to the details of my journey through Siberia.' I sought to reassure him that I was accustomed to having my word challenged, and that it did not shake me, nor my belief in what I was doing. 'There will always be those,' I went on, 'who out of jealousy or perhaps out of some personal malice, will seek to cut down those who must stand tall for something that is dear to them. Rest assured, Reverend, I have already withstood slanderous accusations whilst on my tour, both directly and through the newspapers.'

'Of course, regarding the monies raised... Yes, I am aware of this, and as you know I have defended you publicly on this matter. And as to the charge that any part of your account of the mission is... exaggerated...'

'Falsified, Reverend Francis. Might as well say it. I am called a liar and required to defend myself regardless of the fact that these claims are unjust and utterly without foundation.'

'And you have done so successfully,' he said, nodding, a little relieved, I think, to be able to acknowledge his admiration for me on this point. But then he set down his spoon in his saucer and stared hard into his bone china teacup. 'I am sorry to say the matter on which I am compelled to speak with you is of an altogether more delicate nature.'

We both sat perfectly still. The low, colourless light of the day and in the room seemed to match the feeling of dread that now descended heavily upon me. I looked for a question to put to him, a way in which to challenge what I feared I knew was coming, but I had neither the courage nor the words. The silenced stretched to breaking point and then he spoke again.

'I have received letters. Letters which, when I questioned their authenticity and truthfulness, well, they appeared to be genuine.'

'Might I know the author of these letters?'

'They were sent on to me by Mrs Hapgood...'

'Ah, that woman.'

'...and the letters themselves were written by a journalist employed by the *Wellington Times*,' he explained, and then paused.

'I have had dealings with the newspapers of New Zealand many times before, Reverend. They have never succeeded in ruining me yet, thought that seems their aim. No doubt in Mrs Hapgood they have found a willing conspirator, for she declared herself my enemy from the outset.'

'The other letter was written by a woman.' He hesitated again, and the hiatus was filled with the skipping of my own heartbeats. 'Her name is Mrs Ellen Duff Hewitt.'

For a moment I could not think rationally, only endure the turmoil bubbling up inside me. There could only be one reason Nell would write a letter about me and not to me. I waited. Reverend Francis put his cup down on the table in front of us and placed his hands on his knees as if bracing himself for what was to come.

'Please understand,' he began again, 'that I have always held you in the utmost esteem, Miss Marsden. I have ever been your supporter, and will always be somewhat in awe of what you have done. It is because of my respect for you that I find these accusations so impossible to believe, and yet I cannot ignore the weight of evidence.'

'Evidence?'

'Mrs Hewitt is able to reinforce her statements with dates, names, places, identities of other people who were involved.'

'You have only her word, still.'

'Her most damning evidence must surely be in what she confesses to herself, for no woman would lightly, nor even maliciously I believe, ruin her own reputation without cause. No woman held in high regard by those who know her, such as I understand Mrs Hewitt to be, would sacrifice her own good name without truth as her witness. It is no small thing, after all, to lay oneself open to the charge of having had an immoral relationship.'

I had known the reverend for some time, and I do not doubt that what he expected from me was a vociferous denial. Strong words of indignation, refuting these calumnies and slanders. What he got, instead, was the weeping and sobbing of a woman distraught and broken by shame. I folded forwards, my cup and saucer dropping to the floor, tea spilling forth, as I clutched my arms around my stomach to prevent myself falling apart utterly.

Reverend Francis did not reach out a hand and place it on my shoulder in an attempt to comfort me. Rather I felt him recoil. It was a small but significant movement, as he shifted his position minutely, already eager to put a distance between himself, the good clergyman, and this sinful, shameful woman.

'Nurse Marsden,' he said at last, though his words were barely audible above my sobs. 'Am I to understand that you do not deny these claims?'

'I tried to atone!' I wailed through my tears. 'After Rose everything I have ever done has been in God's service!'

'Rose? I am not familiar with that name...'

'I knew Nell would help me with my mission. I had no money. No one else would support me. And what was to become of Mama if I did not find a way, find someone to assist us?'

'So you admit that you and Mrs Hewitt were... sinfully intimate?'

'I needed her. Not for myself, I did not desire her. I needed her support. Who else was there?' I turned my face to him, but my despair only deepened when I saw revulsion in his expression as he watched me.

'But, surely, you might have gained Mrs Hewitt's assistance without, well, without giving in to your baser desires.'

'I tell you I have never desired anyone besides Rose! It was Rose that I loved. I tried to give her up when Jessy was jealous, though she and I never became close, not in that way.' I gulped air, trying so very hard to steady myself, to explain myself, for I badly needed the reverend to understand. 'And then I met Nell, and I knew what she wanted. I don't deny that. Perhaps I should not have encouraged her feelings for me, but I reasoned we could help each other. Do you see? She was so very lonely, and I offered her a warmth that had been missing from her life for so long. She in turn could remove from me the wearisome problem of how Mama and I were to live.'

'You mean to tell me you manipulated this grieving widow, you played upon her confusion and her loneliness, in order to obtain her financial support?' The shock in the reverend's voice was unmistakeable.

'Oh, it was not as you describe it, you must believe me. Nell was happy with me. I made her happy. She became devoted, and she willingly supported my plans for my mission. She drew great happiness from being a part of what I was trying to do. I could never have reached St Petersburg without her assistance.' I took a handkerchief from my pocket and attempted to dry my eyes and control my tears.

'It seems to me,' the reverend spoke without looking at me now, 'that Mrs Hewitt is a good woman... was a good woman. I believe as such she would have helped you out of good Christian kindness. She would not have seen you or your mother penniless and on the street in any event. There was no necessity for you to use her for your own personal gratification in the way that you did. You knew full well that what you were doing was a sin. Could you not have found the strength of will to deny yourself?'

'I denied myself Rose! I gave up my only chance of true happiness. I never loved another, nor ever will. Whatever I shared with Nell was what she required of me, never for my own fulfilment. Nell would have me; she would not have given money to the mission otherwise. I did not take her for my own desire, for she kindled none in me, only affection. Whatever I did was in order to do God's work.'

'Nurse Marsden, that is an outrageous thing to say! To claim God would have wished you to commit a sin in his name is blasphemous!'

'Surely you can see my motives were honest, were good?'

'I see a woman who preyed on someone vulnerable for her own ends,' he insisted, getting to his feet.

I threw myself onto my knees before him. 'But if you cannot see the good in what I did, I know that He will! He sees into my poor, imperfect heart, so that I know He sees the truth. And I know He will forgive me. He will forgive me, Reverend, will He not?'

But Reverend Francis did not reply. He merely stood, looking down at this heartbroken, sinful wretch, and his face told me that he believed I was wrong. I was wicked. I was immoral. And God would never forgive me, no matter how far I travelled, no matter what I faced in His name, I was forever lost.

At the end of that day's ride we came to a clearing in the trees. The heat of the day was lessening slightly, but still we were all greatly fatigued by it, so that the men were cheered by knowing we could now stop and make camp. I myself was overjoyed – not simply for the imminent rest, but because we had at last reached those lepers rumoured to be living in the area, and whom I had begun to fear we might never find. Their settlement was so remote as to be hidden from any who did not know of its existence, and even then all the skills of our guides had to be employed for him to lead us to it.

There were two *yourta* set beside a small lake, so that at least the outcasts had water and even fish. There their luck ended, however, for nothing else about their existence could be described as good. These tiny houses were constructed of tree trunks fastened with wooden nails and covered with cow dung. the floor was earth. The single window in each was covered only with calico, providing little light, no warmth in winter, and scant air in summer. From the hungry mosquitoes and flies there was not protection to be had other than more cow dung and fish oil smeared over their bodies. I leave you to imagine the smell and the degrading appearance this gave to the lepers.

As we approached, a small crowd began to gather outside the hovels. Some came limping, some hobbled on sticks, others all but dragged themselves, their limbs and faces horribly affected by the disease which had cursed them to banishment. They peered at us with anxious curiosity, even amazement, those of them who still had their eyesight. I was given to understand, later, that they believed I had been sent by God, and certainly any who saw these poor abandoned people would never again question my having devoted body and soul to this work.

I ordered our things to be unpacked and we spread them upon the ground. The priest offered first a prayer of thanksgiving, and then one for her Imperial Majesty the Empress. As always, the local people were astonished to see the picture of their dear Tsarina, and revered it almost as if it were an icon. And who could chastise them for this? For without the assistance of Maria Feodorovna the help that I now brought for them, and the hope for their future, would not have reached them. While we distributed the gifts many of the faces showed clear delight, while others at last lost their look of fear and moved to expressions of confidence. Surely such a scene was worth all the hardships of my long journey. It was heartbreaking to think that some of the worst afflicted would not live to reap the benefits of the new hospital that I was determined would be built for them. They at least were comforted by the fact that others would, and this thought gave them some peace.

How to describe those *yourta*? I think it is best put by quoting from the documents of the officials who were sent to inspect them, the medical inspector, Mr Smirnoff, and the *tchinovnick* Mr Shachourdine. They both have much to say on the hardships the terrible living conditions imposed on people who were already suffering. They claimed that the dwellings were small, and almost devoid of light, and that the atmosphere was so infected by the conglomeration of lepers and the exhalations of rotten fish, that one would be quite suffocated upon entering them. Often the inspectors had been beaten back by the fearful stench coming from these hovels, as in many instances they housed dead bodies that had not yet been removed to makeshift graves outside. For if a person is scarce able to drag himself from one place to another, how can he bear the weight of another?

I saw for myself that the lepers were clothed in rags and rotting animal skins, all of which were infested with vermin and so bound with filth that they could not have been washed in years. These garments were given to them by the charity of villagers, but were

224

only passed on when in a state of tatters. The recipients, having few fingers between them, had not the ability to mend their clothes, so could do nothing to improve their condition. They had no beds nor linen, but only boards placed on trunks, arranged around the inside of the *yourta* as tightly packed as could be, head to toe. There was no separation of the men from the women, nor from the children.

While we were there I asked about these children, and each had their own tale of woe to tell. Some had been declared lepers and sent into the forest, so one or both parents had come with them, refusing to be separated from their child. Others had been so small when their mothers had been diagnosed that they had been taken into exile also, and grown up knowing no other life. Others still had been born to the lepers in the settlement. Inevitably, most of those who began clear of the disease also caught it after many years of living in such close proximity with those who were already infected. It distressed me to think that, had they had proper sanitation, ventilation, and good nursing care, most of those same family members need never have fallen victim to leprosy at all. All were condemned to this pitiful existence for the ten or more years before the illness overtook them completely and they were released by death. My resolve to see them lifted out of this purgatory doubled in that very moment!

'Are you sleeping still? Miss Marsden, are you awake?'

The voice is familiar to me, though I cannot immediately place it. Not a nurse, I am certain of that, for the tone is quite brusque, and without a trace of care. I blink against the light of the room, the sunshine glaring off the whitewashed walls. As soon as I can see the woman's face I know who it is who has come to me, though I cannot imagine why she would trouble herself.

'Mrs Hapgood,' I make a point of speaking as strongly as I am able, though still I hear from my own mouth the voice of a feeble, elderly woman. My detractor, though I know her to have been dead some years, stands before me with any amount of lively vigour. 'This is unexpected,' I tell her.

'You surely cannot think I would leave the matter unsettled,' she says moving closer to my bed. She is dressed in a smart grey jacket and skirt. Tweed, I think, with not a scrap of silk or lace to soften the severity of the look. Even her hat was chosen for neatness rather than style, and sits pinned tightly onto her regimented curls. After all this time, all these many years, there remains about her an air of disapproval that I do not believe anything I have done warrants. Though it may be more what I *am* rather than what I *do* that so provokes the woman. I have never been certain which.

'You all but achieved my ruin, madam. What more can there be for you to do?' I ask.

'I want to hear you admit to your misdeeds, all of them. I want to hear you speak the words.'

'Ah, I see you still regard yourself as judge and jury where I am concerned.' I shake my head, or at least, I try to do so, but I fear the movement is so slight it goes unnoticed. 'I do not believe there is anything I have done that requires me to confess it to you.'

'Oh, but you have.' She holds up some pieces of paper. No, not pieces, but cuttings, from newspapers. 'It is all here, all but your own word of confession.'

'You have always contented yourself with the words of others in regard to my actions; why would that not be sufficient for you now?'

'Here...' she shakes out the pages until they are fully unfolded. 'Listen. Listen to what was said and then, once and for all, I challenge you to deny it. For now I think you will not. I think you dare not.' She searches down the columns and then begins to read.

'Yes, here it is, in the *Evening Post*, dated October 1894. *Exposure of Kate Marsden*.'

'Well,' I say, 'that is a plain headline indeed.'

Ignoring me, she reads on. '"The scandals in connection with 'that sweet woman' Miss Kate Marsden have at last culminated, I am thankful to say, in the complete exposure of the lepers' friend."'... the Special Correspondent goes on... after your return to St Petersburg, how does he put it, ah yes, "laden with plunder from the Chicago Exhibition... decided to take action with regard to the charges against her." And he cites, of course the letter from Reverend Francis. How you sought to dupe that poor man!'

'I never lied to the good Reverend,' I insist.

'Indeed it might be he was one of the few to whom you eventually told the truth!' Mrs Hapgood snapped. 'Even if you did deny doing so later on. His own words condemn you, in this very article in this very paper. "Sir – An acknowledgement of the truth of the gravest of the charges against her has at last been made by Miss Marsden... " The correspondent then continues his own account. "For over eighteen months Miss Marsden travelled about the Continent, enjoying capital times, raising money for 'my lepers'. Many great ladies were touched by her cheerful self-abnegation in wishing to bury herself forever in the wild north land to nurse loathsome lepers. Among others, the Empress of Russia granted the heroine an interview. This made Miss Marsden in Russia..."'

'Dear Maria Feodorovna. Such a kind and gentle heart.'

Mrs Hapgood took no notice of my interruption. '"...and she had several more pleasant months both in Moscow and St Petersburg. Ultimately, however, it became necessary to at a least make a show of looking up 'my lepers', so in 1890 she visited Siberia."'

'No, it was 1891.'

'"In less than six months Miss Marsden was back in London, full as an egg of adventures and with quite a changed programme. Before, she said, the nursing of the lepers could be commenced, hospitals and a settlement would be necessary. For these she proposed to collect more funds. Some tiresome persons now began to ask what became of previous moneys given Miss Marsden. In lectures and interviews one heard any amount concerning Sister Kate's adventures in the past and intentions in the future. What, however, one did not hear was how 'my lepers' had benefited.'" Mrs Hapgood lowers the page for a moment. 'From the very beginning you would not face these challengers, would not answer these questions. Instead, what did you do? You ran to Chicago!'

'My time in Russia was over a year and a half, this journalist is playing fast and loose with the facts.'

'Ha! That you should say so! And here is another who unearthed your secrets.' She drops the first newspaper to the floor and unfolds another, jabbing her finger at the article she selects to read to me, and I am powerless to stop her. 'This in the *New Zealand Mail*, dated March 3rd 1893, a letter published that was written by none other than your old friend – poor misguided creature – Ellen Hewitt. She denounces you, leaving not an inch of room for doubt at your true nature. Listen again, "I may state that I went home with Miss Marsden on the same steamer, that she lived with me in London, that I travelled with her on the Continent, and know far better than most people her true character. Believing her to be a truly Christian woman, I lent her several sums of money amounting to nearly £200, not a penny of which has been returned, and I am sorry to say that from what I saw of her on the Continent, and what I now know regarding her I cannot but grieve that so many good people in England have been guiled into believing her to be a modern Christian heroine, whereas she is, I am afraid, merely a self-serving woman."'

'You and I are, unusually in agreement,' I say, 'for I too think of

Nell as poor, but not for the reasons you might put forward. I am sorry for her soft heart, and for her disappointment, but I never treated her badly.'

'Others might see it differently,' she goes on. 'Not least the woman herself, were she here to speak. In her letter to the paper she said more: "Other people give their money, other people give their work, Russian sisters go to nurse the lepers, and Miss Marsden takes all honour and glory – for what? For having found 75 lepers in Siberia. Those who have known Miss Marsden since she took up the leper cause much agree with the opinion expressed in this paper previously that *the lepers have done more for Miss Marsden than Miss Marsden has done for the lepers!*"' Mrs Hapgood throws this report onto my bed and glares at me. 'What must you have done to this woman that she should wish to expose you so?'

I manage a smile now. Though I know it to be a lopsided, ugly thing, it is born of a memory of my fondness for Nell, and out of pity, too. 'I failed to love her,' I say.

She utters a note of mirthless laughter. 'Love! And see here...' she produces another from her apparently endless supply of vitriolic reports.

I give a sigh. 'These were sufficiently painful when they were new for me not to require hearing them again all these long years later,' I point out, but she is not listening.

'This in the *New York Evening Post*, April 1893, where your book is referred to as "Philanthropy on Horseback." Ha! "Anything more absolutely devoid of literary merit, grammar, or claim to attention from the intelligent public than this volume, it would be hard to find."'

'Fortunately, the public largely disagreed with that critic, as sales of my book attested.'

'His concern was not only with the quality of your written work.

He takes issue with its veracity on many counts. Here he says, "She complains of the wretched *yourta* where they occasionally passed the night... yet a folding bed was set up for her every night in a single room at the posting-stations all the way across Siberia reserved for her exclusive use..."'

'What nonsense this all is. Where was this correspondent that he saw such things? Was he perhaps disguised as one of my guides? How else could he have known precisely what conditions I endured on that journey?'

Mrs Hapgood draws herself up now, a thin smile of triumph playing across her face.

'He might not have been there himself, but he has quoted the words of one who was.'

'Who?'

'None other than Special Commissioner Sergius M Petroff. You cannot deny recalling him, surely?'

'Monsieur Petroff? Certainly I remember him. I remember his wholehearted support during all the time he travelled with me. I remember how helpful, how conscientious he was. I remember also quoting from his very own reports on the conditions in which we found the lepers. He would say nothing other than the truth, which is what I recorded in my book. As you well know, he has put his name to the appendices I included in it.'

'It seems he had a change of heart. Perhaps, like many others, he was unable to withstand the forcefulness of your character whilst in your company. Once returned home, however, it appears he was also returned to his senses.'

'Monsieur Petroff was a serious minded, capable man, in a position of some trust, as *tchinovnick* to the governor. Do you truly believe he would allow himself to sign a document he did not regard as truthful, merely to please me?'

'This article,' here she holds up the newspaper once more, 'makes it plain what he believed, and to what degree he disputed your version of events. The correspondent continues, "Miss Marsden complains that she could never undress herself during the months of the journey from Viliusk. Mr Petroff replies that her folding bed and mattress coverlet and clean sheets, pitcher, basin, brushes, combs, sponges, bags of clothes and other necessities were carried into her tent every day; that she had full opportunity to undress and rest; that she put on her best gown on several occasions..." Not the picture you painted us at all, that's clear. As for the food... "Mr Petrol declares that Miss Marsden brought from Irkutsk bouillon, potted roast beef, reindeer tongues..."'

'Reindeer tongues!'

'"...dried vegetables for soup, prepared coffee, condensed milk... In Yakutsk she bought raisins by the box, prunes and grapes. They had also buck-wheat, wheat, pearl barley, mustard, spirits and cognac. In addition they bought wild game frequently, and often had so much duck and fish they were quite unwell from the eating of it." What do you say to that?'

'I say Monsieur Petroff seems to have been on an entirely different journey to the one I undertook. He appears to be describing a picnic, rather than an expedition!'

'Why would he lie, Miss Marsden, tell me that?'

I feel a heavy weariness descend upon me. Such is the weight of attempting to convince someone of a truth they are resolutely determined never to yield to.

'I am very tired,' I tell her, my voice losing what little strength it earlier had. 'Too tired.'

But Mrs Hapgood has not yet finished with me.

'There is more.' She shakes her head at me, and almost bestows an expression of pity upon me. Almost, but not quite. 'Perhaps the most damning statement yet,' she says. 'The article concludes with this; "Mr Petroff denies most positively that they ever found a dead leper in any house among the sick, or even one near to death; that any lepers ever offered Miss Marsden their repulsive food, or that she controlled herself to the extent of eating it." He goes on to note that you were so overcome at the sight of the first leper dwellings that you never, in fact, ventured into any thereafter, but sent him in to do so. Where is the brave and Godly Nurse Marsden in that account?'

'Why don't you leave me in peace? Your campaign to ruin me was a great success, after all. Can you not be content?'

'I want to hear you confess! I want to hear from your own mouth that you are the fraud and adventuress I know you to be.'

I close my eyes. I have not the strength left to fight for my name. 'Let history make of me what it will,' I tell her. 'I can do no more about it than I have done. God knows the truth.

Tonight I am utterly unable to sleep. I have often lain in the embrace of the dark hours alone, unheard, the nurses busy with louder patients. I would like to sip some water, but to reach the carafe beside my bed, lift it, and pour a glassful is as impossible for me as leaving this bed. I stretch out my one good arm. I can touch the glass, just, but... no, I cannot take hold of it.

'Miss Marsden? Let me help you.'

It is the young nurse, the cheerful one. I am fortunate indeed. I mumble my thanks.

She smiles at me, accepting my slurred words, propping me up against the pillows and then pouring water for me. With great care she puts the glass into my hand but does not let it go. Instead she wraps her fingers around mine and guides it to my mouth. I am able to sip, and not a drop is spilled. It is these tiny gestures, full of care,

232

full of awareness of the needs of the patient for some control over a fading body, which mark out a true nurse. I am as comforted by her actions as I am revived by the water.

'Thank you,' I mutter again.

'If you are not sleeping, shall I switch on your reading light?' When I nod she does so, adding, 'There, a little more cheerful than sitting in the dark, isn't it? Only an hour or so until dawn. I shall call in on you again when I have finished my rounds.'

I watch her go. I cannot remember if she knows of my past. Some of the nurses do. I have heard them speak about me as if I were not present in the room at the time. I am, to some, an object of curiosity. I suppose that is preferable to the complete obscurity into which I have fallen in my later years.

Did you enjoy your notoriety then?

I did not. And yet, as long as I was in the public eye, so was my cause.

But there was a danger of damaging that cause wasn't there? People, places, things connected to you might be tainted by that association. Other people – the ones who might have given you money or talked up your mission – well, they turned away because they did not want to risk their own good name.

Some did. Not all. Queen Victoria herself never forsook me.

Though her advisors dearly wished she would.

I was asked to court a second time, you know? That was such an honour, and quite without precedent. Her Majesty personally asked for me to attend.

You bought a special dress.

Yes, of course, I had to look my best. I could not stand before the Queen in something dowdy and poor, it would have been an insult. For my appearance at court, I bought a new dress. Navy blue it was, and very fine.

'A very expensive one, no doubt,' says a voice from the corner of the room.

'Nell? Are you here?'

Only Nell would bring up the cost of the thing. Everything was always about money with Nell, wasn't it?

'No, that's not true,' I insist, forgetting for a moment that only I can hear Rose whispering in my ear. She will not speak to Nell. 'Step forward so that I can see you. Won't you come closer, Nell?'

She moves into the light of the little lamp. She has not changed since the last time I saw her, in Paris. Or was it Berlin? She is every bit as elegant and poised as I recall.

'You look very well,' I tell her.

Her face is set in a stubborn frown. I see she has not forgiven me yet.

'Time did not mend,' she says. 'You left me and never looked back, and time did not mend, as you said it would.'

I know that there is nothing I can say that will change how she feels. Not now. Not after all this time. I could not return the feelings she had for me. I had been fond of her, but in the end she had come to see that fondness as a thing worthy only of her contempt.

'I am sorry that I caused you so much distress,' I tell her.

A sudden movement at the foot of my bed makes me start. 'Jessy!' I cannot keep the shock from my voice, for she appears to me as she must have looked after suffering a lengthy death from cholera. The ravages of the disease left her with red, sunken eyes, hollow cheeks, and a blue tinge to her mouth.

She does not speak to me, but addresses Nell.

'You were content to see me abandoned to suit your plans,' she tells her. 'You did not stop to think what would become of me when you gained Kate's affection, and took her away from me.'

This causes a snort from Nell. 'You cannot imagine that she

would ever have loved *you*! You were only ever useful. Your house. Your money. The fact that you were a nurse and might join in her wild adventures. These were the reasons she gave anything of herself to you at all.'

'And you believe you were different?' Jessy strides forward as best she can on her weakened legs. She is full of rage, and does not flinch when Nell draws herself up to stand strong and proud in front of her. 'She used you,' Jessy hisses, 'just as she used me. Just as she used everyone!'

Nell shakes her head. 'We could have been happy together, she and I, if only she could have settled for an ordinary life. But no, she had to be off, charging across the world, seeking something that would make her name, that would finally elevate her in society, that would give her some proper standing in the world.'

My goodness, see how they loved you!

'Please,' I try to make myself heard, but the two women are shouting at one another now, both of them venting their fury, neither truly listening to the other. 'Don't quarrel,' I beg them, 'There is nothing to be gained by angry words after all these long years.'

Such fury! See what passion you still ignite, Kate.

'Hush!' I say, as much to Rose as anyone else. And now I can see another figure. Sitting in the chair on the other side of my bed. I turn with difficulty, for this is my stroke-ridden side, and these limbs will no longer respond to my urgings for movement. Now I can see who it is. 'Mama! Mama, you should not have troubled yourself to come.'

'Why would I not come and see my own daughter? What other daughter have I living?' She sits with her chest puffed out and her stout arms crossed in the way she always did when she wished to show her disapproval. 'I fail to see what business *they* have here,' she says, wagging a finger at Nell and Jessy.

'Mama, they are my friends.'

'Friends!' chorus all three of them, as if the word tastes of poison in their mouths.

Oh dear. I don't think they wish to be soothed. I believe they are enjoying their rage. I don't think you will part them from it, whatever you try.

'I am too tired to try,' I say, though in truth they are not listening to me any more than they are listening to one another. 'Have you come here only to show your anger? Have you nothing else to say, after all this time?'

I feel a feather-light touch upon my arm and look up to see the beautiful, serene face of the Maria Feodorovna smiling down at me.

'Tsarina!'

'Now, now, Katerina,' she says gently, her Russian accent softening the edges of her words and slowing them down. 'You look so pale. Not at all like the brave Katerina who stood before me in St Petersburg and spoke with such excitement about her plans.'

'I was young then...'

The Tsarina looks sad. No, not sad, disappointed. 'Such a pity,' she says, 'that you were not as you seemed at first. How could I receive you at court again? Once your secrets were known...' She steps back and begins to fade from view.

'Wait!' I reach out with my trembling hand. 'I do so want you to understand!'

Beside me I hear my mother tut and huff. 'Tsarina this and Queen that, what business had you mixing with such people?'

'They wanted to help me, Mama. They wanted to do what they could to see that my mission succeeded.'

'Your mission!' Isabel Hapgood's shrill tone is unmistakeable. 'Your journey of whimsy and invention! You never took a single step but that it benefited yourself. Those wretched lepers were nothing more than a means to an end for you.'

'That simply is not the case,' I insist. 'The hospital was built. The houses of my poor lepers, the church... it is there still. It is as I promised it would be!' But no one is listening. They are all clamouring and arguing and speaking over one another, determined to make their point, covering old ground with their hurt and their spite. There is even the wretched Desmond Mackintosh here now too, waving a newspaper in my face, shouting his questions at me. Journalists never tire of their pursuits, least of all when they feel personally affronted. He likes to blame me for what happened to Jessy, thinks it makes him less culpable for her fate although he offered her no help when she needed it. His mistake is in thinking he could make me feel any more guilty than I already do. Poor Jessy.

'Tell us about your so-called accident!' he demands. 'Why did you take out not one but two insurance policies only a short time before you sustained your injuries? Why have you not fully answered charges of embezzling funds raised in the name of the lepers you claimed to care for? Why did you drop the libel case against your detractors? Was it because you knew they had found you out and you could not win? Tell us!'

The others seem to take up the chorus, shouting, bullying, their angry faces and aggrieved souls appearing to fill up the entire room.

At last I see Rose's face, sweet and lovely.

'Oh, Rose!'

She looks so very sad that I fear my heart will break all over again. I wish that it would, so that I might be released from this prison of a body.

You could have stayed with me, Kate. None of this need have happened, and I know we could have been happy together. You should have stayed with me.

It was many years after my trek that I returned to Yakutsk. My memory is so confused on so many points of my life, but that visit is as vivid, as clear, as true to me as if it had happened only a matter of days ago, rather than decades. Perhaps I should have stayed there. Lived out my years in obscurity, yes, but surrounded by my success, my gift to the outcasts, my monument to God's will.

I arrived on a pellucid summer's day, with air so pure it enriched one's very soul with each breath. As ever in the far reaches of Siberia at this time of year, such perfection was blighted by the constant and unwelcome attention of myriad mosquitoes. If I had forgotten how bothersome they were, I was reminded the moment I stepped from my carriage, and thereafter constantly by their relentless biting and whining.

'Sister Marsden, welcome! Welcome!' The diminutive figure of Mister Mateev, the Minister for Health and Community, greeted me effusively, bobbing something between a bow and a curtsey at thirty second intervals. 'Such an honour! Such an auspicious day for Sosnovka!' he beamed, his imperfect teeth failing to dim the brightness of his smile is his nut brown, round face. An even smaller man shadowed his every move, working a horse-hair switch ceaselessly in a losing war against the mosquitoes.

'The honour is mine,' I assured him, shaking his hand, attempting to pay him deserved attention, but unable to keep my eyes from lifting to the spectacle of the buildings before me. It was not that they were grand, for they were not, it was what purpose they served and how they had come into being that made them so very important to me.

Mister Mateev uttered harsh words at his aide, evidently directing him to protect myself, so that thereafter I endured the tickling whiplash of the switch, which was at least a preferably irritation. My host babbled as he led me towards the hospital, keeping up a torrent of information regarding the extensive nature of the completed building works, the quality of the nursing staff, the high standards of care available to the lepers, and so on. I confess I heard little of what he said. My mind was taken up with coming face to face with what had for so long been nothing more than a vision. I felt my heart leap beneath my breast. At last I was to witness for myself the blossoming and fruition of that seed planted so many years before, so many thousands of miles distant.

Sosnovka is a village, nothing more, in the remote and little known region of Viliusk, with its eponymous town. The settlement comprised mostly of peasant farmers, with the bare minimum of amenities and attendant businesses. The landscape was more *taiga* than tundra, though the forests surrounding the village were not as dense nor extensive as most of those I had travelled through. Indeed, this was an important consideration when I had identified the spot as the ideal location for the leprosarium. The slender birches and feathery larches stood as shelter and provided lumber without being so vast and abundant as to encroach upon the clearing. The entrance to the settlement was proclaimed by a sign spanning the width of the road, held aloft by two wooden posts, at a height to allow the passage of laden wagons. The lettering, in Russian rather than the local dialect, proclaimed this to be the Sosnovka Leper Hospital, with an inscription beneath declaring it to have been gifted "...by the dedicated actions of Sister Kate Marsden, the gracious kindness of the Empress Maria Feodorovna, and the merciful will of God". The scent of larch needles drifted up to me as I trod them underfoot. A small step through the modest portal, but the ultimate one of such a journey. My head swam with the excitement of the moment.

'This avenue,' Mister Mateev was telling me, 'leads, as you will see, past the treatment room on the right, and the kitchens on the left. Here the afflicted may receive both medicine, nursing care, and sustenance. Behind these buildings are the patients' own dwellings, and you will notice, Sister Marsden, the buildings on the other side of the stream which are the houses of our noble doctors.'

I followed the direction of his sweeping gesture. How delightful it all was! Had I not been told its purpose I could not have discerned it. This was no ramshackle, make-do place in which to deposit the unwanted and leave them to live or die as they might. This was a community, a tiny village in itself, planned and executed with great thought and care. The houses were of wooden construction, single storey, the logs of their walls sturdy and expertly hewn, and would withstand the wicked winters, while keeping out the worst heat of the summers. The doctors' houses were only a little larger and smarter than those of the inmates, but had the advantage of being set at a slight distance on the other side of a sparkling stream. There was a broad wooden bridge connecting the two areas.

'And here, Sister Marsden, if it pleases you, we have our school,' said Mister Mateev a little breathlessly as he led me on, indicating a capacious building surrounded by a picket fence and boasting a bell. At that moment the door opened and two dozen children filed out, skipping and chatting happily as they made their way towards the kitchen building for their midday meal. Some bore the scars or disfigurement of the dread disease, but others appeared free of it. Seeing them was a salutary reminder of how the families of leprous adults would often have no option but to share their parents' banishment, even if they themselves were not afflicted. Of course, the conditions in which they then lived meant that most would catch the disease, or else fall victim to the deprivations or starvation of their outcast existences. Here, those who needed it would receive treatment, and those who came with their stricken families would have a safe place to live and be raised healthy and educated. I clasped my hands together, my heart bursting with the wonder of it all, as a small boy passed by, pausing to smile quizzically at this tall, foreign lady who appeared to be on the verge of tears. As indeed I was!

And then I saw it. At the end of the curve of the avenue, positioned so that all led inevitably to its tall double doors, stood the church. Here the architects had allowed themselves the luxury of some beauty, even if on a modest scale. It was, I thought then and have not had my mind changed since, one of the prettiest places raised to God's glory that I had ever seen. The timber had not been left raw as in the other buildings, but planed and smoothed and painted to give a more refined finish. There were two stories to the main section, with long, shuttered windows, also prettily painted. There was a section for the nave at one end, and a belfry at the other. Atop of each of these thirds was a golden poppy-head dome, finished with a golden cross, all glinting and flashing in the dazzling Siberian sunshine.

'Oh!' I whispered, to myself, perhaps, to Mister Mateev, certainly, but nonetheless to God. 'Thank you!'

At that moment there came sounds of a commotion behind me. Turning, I found the avenue was now thronging with people. A veritable crowd was forming, with patients, children, nurses and general workers emerging from every door. Word of my visit had spread, and everyone, it seemed, wanted to get a good look at the curious English woman in their midst.

Mister Mateev called out to them, speaking in the impenetrable Yakuts language that seemed to fall over itself with each successive word. The crowd listened, and then, hearing my name repeated, seeing the minister's effusive gestures and expressions, they began to gasp and chatter and then to cheer. Gaining confidence they pressed forwards so that they surrounded me, though long practice had clearly taught them to keep from making physical contact with a stranger. At first glance there was much suffering – many bandaged faces and shortened limbs and people without sight or fighting pain. But closer inspection showed faces full of hope, of acceptance, devoid of fear, filled with contentment. Louder and louder they cheered, trying out the unfamiliar sounds that made up my name until their clapping was drowned by a happy chanting that lifted me heart and soul.

"Seester Moorsdyin! Seester Moorsdyin! Seester Moorsdyin!"

How we succeeded in entering the nurses' dormitory without being seen I shall never know. My fear of being apprehended rendered me silent and cautious, but Rose appeared to find the whole business an adventure, and had to suppress giggles throughout. As we finally burst through the door into her own room she fell into gales of laughter which I was certain would be overheard.

'Rose, for heaven's sake, have a care. If someone were to hear us...'

'They will not,' she declared, taking off her hat and grinning at me. 'And if they did, what is there to find objectionable in the sound of laughter?'

'Objectionable, no, nothing, but surely at this hour a little... odd.'

'Well, you might be right about that,' she nodded. 'And this room gives one very little to smile about, let alone laugh.'

She closed the curtains and lit a lamp on the table beneath the window. It was indeed a cheerless space. Aside from the small table there were two wooden chairs, a washstand with bowl and water jug, a wardrobe that had evidently been selected for its size rather than charm, a threadbare rug upon the floorboards, a mirror, and two narrow beds. Here and there an attempt to brighten the place had been made – a small vase of flowers, a picture of the sea, a scarf over the back of a chair – but it remained fairly grim.

'Where is your room-mate?' I asked.

'Working a night shift, poor thing. Don't worry about her; she is the most conscientious of nurses and would not dream of leaving her post until eight o'clock tomorrow morning. We will not be disturbed,' she said, as she gently removed my hat.

There was no stove in the room, so that what heat there was came from the hot water pipes that ran along its length. I felt myself shiver, but I was painfully aware that this was as much because of nervous excitement as it was because of the cold. Rose noticed my discomfort and took my hands in hers, smiling at me.

'Rose, with you I am quite transformed.'

'You cannot always be Sister Marsden, in charge of the world, responsible for everyone's health and well-being,' she laughed.

'Indeed, in your company I am not!'

'Good!'

'I am reduced to a young girl, awkward and blushing.'

'And that is what I saw in you, the very first time we met,' she said. 'I saw through all the starch and sternness. I saw behind the fierce gaze of the renowned nurse, and I saw someone lonely and tender. I see her still, that girl. Where everyone else sees only a woman, capable and efficient.'

'That is what a nurse must be, after all. And I have a post that requires me to be... a certain manner of person,' I said, my breath catching as she began to unbutton my coat for me.

'Well here, with me, tonight, you are not a nurse at all. You must put all of that right out of your mind. In fact, I expressly forbid any mention of nursing, or mothers, or any kind of responsibilities. Here it is just you and me. The whole world has vanished. Only you and I remain. Together.'

She finished unbuttoning my coat and slid it off my shoulders. Even in the dreary surroundings Rose looked so very pretty. I had

243

thought, at times, that my opinion of her was coloured by the hours we spent on picnics by the river, and that somehow my feelings for her could not thrive in the mundane everyday. Of course there was Rose the nurse, who brightened up the wards with her smile and her easy way with the patients. But that other Rose, secret Rose, *my* Rose – I had begun to think perhaps she existed only in that sunlit glade, beneath the leafy tree, beside the sparkling water. I was so moved to discover that this was not the case, that I felt tears spill from my eyes.

'Tears, Kate?'

For a moment she was disconcerted, afraid, I thought, that I had changed my mind and did not want to be with her. I clumsily attempted to make my feelings clear.

'I do not deserve such happiness,' was all I could mumble.

She leaned forwards and kissed away my tears!

'Does not everyone deserve to be happy?' she asked.

The feel of her soft mouth against my face sent tremors of delight through me. Such sensations, such a response to her touch served only to make me feel more wicked, more sinful.

'But Rose, how can we... how can I? It is wrong...'

She placed her hands on my shoulders and fixed me with her strong, beautiful gaze. 'Is it wrong to be loved? Is it wrong to love? Kate, you give of yourself day in, day out, caring for others, tirelessly fighting for the weak and the sick. You have done so all your life. You have nursed soldiers in terrible wars, you have nursed your brothers and sisters to their very end, you have travelled halfway around the world for the sake of those who needed you.'

'I only do what I believe God wants me to do.'

'And is it part of God's plan for you to be lonely and miserable? I don't think much of your God if it is.'

'But what we want, what I feel... it is a sin, Rose!'

She shook her head. 'You once told me – when I asked you why you are so determined to seek out the most shunned, the most reviled, the most wretched of people – you said it was because someone needed to care for them, because it was the Christian thing to do, for we are all God's children. *All* of us, Kate. And that includes you, exactly as you are, in every respect. Do you not see that?'

She waited for me to answer. The air about us seemed to crackle with the importance of the moment, and yet I could not speak. I could not. I thought about what she had said and more than anything in the world I wanted to believe that she was right. In the end, I had not the will to believe otherwise.

⚇

I remember the snow was silver beneath that arctic sun. A sun that had scarcely the will to raise itself above the ever distant horizon. Its rays washed not golden like the summer sun of childhood, but thin, cool, sharp, bathing the landscape in a chill light that did not warm or cheer. This silvery snow appeared to me not pretty, but sterile, spurning life and all living things. As clear a warning as any could be that this was not a place for frail, warm-blooded creatures

⚇

Will God forgive me? Have I atoned? I know Him to be merciful and loving, and because He can see into my heart He knows I am sincere in my love for Him. I am stripped bare before His eyes, and that is, if I am to be truthful, what terrifies me. For there beside my steadfast faith sits my greatest sin, for the same heart that loves my Lord so dearly has also loved where it should not. Oh, what it was to have been cursed with such a tender heart! And I have paid a high price for listening to the fluttering beat of it. I do not believe that my traducers acted only out of some professional jealousy, nor because they truly concerned themselves with the tiresome details of monies I might or might not have benefited from. Such vitriol as I was shown, such loathing, that was born of something altogether more personal. The men who vilified me I think acted out of fear, for a woman like me assails their treasured position in so many ways. And the women who set themselves against me? Ah, their reasons for doing so were more complicated. Did some rail against me, against the truth of me, out of an instinctive disgust? Did my behaviour shame our sex? Perhaps. Perhaps. But it seems to me there were others to whom I held up a mirror, and they did not like what they saw. To be so afraid of one's own heart is a terrible thing. I would not, could not, deny my true nature. I kept up a pretence because there was no other course open to me, and yet I need not have troubled myself. In the end conjecture, speculation, gossip, slander, these were enough to condemn me. And Nell, of course. Poor unhappy Nell.

At last there is a peace in this room the quality of which I have not known here before. They have all gone, even Rose. Was she right? Could we really have had a life together? I do not believe so, for there were too many things against it.

They found her clothes on the grassy river bank, beneath the broad tree where we shared so many precious hours. She had eaten a picnic, all by herself. It was early summer – I can picture how pretty the place would have looked – and the river was full and fast-flowing. They found her body a little way downstream, caught in the eddy of a deep, cool pool. A tragic accident, was how it was reported. But Rose was a strong swimmer. I know why she went into the water that day and did not come out.

And now she has left me completely. All the others have gone too. I have seen the last of them all. I am to leave this life alone, it appears. No matter how I loved, or whom I loved, at the last I am alone.

The light of the room seems to me to be dimming, though I know it to be a sunny day. It is as if the very space is shrinking around me, blurring and softening. And into this twilight comes a figure, soundlessly, wordlessly. It is hard to make out who it might be, for my eyes are failing quickly now, and the visitor is shrouded in strange clothes. No, they are not clothes, rather they are rags. These ragged pieces of cloth and frayed garments are swathed about his head, half covering his face. It is his gait I recognise now. The shambling shuffle of a leper, one painful faltering step after another, arms held across his body to protect his fingerless hands. As I watch he makes his halting progress across the room and slowly, awkwardly lowers himself onto the chair beside my bed. For a moment he does not move, and the only sounds in the room are of his shallow breaths and my own whispering ones.

At last he turns towards me. Still I cannot see his face, but I know only too well what I would find there if it were revealed to me. It is a blessing, a mercy perhaps, that his scarred and disfigured features are obscured. He does not speak. Carefully, slowly, he lifts his shortened hand, which is wrapped in a blue-grey remnant of fabric. As I watch he lays his hand upon mine. And I feel my body lighten, my own pain vanish, my sorrow melt away. In the end, I am not, after all, abandoned. And as I close my eyes, I am content.

Reprinted by kind permission of The Royal Geographical Society (with IBG).

The hospital and refuge that Kate worked so hard to establish was indeed built in Sosnovka and opened in 1892. It was run by the Russian Sisters of Mercy, and provided care for lepers gathered from hovels such as those Kate found. For decades it was the place to where people afflicted with the disease travelled from all over Siberia. In Kate's hospital they found treatment, companionship, and a place of safety. It closed in the 1960s once modern understanding of leprosy meant it was no longer needed.

Kate's reputation never recovered from the scandal which dogged her footsteps wherever she went. Despite her work for the lepers in Siberia, being made a Fellow of the Royal Geographical Society, helping to establish the Bexhill Museum, and setting up the St Francis Leper Guild, she never found acceptance in her own society again. She died penniless in Wandsworth Asylum, her mind disturbed by dementia. Her grave in Uxbridge Cemetery has no headstone to tell of her achievements.

Her book, *On Sledge And Horseback To Outcast Siberian Lepers*, successfully raised both awareness of the disease of leprosy and funds for the hospital. In the town of Sosnovka there is a statue erected to her memory and a street named after her. In 1991 a 55 carat diamond found in Yakutsk was given the name 'Sister of Mercy Kate Marsden'.

ABOUT HONNO

Honno Welsh Women's Press was set up in 1986 by a group of women who felt strongly that women in Wales needed wider opportunities to see their writing in print and to become involved in the publishing process. Our aim is to develop the writing talents of women in Wales, give them new and exciting opportunities to see their work published and often to give them their first 'break' as a writer. Honno is registered as a community co-operative. Any profit that Honno makes is invested in the publishing programme. Women from Wales and around the world have expressed their support for Honno. Each supporter has a vote at the Annual General Meeting. For more information and to buy our publications, please write to Honno at the address below, or visit our website: www.honno.co.uk

Honno, 14 Creative Units, Aberystwyth Arts Centre
Aberystwyth, Ceredigion SY23 3GL

Honno Friends

We are very grateful for the support of the Honno Friends: Jane Aaron, Annette Ecuyere, Audrey Jones, Gwyneth Tyson Roberts, Beryl Thomas, Jenny Sabine.

For more information on how you can become a Honno Friend, see: http://www.honno.co.uk/friends.php